EMBERTON

EMBE

RTON

PETER
NORMAN

Douglas & McIntyre

1 2 3 4 5 — 18 17 16 15 14

Douglas & McIntyre (2013) Ltd.
P.O. Box 219
Madeira Park, BC, Canada V0N 2H0
www.douglas-mcintyre.com

Edited by Caroline Skelton
Text design by Mary White
Cover design by Anna Comfort O'Keeffe and Carleton Wilson
Printed and bound in Canada

Cataloguing data available from Library and Archives Canada
ISBN 978-1-55365-554-1 (paperback)
ISBN 978-1-55365-784-2 (ebook)

We gratefully acknowledge financial support from the Government of Canada through the Canada Book Fund and the Canada Council for the Arts, and from the Province of British Columbia through the British Columbia Arts Council and the Book Publishing Tax Credit.

Dedicated to the memory of
Robin Baker, 1949–2002

Prologue

Dusk advanced on the city. Clouds curdled overhead, and when the wind picked up they did not disperse, but rather knit themselves tighter together. The last strands of Sunday traffic glowed along the thoroughfares. The weekend was waning, drawing in like the inhalation of water before the big wave.

In a venerable business district stood Emberton Tower. Newer skyscrapers had sprung up around it, but it remained an impressive edifice. Slabs of limestone fleshed out a twelve-storey steel skeleton, with a penthouse perched on top of that. Built early in the last century, with authority and grandeur as the intended effect, Emberton Tower was solid, thick, reluctant to crumble—to crumble visibly, that is. Inside, hairline cracks spread, stone corners eroded like edges of cake, pipes and rebar bent imperceptibly from true.

The wind gathered strength. Traffic lights strung from cables swayed and jounced. Scraps of paper hurried along the pavements. The wind found chinks in the Emberton facade, gaps along the seams of windowpanes, ruptures in the blocks of stone. Incrementally, it nosed into the Tower's interior, making expeditions down the polished hallways, under the cracks of doors. The building's rheumatic interior stirred, very slightly, with the life of the outside world.

But only slightly. A stolid dankness infused the Tower. Age and immobility reigned. The air could get in, but there was very little it could do. Very little it could change.

On these thirteen floors—and in the layers of cellar below them—the Emberton Dictionary was contrived. A respected lexicon, with new editions churned out twice a decade from the clanging printers two storeys underground. Here, the language was harvested, sifted, suitable words for inclusion chosen; definitions were crafted and tested and refined; etymologies were parsed, pronunciations codified, hyphen breakpoints determined. On the twelfth floor, senior editors, the captains of language, chose what to include and what to cast away, which turns of phrases to accept and which to condemn.

Although it was Sunday evening, Emberton Tower was not deserted; along its aged face, the occasional window was alight. A weekend janitor buffed the lobby's marble floors. On the seventh floor, a definer toiled over the stack of words he'd failed to finish during the week: *Lanyard. Lapilli. Lappet.* He was hungry. He reached for a sandwich, turning from the glass surface of his chunky old vacuum-tube screen. Had he kept his eyes there a few seconds longer, he might have observed a reflected movement in that glass, a shadow passing through the hallway outside his office.

The shadow belonged to an old man. How many years had withered him? He barely ambulated; rather he seemed to glide, or float, or flit—less a solid man than an idea or an impulse. His cane touched the ground only sparingly—the old man placed hardly any weight on it. A lanyard round his neck held a shiny black passcard that allowed him into every corner of the building—or at least to every corner officially acknowledged in the blueprints, on the security computers, on the diagrams registered a century ago at city hall. Clinking dully in his pocket was a large ring binding three old keys. With these, his access to the whole Tower, to every level of cellar, was complete.

He slipped into an elevator. It rattled into motion, dropping him down the Tower's spine, vertebra by vertebra, until it halted three storeys below ground. The doors parted to reveal a metal grid that had to be pried apart by hand—down here, the system had not yet been modernized. The old man separated the grille quickly, easily, as if those iron jaws were light as balsa. Indeed, as the old man stepped into a dimly lit corridor and strode forth, he seemed to be gathering strength. One of the antique keys on his ring opened a small wooden door. He stepped into a new corridor, this one of hewn rock. It sloped downward, lit by sulphurous torches mounted on the walls. The old man began his descent.

Halfway done buffing the lobby floor, the janitor switched off his machine. Time for a smoke. He paused at the revolving door. A low grumble was audible. Ever so faintly, the floor shook. The ventilation ducts along the room's perimeter gave a subtle gasp. The janitor shook his head. He'd worked at the Tower long enough that such disturbances did not startle him anymore—but they still left him uneasy. The cellars were beyond his custodial jurisdiction, but curiosity gnawed. What happened in those depths that made the Tower judder and moan?

Oh, well. At Emberton Tower, he'd learned, curiosity

was unwise. Nicotine was a far safer indulgence. Patting his pockets to check for his smokes, he shuffled to the revolving door.

Directly outside, gazing up the height of Emberton Tower, stood a young man. His business attire was inexpensive: an overcoat that didn't quite have the solemn heft it should; drab trousers; scuffed shoes. His hands were buried resolutely in his pockets. At first he was motionless, but then his mouth started working—speaking, it looked like, even though no phone was in his hand, no wire protruded from either ear. He was talking to himself. His eyes met the janitor's. A startled look came over him. He lowered his face and stepped quickly away.

The janitor watched him go, then stepped out for that smoke. As he passed through the revolving door, another groan trembled from the depths of Emberton Tower.

Chapter 1

Lance Blunt trudged up the steps from the subway station. It was raining, sort of—these droplets didn't fall so much as hover. He stopped to get his bearings. All around him stood glass towers, shoulder to shoulder, their panes reflecting a bruised sky.

Lance drew his overcoat tighter around him. It was scratchy at his neck. Twenty bucks at his local thrift store. Not exactly a great fit, not the most impressive garment all around, but he had to be careful with his remaining funds.

Disregarding the street signs, he tried to follow the route he'd memorized. He had even practised, twice, on the weekend, once on Saturday and once on Sunday, riding the subway to the correct spot, ascending to the appropriate exit, tramping through the sequence of streets that led to Emberton Tower, speaking under his breath to memorize the path and its landmarks. But today was Monday, and the streets were crowded. Today, he had to battle this jostling tide, which even now pulled him the wrong way, drawing him away from the intersection. And the weekend weather had been more helpful; today's drizzle made everything harder to see. Lance's dress rehearsal had been no sweat. The real thing was another story.

He swam against the current—almost literally swam, his arms helping propel him past the bodies coming the other way—and got to the intersection. Go straight? He glanced back at the subway entrance to get his bearings. Yes, he was in the right spot: the dark mouth of the tunnel faced him directly.

With a jolt, he was moving forward. The light had changed, and a new current of bodies compelled him across the intersection. He stumbled to the curb and came to a newspaper box. He crouched beside it, pretending to read the headlines, but really he was taking a breather, mentally rehearsing the route one more time.

"Excuse me."

Lance stood abruptly, bumping into a tall man in impeccable business attire. He wore a grey fedora, droplets of drizzle furring it, the brim hiding his face in shadow. A coin glinted in one hand. "Are you buying the paper?" he demanded. "Or trying to read it for free?"

"Sorry," said Lance, stepping out of the way.

The man stepped forward without a word. His face was visible now, a scornful gleam in the eyes. As he pulled open the door and reached into the box, a tremor moved through the ground. A minor earthquake, or likelier yet a subway train passing beneath Lance's feet.

"Look here." It was the man again, now prodding Lance's shoulder and showing him the folded newspaper. "Do you see anything wrong with this?"

Lance did not. He shook his head.

This appeared to distress the man. "What's happened to me," he muttered, before backing into the crowd.

Lance's watch showed five to nine. He tried to hurry forward but got caught in a knot of people who weren't moving. They huddled as one, facing away from the road, necks craned. Following a pointed finger, Lance saw a billboard mounted over a parking lot. Murmurs passed through the group. Lance couldn't see what the big deal was: it was a normal billboard, a picture of a couple on a tropical beach, probably advertising some vacation package. The bodies were attractive in their swimsuits, and the beach was scenic, but nothing really set this ad apart.

Edging around the crowd, Lance got to an empty stretch of sidewalk and exhaled in relief: straight ahead of him, Emberton Tower loomed through the shifting mist. Crowded by newer, taller office blocks, it stood out like a partially severed pinkie.

The Tower's entrance was flanked by columns. In the central archway was a revolving door, glass panels with brass trim, whirling as workers pushed through. Lance gazed up the height of the Tower. Its top was hidden in mist.

The air pressure shifted subtly as Lance stepped into a polished lobby. The marble floor gleamed, spattered though it was with downtown grit. To one side was a stone fireplace with plush armchairs arranged in front of it. Opposite that was the security desk, where a man in a peaked cap stared into a bank of surveillance screens. A cluster of employees, their coats and hair beaded with moisture, stood before the elevator doors as flashing numbers marked the progress of the cars.

"Sir?" The security guard had come from behind his desk and was making for Lance, his boots tapping on the marble floor.

"Hi," said Lance.

"What is your business here?"

"Fourth floor. I have an interview. For a job." Sweat itched along Lance's neck where the collar of that stupid cheap overcoat pressed against it. "In the department."

"The department, sir?"

"The one on the fourth floor."

In the shade of the cap's peak, the guard's eyes glistened.

"Sales and marketing," said Lance. "I have an interview there."

"Come with me, please." The guard led Lance across the lobby. At the security desk, he busied himself at a keyboard. "So you would be... Lance Blunt, correct?"

"That's me."

The peaked cap nodded once. "You're free to proceed."

The elevator was crowded. Most of the people in it were dressed more casually than Lance—but this was to be expected; the marketing department was sure to have a more businesslike culture than the rest of the Tower. These people were... what was the word? *Lexicographers*—probably not a suit-and-tie line of work. A few carried satchels or briefcases; one had a stack of books propped on a forearm. Another jabbed at a handheld device. "Signal's gone," he muttered, looking around. "What the hell?"

"You must be new," someone remarked. Quiet laughter passed through the elevator, as if this were an old, familiar joke.

The door moaned, lurched, and started to close. But at the last second a hand appeared in the shrinking gap. The door grumbled back open.

The crowd inside shifted and stirred, making space for one more. A young woman, mid-twenties. Her eyes were emerald green. "Thank you," she said with a nervous nod.

14

Her face was pale and serious, her shoulder-length blond hair unkempt. She clutched a stack of books to a threadbare brown cardigan. Lance found her breathtaking—and her disordered hair, her humble clothes, only magnified the effect. She was absorbed, Lance imagined, by valuable work, not by vanity. And if surfaces did not obsess her, maybe she was free of the usual surface judgements.

As she squeezed in beside Lance, she smiled—briefly, just to acknowledge he'd shuffled aside to make room—then turned serious and looked down at the ground. All the way to the fourth floor, she did not look up again.

Over the years, Lance had trained himself well for moments like this. Immediately, without mercy, he snuffed the spark of interest, buried his attraction in the bottom of his throat, swallowed hard to keep it locked down there. He performed the necessary mental exercise: imagined what might happen if he got to know her and then asked her on a date and she said yes; visualized the minefield of locations he would have to navigate—restaurants, coffee shops, movie theatres with sixteen titles on the marquee. The question of not being able to drive. The question of meeting her at her home, finding the place. There were a thousand ways it could go wrong, and finally he would be forced to divulge the truth about himself—and no matter how kind, how sweet, how hopeful or optimistic she was, the girl would balk. Like that time in the restaurant with Marie. That was a tough night. He'd held out hope with Marie; she was warm and effusive, and somehow she'd agreed to a second date. But her expression when he made his revelation—not cruel, not judgemental, but scared. The calculations under her eyes, weighing his limitations, sizing up the odds of a decent future. Even a short-term future would be fraught with embarrassment.

Any girl would be a long shot. But here, where the dictionary was made? For now, if not forever, any woman who worked at Emberton Tower was going to be out of Lance's league. And this one, hoisting in her arms the biggest pile of books Lance had ever seen a person carry— surely she was the longest shot of all.

The bell dinged, and a red 4 lit up above the door. Before stepping out of the elevator, Lance allowed himself one last glance at the curve of her neck, the strands of blond hair that fell over it.

Lance had not spent a lot of time in offices, but the ones he had seen were flimsy: thin, swaying dividers; makeshift workstations; furniture hastily assembled with Allen keys. But the fourth floor of Emberton Tower was a warren of proper offices—no cubicles in sight. Everything here was solid, old. Actual walls. Rooms with doors. Substantial furniture, built to endure and bought for significant coin. A century had gone by, and this floor had barely changed.

Most of the offices were occupied. The marketers within were busy folding jackets over chair backs, or rummaging in purses, or squinting at computer screens. They all looked sixty or older.

You can't miss my office, the department president, Ms. Shillingsham, had told Lance over the phone. *It's at the end of the corridor. Walk straight.*

Her door was open a sliver. Lance heard a conversation in progress. He paused at the threshold. The voices were being kept deliberately low, and only the occasional phrase popped free: "The meaning was clear..."; "But he's not even…"; "…have no choice." Not much to gain by standing here, secretly listening. Lance knocked.

The voices stopped short. Then Ms. Shillingsham's, which he recognized from their brief chat on the phone, chimed forth, suddenly peppy: "Come in?"

She was seated behind a large mahogany desk—a nice piece, hefty, in the Regency style. She kept almost nothing on top of it: a flat-screen monitor, a keyboard and mouse, one fancy pen erect in its holder. The rest was all burnished surface. Ms. Shillingsham herself was a woman of around sixty. She wore a maroon blazer; perched crooked on her head was a matching pillbox hat. Her silver hair was cut straight, just above her shoulders. But her most remarkable characteristic was her thinness. Her cheekbones made shadows on her face. Her hands were all talon, the nails painted to match the clothes.

A man sat across from her, his back to Lance. His head was streaked with thinning white hair, and below that was a series of ever-bigger rolls: round neck, round upper back, round lower back. His whole body appeared shaped from dough. He turned to Lance. Two dark eyes were pressed into the yeast of his face like raisins.

"It's nice to meet you in person, Lance," said Ms. Shillingsham, leaning over her desk to shake his hand. "This is Mr. Furlanetti, vice-president of sales and marketing." Mr. Furlanetti's hand was soft and profoundly squeezable, like a stress ball.

Lance took the unoccupied chair. Through his thin trousers, the seat made his legs itch. It was upholstered with the kind of material you might use to make durable carpet.

"Well," said Ms. Shillingsham. "Where to start? It's been a while since we've conducted a job interview. This department hasn't hired anyone for a long time. The last one would have been... Well, a while ago."

"Stable," said Mr. Furlanetti. His voice oozed out as if through a mouthful of molasses.

"Yes, Mr. Furlanetti, that's a good way to put it," agreed Ms. Shillingsham. "We have a very stable and devoted team. Truly devoted. Willing to give whatever it takes. And so we don't see a great deal of turnover. You could say our department has a lot in common with an inept panhandler."

"Sorry?" said Lance.

"We don't see a lot of change."

Mr. Furlanetti made a series of noises. Lance wondered if something had become lodged in the man's throat, but no—Mr. Furlanetti was laughing. Or, more accurately, he was making the noises that laughter was supposed to consist of. "Ha," he said. "Ha. Ho. Ha." His doughy torso trembled.

"So you may well wonder," continued Ms. Shillingsham, "why such a stable team would be looking for a newcomer." She blinked at Lance.

He realized he was meant to respond. "Oh," he said. "Yes."

"Lance, this opening, this new position in the department, it wasn't really our idea."

Mr. Furlanetti shifted in his chair to stare at Lance.

"The request," said Ms. Shillingsham, "came from rather high up—from the upper floors of the Tower, in fact. Normally we don't seek youthful personnel. But I suppose our senior editors are worried about the future of the dictionary. How does a big, heavy, inanimate reference book survive today's plugged-in era? How does it stay remotely relevant? They want us to take this fusty old thing..." She pointed to a heavy wooden bookshelf, where a copy of the Emberton Dictionary stood at attention. "... and make it hot." She glanced at Lance, perhaps to check that she was using the right terminology. "We need someone who can make Emberton sexy!"

Lance had no answer. As far as he could tell, Emberton Publishing had all the sex appeal of a tracheotomy.

"On the other hand," she continued, "it's important that the successful candidate respect the Emberton traditions. We are a venerable institution."

"Oh, I do!" said Lance. "I totally do. See, when I was a kid, in my family—we didn't have so many books in the house. Not what you'd call a book house."

"Not a house of books?" rumbled Mr. Furlanetti. Lance was surprised to hear so many words in a row come out of the man. They seemed to emanate from deep within his core, like the rumblings of liquid rock far beneath the earth.

"No," said Lance, nodding. "Not a house of books, not at all. There was a big Bible, but no one opened that except my mother, when she was worried about something. She'd get these terrible anxieties, and... Anyway, plus there were some paperbacks, spy stories or mysteries or whatever. And then there was the Emberton Dictionary. My dad, he worshipped that thing. Kept it in this case with little glass doors. Anytime they said a word on TV that none of us understood, Dad would send me over to fetch the Emberton so he could look it up. He'd read out the whole deal: correct pronunciation, definition, even the... what's it called, where the word came from. The etymology."

Ms. Shillingsham and Mr. Furlanetti were absorbed in the story. This is what happened when Lance got in his groove, relaxed a bit, and started really talking to people. The words came easy, and something in the way he spoke got people wrapped up. It wasn't the actual ideas—he hardly ever had anything important to say—but it was his manner, his face, his voice and eyes, his... what did you call it... his *cadence*.

"Dad used to tell me, 'It's all there, son. The whole of the language lives inside that book. Key to every door.'"

Mr. Furlanetti's stomach was gurgling; otherwise, the office was silent.

"Well," said Ms. Shillingsham at last, "I can see that you have the appropriate reverence. Good. So." She sat up straight and placed her palms on the desk. "Have you brought a resumé?"

Lance hoped the heat that rushed to his cheeks did not burn visibly. He wrestled to keep his voice steady. He'd rehearsed this a dozen times.

He looked Ms. Shillingsham straight in the eye. "Of course," he said. He bent forward, gripped the handle of his briefcase, and summoned his willpower. He hoisted the briefcase onto his lap and undid the latches. It opened away from him, its raised half blocking its contents from Ms. Shillingsham's view. Mr. Furlanetti, if he'd wanted to, could have leaned over to peer in, but he was staring at his hands, which were folded on his lap like a pair of over-stuffed calzones.

Lance tried to maintain the cheerful air of someone eager to present his impressive and beautifully crafted resumé. He rummaged carefully through the items in the briefcase: two file folders holding random papers he'd found in the recycling bin of his apartment building; two glossy magazines dispensed for free from boxes at bus stops.

He let his smile fall away as his rummaging turned frantic. He looked up from the case with what he hoped was a convincingly panicked expression. "Gee, Ms. Shillingsham, I... this is crazy. It's not... I can't find it in here." Now he allowed the blush to come, because at this point it was appropriate. "I'm so embarrassed. I was sure it was in here. This morning I packed it, and—" He tried to swallow but found he lacked the spit. "Not a good first impression. I'm so sorry."

Mr. Furlanetti's eyes seemed to glisten greedily as he watched this performance, but Ms. Shillingsham waved aside Lance's apologies. "No need to worry, Lance, these things happen. It's only a piece of paper, after all."

"Yeah, sure, but I spent two hours really making—" Lance felt bad. He hated to lie. But what else could he do? Later, if he was lucky, there would be time for truth and explanation and apology. But first he had to get hired.

Ms. Shillingsham smiled warmly. "I'm sure the resumé was wonderful. But we'll have to be content to imagine its glories. Meanwhile, you're here in the flesh. How about you tell us what the resumé says?"

Lance's blush abated. He'd played it perfectly. "That's nice of you," he said.

She liked him. It was clear now. He'd turned on his particular form of charm, which basically consisted of appearing helpless or inept and then apologizing in an open-hearted way—after all, he did feel genuinely apologetic, genuinely unworthy, almost every second of every day. It was particularly effective with people who wanted to mother you, tuck you under a kindly wing.

Mr. Furlanetti did not look so charmed. Maybe he preferred that his boss's good favour be reserved for him.

"Lance," said Ms. Shillingsham, "between you, me, and the doorknob, you don't have much to worry about. You're doing great. And... well..." She looked at Mr. Furlanetti. Excitement seemed to ripple through his doughy folds as some sort of communication passed between the two of them. "Competition for the position is not especially fierce. When we wrote the classified ad—"

"Ad?" interrupted Mr. Furlanetti. He looked ready to develop the question, but was silenced by a stern glance from Ms. Shillingsham. Lance, for his part, had never seen an ad. He had learned about the position through a more mysterious process.

"When we wrote the classified ad," continued Ms. Shillingsham, "we may as well have said this: 'The successful candidate will arrive for the interview no more than sixteen hours late, demonstrate reasonable personal hygiene (deodorant optional), refrain from referring to the female president of the department as *Sir*...'"

"Ha! Ho!" Mr. Furlanetti gave a reasonable imitation of someone choking, one by one, on a series of wine gums.

"'...and will not appear at the interview wearing a machete blade through each ear.' So far, Lance, you're in the lead." She waited out Mr. Furlanetti's final dollop of laughter. "So. Your experience and qualifications."

Lance tried to put the best possible spin on the situation. He admitted that in his working life so far he'd held only one real job, which he'd lost when a big conglomerate bought out his employer. He stated truthfully that he could be relied on to stick with a job once he had it. He was not a... what did they call it with criminals?... a *flight risk*.

He did not explain how his years of working for his own father had dragged on and on despite his father's efforts to

22

land him another job, get him *on his own two feet.* He did not divulge his father's repeated and frustrated attempts to help his son improve his job market value by paying for him to take courses—remedial classes, tutors, professional development seminars.

Lance did tell Ms. Shillingsham that his position—furniture salesman—had involved extensive interaction with the public, that he was well-liked among customers, many of whom came back again and again and asked for him by name, and that his numbers were consistently excellent (compared to those of the other salespeople, who came and went and rarely stayed more than a year, who often tangled with Lance's father in his cantankerous moods, which became more frequent and corrosive as his illness progressed).

He did not explain that charming the customers was all he was good for, that the practical aspects of the job—administration, paperwork, warranties, delivery arrangements, follow-up, returns, and exchanges—were handled entirely by his father, which of course caused resentment among the rest of the sales team.

So basically what Lance did was paint a pretty good picture of his eight years at Blunt Furnishings. And somehow avoid mentioning the company name. It was bad enough that he'd had only one job, that the hypothetical resumé would barely stretch to half a page. No point revealing that the employer was his dad, and the employment an act of fatherly protection. As Lance's dad used to say, *Always tell 'em the truth. But never tell 'em the whole truth.*

When he was done, a stillness came over the room. Mr. Furlanetti gurgled in his gut. Ms. Shillingsham tilted her head. "Well," she said, "I like what I see."

"References," gurgled Mr. Furlanetti.

"Well..." Ms. Shillingsham twisted her mouth in an *I'm not sure we need to worry about that* expression.

Mr. Furlanetti shrugged, and whatever he said next was mumbled toward his own lap and lost to human ears.

Ms. Shillingsham smiled. A burden seemed to have lifted from her. "I guess we have only one question for you, Lance: how soon can you start?"

Lance's heart thudded. He looked again at the bookshelf, at the Emberton Dictionary's massive leather-bound spine, behind which lived all the words in the world. If he could absorb its contents, learn its trove, who knew what he might become? A functioning citizen. A man of competence. The sort of guy a book-wielding girl in the elevator might want to date, fall in love with, be made joyful by... He grinned and waited for his breath to come back, and he opened his mouth, and one word soared out on a surge of relief: "Tomorrow!"

Mr. Furlanetti slouched further into his chair. Ms. Shillingsham beamed. "Terrific!" she said. "Come in at nine. I'll have the paperwork ready."

Paperwork. Lance's ribs clenched like a fist.

Whatever. Deal with it. He'd made it this far; he'd be able to figure out the rest. There were going to be hundreds of obstacles like this, hundreds of rude surprises, hundreds of paperwork moments. He'd have to steer through them. It was his only hope. Pouring all the cheer he had into his voice, he answered: "That sounds awesome."

Mr. Furlanetti escorted him back to the elevator. Corkboards on the corridor walls were cluttered with notices and posters. Fire hoses were coiled behind glass with instructive decals stuck on. Through the open doors of offices, Lance could see books lined up on shelves, documents in neat piles, computer screens showing rows of text.

If everything went well, all of these things, in time, would lose their mystery. Like in that passage Lance's mother used to read aloud from the Bible: the scales would fall from his eyes. He had been blind, but now he would see. *Amazing grace*, she used to sing, helping him to sleep when he was a nervous tot. *How sweet the sound.*

Through those early years at school, before he was rescued by his mother's decision to tutor him at home—and for all her attempts to help, for all his father's entreaties to *get it together* and *it's all in your head*, despite all the adult learning courses his father had shelled out for, Lance had never been able to grasp that crucial basic knowledge that most everyone else enjoyed so effortlessly, that the happy and employed and competent people of the world called upon, day in, day out, without breaking a sweat: Lance could not read.

And yet here, at Emberton Tower, someone was ready to show him how. He didn't know who, and he didn't understand why, but a promise had been made. Somehow, if he could stay at the Tower long enough, the promise might be fulfilled. His life might be transformed.

After pressing the down button, Mr. Furlanetti grabbed Lance by the forearm. His grip was alarmingly strong. He opened his mouth to speak, but the words did not arrive immediately—first came another round of rumbles from deep within his volcanic core.

Above the door, a red arrow dinged.

"Don't," said Mr. Furlanetti, his grip tightening.

"Don't?"

The elevator door was making a noise suggesting it was thinking of opening, a kind of preparatory clatter.

"Don't be too pleased." More rumbles and gurgles. Lance turned away from Mr. Furlanetti, whose breath was not exactly the breeze you long for on a hot day, and watched as the door slid open. Never had the interior of an elevator been so attractive. "We had..." More gurgling. Lance tried to edge toward the elevator, but Mr. Furlanetti's grip would not let him. "No choice. She lied."

"I don't understand."

"There's no other candidates. We were told to hire you. No choice." A fit of coughing, or some slower, phlegmier version of coughing, seized him. "She lied. We don't need new people."

Mr. Furlanetti's hand opened, and Lance staggered backward into the elevator. He reached instinctively for the button that closed the door faster. But that was not enough to block Mr. Furlanetti's last shot: "We don't need you, Blunt. Be careful."

And with that, mercifully, the elevator sealed itself, and Lance was on his way down.

Chapter 2

The first day of Lance's employment at Emberton
Publishing dawned clear, although the sky had a milky
tinge by the time he pushed through the Tower's revolving
door, and already a cluster of grey clouds was approaching
from the west. As he passed the security desk, the guard
nodded. "Mr. Blunt," he said, by way of greeting. Lance
returned the nod and proceeded to the elevators.

On the fourth floor, Lance thought he saw the
marketing execs—in their offices, folding jackets or
unloading briefcases as before—sneak glances at him. But he
kept his focus straight ahead, toward his destination at the
end of the hall: there was paperwork to face.

As he strode forward, willing the sweat to retreat back
into its pores, trying to dry his armpits through sheer force
of mind, he thought he heard a chuckle. Brief, harsh,
and gummy with phlegm—the sound reminded him of his
father's last days, of Blunt Sr. sunk into his hospital pillows,
seized by a thick, violent cough.

Lance could not see anyone around who might have
laughed at him. Were they hidden behind a door? But

then the noise repeated, softer and more liquid this time, and Lance realized it was too low to the ground to be a person. Beside him, rising to thigh-height, was an old radiator. It would have been white once, decades ago, but now it was a greenish sort of grey. Faint heat emanated from its vertical metal bars, and the phlegmy chuckle gave way to a gentle shushing. A strange compulsion came over Lance: he wanted to find the precise source of that noise, see the water or heated air that laughed and whispered. He could imagine kneeling on this less than pristine floor and dismantling the radiator, discovering which pieces could be loosened by hand, which panels could be pried free, and laying bare the liquids and gases that made this thing work.

Lance gave his head an abrupt shake, dislodging that silliness. He faced enough challenges coming to work here; no point becoming a rampant daydreamer to boot. He looked around to check he hadn't been spotted gawping like a simpleton at a straightforward radiator. Sweat began again, profuse and hot and unwilling to be wished away. So he gave in to its will, hoped the damp wouldn't show through the weave of his jacket, and continued down the hall.

Ms. Shillingsham was wearing a lime-green blazer. Its heavy cloth and shoulder pads helped fill out her emaciated form. Again today, a small brimless hat matched her jacket. She smiled as Lance entered. "The new recruit! Good morning, Lance."

No Mr. Furlanetti this time, so Lance had two chairs to choose from. He noticed the printed papers stacked in front of Ms. Shillingsham and, as if they were radioactive, instinctively chose the farther chair.

"We may as well get straight to business," she said. "Mr.

Furlanetti should be here any moment—I guess he's been delayed. So let's you and me go over this contract."

Lance couldn't find his voice. He nodded instead.

But rather than pushing it across the desk for him to look at, she picked up the stack of papers herself. "Well, I guess..." Her expression was like that of a wine taster assessing a complicated swig. "See, the thing is, Lance, you may find this contract a bit different from other contracts you've seen."

"Sure, no worries." Lance had not seen any others, but he decided that point might be better left unstated.

"I think, rather than... Well, Lance, if you feel you can trust me, rather than going into all the ins and outs... I mean, *golly*, how boring do you want your first day to be, anyway? Rather than covering it all right now, how about I give you the executive summary, you sign up now, and then you take it home later for more of a full perusal."

Lance tried not to betray his immense relief. "Okay, I guess."

"And believe me, Lance, if you see anything... I mean, take it home tonight, make sure you know what you're signing up for. How about this: I won't file it until tomorrow. If you see something you don't like or don't understand, let me know and we'll change it. How does that sound?"

"Reasonable," said Lance, as calmly as he could.

"Great," said Ms. Shillingsham. "The executive summary is..." And she laid down a bunch of terms. What stuck out for Lance was the salary—more than he needed for his present purposes. He'd be able to cover his rent and daily necessities and meanwhile see if he could do what he ulti-mately came here to do.

"Aha!" cried Ms. Shillingsham, grinning past Lance. He turned to see Mr. Furlanetti slouching through the door. "The man himself! Come in, come in. Lance and I are finishing up the paperwork."

"Just," said Mr. Furlanetti.

Ms. Shillingsham waited for more.

"Just late."

"Yes, Mr. Furlanetti, that much we gathered." She was trying to be stern, but Lance could see it was a real effort—behind that facade, poorly hidden, Ms. Shillingsham was concerned for her colleague.

"Because uh. Because of. Of. Because."

Her concern dissolved her boss-face. "Mr. Furlanetti, do you need some... time... to...?"

"No. All right." He wiped his mouth, from which a grey fluid had begun to leak. "All right now." His breath rattled in his throat. "I'm okay." He smiled at Ms. Shillingsham, then looked at Lance, letting his smile collapse. His jowls quivered as he lowered his bulk into the empty seat.

Ms. Shillingsham kept her gaze on Mr. Furlanetti a moment longer—Lance suspected a private conversation between the two was forthcoming—then riffled through the contract, plucking free a single sheet. She laid it flat in front of Lance, who leaned forward to inspect it. Mr. Furlanetti leaned forward too, staring intently at the sheet, which Lance did not like. He'd have to perform under pressure.

"Initials here, here, and here, please." Initials Lance could handle; single letters were never a problem. *L* and *B*. Done. "Perfect. And sign there, at the bottom." Signatures were a godsend because everyone, Lance's father had explained, signed their name as an illegible scrawl. Lance laid his own personal hieroglyph on the page, making sure it started with something resembling an *L*.

"Terrific. Now Mr. Furlanetti and I will sign our bit."

Each of them bent over the page and scribbled on it.

"Again here," said Ms. Shillingsham, producing an identical sheet. The process repeated, and she divided the stack in two, handing half of it to Lance. "For you," she said. "As I say, let me know first thing tomorrow if anything seems amiss, and I—" She waited for a particularly loud rumble from Mr. Furlanetti's gut to subside. "And I will take care of it."

While Lance put the papers in his briefcase, Mr. Furlanetti said, "The tour?"

"Quite right," said Ms. Shillingsham. "You'll be getting a little tour this morning, Lance. The better you know this place, the better you'll know the product, and the better you'll be at selling it."

"Sure thing," said Lance.

"Of course, the Emberton team is very busy, so we should try not to bother them too much with questions and so on. And, of course, we won't endeavour to cover the *whole* Tower! Goodness, what are we, simply *built* of spare time?"

"Ha," said Mr. Furlanetti. Then, after a pause: "Ho!" He was returning to normal.

"No," Ms. Shillingsham continued, "we are not built of spare time. Each of us has a plate, if I may make a metaphor, and on that plate there are many food items."

"Yes," said Mr. Furlanetti.

"Following the tour, we'll get you installed in your office. Someone will set you up with email and whatnot. Although…" She bit her lower lip.

Mr. Furlanetti made a noise that might have been a growl.

"This may sound fogeyish to a young person like yourself, but you'll find that in this department we don't much go in for the email."

"No," agreed Mr. Furlanetti.

"We prefer to meet. Face to face. Talk things over in person."

"Oh, hey, no problem," said Lance, wiping away a trickle of sweat from his hairline. It had emerged at the first mention of email. "Actually, that suits me really well. I'm more of a talker too, myself."

"Well." Ms. Shillingsham beamed at Mr. Furlanetti. "Isn't that nice to hear. A young man who isn't all hung up on the, you know, the, uh, chat rooms and texting and whatever else you do. Nonetheless!" She thrust her index finger in the air; a shaft of sunlight from the window behind her made it glow slightly red. "Nonetheless, we do try to keep up with the times. After all, Lance, that's why we need a youngster like yourself. Yes, we do march to the beat of progress, and we do have email accounts. And yours will be duly set up. Meanwhile, how about you and I commence that tour!"

Rumbling through a series of noises that evidently indicated farewell, Mr. Furlanetti took his leave. Ms. Shillingsham led Lance to the bank of elevators. "The Emberton brand," she explained as they descended, "relies on tradition. The past is very important here. And one of our venerated traditions is printing the book ourselves, on the premises."

They stepped from the elevator into an underground room with rough concrete walls, lit by exposed fluorescent bulbs. A janitor was swabbing the floor with a mop. A folding yellow sign showed an icon of a stick figure falling on the wet floor. As they sidestepped the sign, Lance noticed the floor was not only wet but also shaking. A dull roar filled the air. Its rhythmic surges were oddly comforting.

Ms. Shillingsham tugged open an orange door and led the way onto a metal catwalk. Lance followed and peered over the railing. Below them was the source of the noise: a jigsaw of hulking machines encased in ladders and platforms. Large rollers spun, plastered with paper; conveyor belts carried new pages and their hoards of text from one workstation to the next; hard-hatted workers ducked in and out of gaps in the machinery, consulted clipboards, uncapped thermoses. A cart slid along rails in the middle of the room, a giant roll of paper perched atop it. The air dripped with the scent of oil and ink. Pipes—red, white, black, reflector-jacket orange—rose from the machines and disappeared into the ceiling.

"Seems expensive," said Lance.

"Indeed. Emberton is a quality product. Not some flimsy paperback college dictionary."

A steady thrum vibrated through Lance's skeleton, and he still found it inexplicably soothing. He was almost disappointed when Ms. Shillingsham returned him to the elevator.

They ascended several floors. "We're going to skip some of the more quotidian departments," Ms. Shillingsham said. "The second floor is building maintenance and so on. Then there's the infirmary on three. Should you have any sort of medical emergency... Anyway. I'm sure you won't."

"We have our own hospital?"

"Helps curb insurance costs."

"Wow. Emberton takes care of everything."

"Indeed," said Ms. Shillingsham. "We'll also skip the fifth floor—HR and the like. Boring. And we won't reach the uppermost levels. No need to bother the editors. Imagine the responsibility—steering the very fate of our language! That's floor twelve. And then, of course, there's the penthouse. The domain of... well, I'm sure you can imagine."

"Sorry, I don't understand."

"Our owner. The man who makes it all happen." Her voice dropped several notches in volume. "Mr. Emberton."

"He's in the penthouse?"

"Yes. I need hardly mention that nobody bothers him."

"Of course."

They got out at floor six. Here, the offices were modernized, the drop ceilings gridded with fibre panels and striped with fluorescent lights. Language harvesters pored over books, magazines, newspapers, computers; some of them watched TV sets or scanned the radio waves through their earbuds, keeping an eye out for new words and idioms, or old ones accumulating new meanings. On floor seven, definers slouched at desks, confronting stacks of cue cards—written on these, Ms. Shillingsham explained, were notes from the harvesters downstairs. The eighth floor handled spelling and pronunciation: more people at desks, more people staring at books and magazines, or tethered to earbuds, or scribbling notes as they watched TV, listening for changes in how a word was written or spoken. Everywhere, a tension dominated, slunk in through the radiators, and settled like a fog over the workstations. Shoulders were set in grim hunches; faces grimaced against the tedium. When Ms. Shillingsham asked questions, the replies were brief and dispassionate.

Bored by the people and their jobs, Lance turned his attention to the Tower itself: the way the ceiling bulged in places; the occasional startling rush of water through an invisible pipe; the stains and scuffs arrayed on the carpets like deliberately unappealing art. The building reminded Lance of an old chair with its upholstery shredded, glutted with rot but somehow comfortable. He felt a nostalgic familiarity with the Tower, as if in some way he'd come home.

"The ninth floor," Ms. Shillingsham announced. "Etymology." She lowered her voice like a tour guide stepping inside a hallowed cathedral. "Here, the very depths of the language are plumbed. The roots unearthed."

This storey reminded Lance of the fourth—since the Tower went up, the decor on this floor had not apparently changed. Ms. Shillingsham took him past roomy offices with high ceilings and elaborate plaster swirls above the doors. All the offices were empty. "A meeting?" Ms. Shillingsham mused. "Perhaps they're all in the boardroom... Oh, here's someone!" They had reached an open door. Beyond, at a desk heaped with leather-bound books, sat the woman who had smiled at him in the elevator.

"What's your name?" asked Ms. Shillingsham.

"Elena Wright." She sounded like a shoplifter confronted by store detectives. Her emerald eyes darted around the room as if seeking an escape route.

"Lovely. Well, I'm Ms. Shillingsham, head of marketing. This is Lance Blunt." Lance waved. "He's just joined us, so I'm giving him a little tour of the premises. Showing him the Emberton ropes. Why don't you tell us a bit about what you do?"

Elena looked panicked. "Well, it's not enormously

interesting. We, um, you know, make sure the etymological listings are in line with the latest scholarship. Sometimes we do a bit of independent research of our own… or at least, I've done a bit of that, but…" She trailed off helplessly. She spread her arms, hoping her surroundings would explain what she couldn't.

Her surroundings were not up to the task. All Lance could see were piles of books on various surfaces. A poster was on the wall, a nature scene with cattle grazing on grassy hills. There was something odd about the landscape, the knuckly hills and sun-drenched grass. Something not quite complete.

"But most of our work is kind of rote," said Elena, deflated.

Lance tried to help her out. "You mean," he said brightly, "rote as opposed to, uh, verbal?"

Elena winced.

"Marketer that I am," said Ms. Shillingsham, "I have to ask: how does your work add value to the Emberton product?"

"Well…" Elena's panic deepened. "I'm not really sure it does."

Ms. Shillingsham was silent, but her concern was palpable. This was not the kind of education she wanted Lance to get. Lance feared she might be about to usher him away. "No!" he blurted. "No, it completely adds value. I mean, when I was a kid…" He inclined his head toward Ms. Shillingsham. "She can tell you. It was the word origins that really interested me."

"Really." Elena's distress was ebbing.

Lance pressed on. "How about you tell us the etymology of one word? A really good one."

Elena's face brightened. "Hmm," she said, new vigour in her voice. "Let me think." Lance's heart soared. But then something happened to her smile—like an imploded highrise, it fell in sections, whole bits of it flattening until it was all gone. She pointed past Lance.

Mr. Furlanetti had arrived. He leaned on the wall, panting, streaks of sweat on his doughy brow.

"Have you run a marathon?" asked Ms. Shillingsham.

Mr. Furlanetti pointed at Lance. "Him."

"Me?" queried Lance.

"Summoned," said Mr. Furlanetti.

"Summoned?" repeated Ms. Shillingsham.

Mr. Furlanetti straightened to his full height—not a particularly impressive move—and fidgeted with his shirt, apparently checking that it was properly tucked in. "Summoned," he said, "to the penthouse."

Silence invaded the room. You could have heard an icicle detach from the ceiling. Ms. Shillingsham's hand flitted to her throat and wavered there. Elena stared at Lance, her shock tempered by something else, something like excitement.

"Okay," said Lance, since no one else was willing to break the spell. "I guess I better get up there."

"Indeed." Ms. Shillingsham had found her voice. It was a high, fluttering one, charged with awe. "You'd best get up there at once."

The twelfth was the nicest floor Lance had seen yet. Fancy mouldings and doorways; a burnished wood floor that squeaked slightly as he passed over it; well-stocked bookshelves and plush old chairs, some with volumes laid on the armrests, bookmarks protruding. Light was cast from elaborate hanging lamps.

No one was around. Before leaving floor nine, Lance had asked how exactly he should get to Mr. Emberton's office, but his companions had been unable to help. "The very top," was all they could suggest; a couple burbles from Mr. Furlanetti had provided the final punctuation.

He wandered past open doors that revealed unattended desks. Each office had floor-to-ceiling shelves crammed with books—standing on end, lying flat, wedged into corners at every angle. Lance wondered whether he'd ever before stood in the presence of so much printed matter.

As he walked by the men's room, the door swung open. The man who emerged wore a tweed jacket over an argyle sweater. He gave his hands two quick shakes. Drops of water shook free. "The automatic dryers," he said. "Always breaking down. Contemptible machines."

"Sorry to hear that," said Lance.

The man leaned forward. "I didn't really need the toilet," he whispered. "I needed to escape the horrors of the editorial meeting. We're assessing possible new inclusions. You would not believe some of the terms my... *esteemed colleagues*"—these two words were hissed rather than whispered—"propose to add to the lexicon. Moronic slang. The most egregious ephemera. *Sext.* Can you imagine? *Bling. Derp.* What kind of idiocy is this?" The man gave his wet hands another shake. "Where, my dear fellow, are the *standards*?"

"Sounds bad," said Lance.

"*Bad?* That's all you have to say?" Squinting, the man assessed Lance. "Well, you're young. I suppose you're continually *sexting.*"

"No, not me."

The man appeared deeply unconvinced. "I don't recognize you," he said, "and I can't imagine you have any business being up here."

"The name's Lance Blunt." Lance would normally have extended his hand at this point, but the wetness of the other man's gave him pause. "I'm looking for Mr. Emberton."

The man took a step back. "What kind of joke is this?"

"No joke, sir. I was summoned to see Mr. Emberton."

Though hardly a tanning salon model, the man had gone yet paler. "That does not happen. Only to the most senior editors, once in a very long while. Where do you even work?"

"Sales and marketing."

A strangled chortle. "Mr. Emberton summoned one of the marketers. One of the... *team*, is that what you people call yourselves? I suppose you engage in *team-building* or what have you?" More hideous laughter. "You're having me on. Why are you really up here?"

Lance was about to repeat his answer when a new voice cut in. A man in a navy blue pinstriped suit approached from the far end of the hall. "Mr. Tradd!" he said. "What now? Recruiting this young fellow for your prescriptivist army?" Turning to Lance, he added, "Don't listen to this retrograde character. He'll try to convince you that *sext* isn't a word. Well..." A significant glance at Lance. "...I suppose *you'd* know. Let me tell you, if we'd had texting when I was a young man..."

"Yes," said Mr. Tradd, "I'm sure your prowess was incomparable—a half-century ago. Your quill-written notes must have knocked the socks off many a trollop. But let's focus on the present, shall we, Mr. Allsop?"

"That," said the man in blue, "is precisely what we've

been trying to tell you in this bloody meeting. Pull your head out of the past and accept the language as it is today."

"We shall resume hostilities in a moment," replied Mr. Tradd. "Meantime, this interloper, who states that his name is Lance Blunt and he works in marketing, has been trying to convince me he's been summoned by the man upstairs. I'm trying to convince him he's mistaken."

Mr. Allsop's demeanour changed. His back stiffened as he turned to Lance; his hands slid free of his pockets. "Well, that is unusual."

"It's beyond unusual," said Mr. Tradd. "It's beyond credible."

"Lance, your name was? Yes? Did Mr. Emberton tell you why he seeks your company?"

"Someone in my department came and told me."

"I say we call security," said Mr. Tradd.

A mean light came into Mr. Allsop's eye. "So I take it, Mr. Tradd, that you've never been summoned yourself?"

"I have not. I suppose Mr. Emberton's never had occasion. Busy man."

"Because if you had," continued Mr. Allsop, "you'd be well aware that Mr. Emberton has his own line of defence. A very loyal secretary guards the gate. She's quite capable of calling security herself." He spoke now to Lance. "You want the next floor up. The penthouse. It has a special elevator. End of this hall, to the right." Back to Mr. Tradd: "If you're correct, and this young man has no business upstairs, we'll see him come back out of that elevator in a matter of minutes. This is not a problem we need to resolve."

Mr. Tradd spluttered.

"We have plenty of problems of our own," continued Mr. Allsop. "Such as bringing you around to a sensible appreciation of a dictionary's real purpose." To Lance: "Mr. Tradd thinks we should control the language, stunt it with his unbending rules. He believes he can jam his thumb in the dam's hole and postpone the floods of change! We're hoping to bring him round before he retires or—God forbid—drops dead." He pointed to the end of the corridor. "Your elevator, Mr. Blunt, is that way."

Chapter 3

It was fancier than the other elevators—buffed mirrors, panels inlaid with mother-of-pearl scrollwork. It spat Lance into a small anteroom. A bare bulb dangled from a cord. Its weak glow attracted a fat fly, which thudded repeatedly into the glass. Beside the door was an intercom. Lance pressed its one grey button. Nothing happened.

The fly's wings droned louder.

Lance tried again; no dice.

The fly's head butted the bulb in a slow, monotonous rhythm.

Lance pressed the button a third time, shifting the pressure so that different portions of its rectangular body were depressed. Something connected, and a hoarse squawk came from the other side of the door. With an onslaught of crackles, the speaker came alive. "Who is it?" asked a woman's seasoned voice.

"Lance Blunt."

"Oh, good. Step on in." The intercom crackled and was silent, and a growl emanated from the door handle. Lance tugged it. He swatted away the fly and stepped into the penthouse foyer.

It was larger than the previous room, but only just. It was certainly better lit: two fluorescent strips did that job, creating the kind of excess glare used to chase closing-time stragglers out of a nightclub. Behind a small desk sat not merely a secretary, but *the* secretary. The one cartoonists draw when they want to communicate the concept of a secretary. A beehive hairdo. A pen behind one ear. Behind pointy specs, raccoon rings underscored her eyes.

The secretary handed Lance a clipboard with a pen attached by a length of string. "Sign," she said.

Lance performed his scrawl on the first available blank line.

"Go on in, hon," said the secretary, her beehive tilting in the direction of a door.

Lance hesitated.

"Something the matter?"

"We haven't, um, ever met, have we?"

"Don't think so. I'd remember a sweet-looking boy like yourself."

"It's just your voice. I know it from somewhere."

The beehive tipped again. "Better you don't keep Mr. Emberton waiting."

Mr. Emberton's office was resplendent with wood panelling, broad old armchairs, and bookshelves showing fat leather spines. The carpet was the colour of dark red wine. On the far wall, large windows were obscured by charcoal blinds. But no, it was an illusion—no blinds were down. The air outside was choked with dark grey drizzle.

The furniture was mostly antique, probably dating back to the earliest days of the Tower. Plenty of Art Nouveau; a pair of ornate mid-nineteenth-century cabinets in bombé form with floral marquetry. But there were newer pieces too, and these—with a strange tilting feeling in his stomach, a blast of fondness for his old, safe existence—Lance recognized as having been in stock at Blunt Furnishings. Two chairs—very nice de Sedes, a few grand apiece—and a walnut coffee table that would have set Emberton Publishing back five large.

Behind a giant desk sat a man so old his wrinkles had collapsed upon themselves and layered like roofing shingles. Features in that face were hard to pick out, but there were dark points where his eyes should be, and a thin, tight slit where you'd expect to find a mouth. His hair was a blazing aura of white. A crisp white collar enclosed his neck; his silken blue tie was impeccably knotted; his jacket, somewhere between blue and black, seemed to swim and shimmer with an oily sheen. He indicated one of the de Sedes, which Lance took.

His voice was surprisingly strong. "Lance Blunt," it pronounced.

"Yes, sir," said Lance.

"Welcome to Emberton Tower."

"Thank you, sir. Really glad to be here."

"Good." Emberton watched Lance. "Do you recognize the chair you're sitting on?"

"I definitely know the make. It's a quality piece of furniture."

"But do you recognize that specific chair?"

Lance twisted in his seat, making a show of examining it. "Can't say I do."

"You sold it to me."

"Really!"

"You did. I was impressed by your demeanour. You're a good salesman."

"Thank you!"

"Furnishing my private office is very important to me, Lance. I want the environment just so." His voice was comforting in its thick flow, like honey added to tea.

"Of course you do, sir. Furnishings make all the difference."

"I don't often venture from the Tower on errands. But I always made sure to go in person to Blunt Furnishings. No underling was going to make that trip for me." Mr. Emberton lifted a decanter from a silver tray and poured two glasses of a gold-coloured drink. He lifted himself from his chair to offer one to Lance, who leaned over the mahogany expanse to take it.

The old man raised his drink and took a sip. Or, more accurately, he poured the fluid into the space between his lips. No flexing of cheek muscles, no motion of the Adam's apple—nothing suggested any of the mechanics of swallowing.

Lance sipped from his own glass, which was heavy and sculpted, the glass chiselled at angles that refracted the light. Once the initial burning sensation of the drink had subsided, he detected a flavour of something like lacquered wood, with a burnt undercurrent.

"I don't mean to pry," said Emberton, "but I under-stand you recently lost your father."

"That's right, sir. Cancer."

"My condolences."

"Thank you." Lance took a hurried sip.

"And your mother passed away some years ago."

"Yes. Also cancer."

"The body. So weak. So easily felled by corruption."
Mr. Emberton shook his head. "I'm sorry for you, my boy.
I too am an orphan, with no siblings to share the burden.
My father, who built this Tower, he hung on for a long
time." Emberton raised his glass as if toasting someone
behind Lance. Turning around, Lance saw a painting hung
beside the office door. A portrait of a stern man with a fat
book propped on his knee. He wore the clothes of a bygone
era, though Lance couldn't say precisely which one—furniture was the only field where he had that kind of expertise.
"Left me when I was forty," said Emberton.

"I'm sorry, sir."

"Well, that was a long time ago. Many, many years now."
Emberton took another sip. "I was lucky I had him as long
as I did. He was able to impart a great deal of knowledge
before his death. You may not believe it, but as a young
man I was not very well suited to this enterprise. Reading,
writing, vocabulary... not really my forté."

Lance tried not to appear too intrigued. "Really?"

"But Father showed me the way."

"Oh." In the uncomfortable pause that followed—an
invisible door had swung shut, sealing off that part of the
conversation—Lance took a heavy swig. For the first time, he
noticed a large painting in a gilt frame, dominating almost
a whole wall. Amazing he'd missed it before; he must have
been too busy observing the furniture. It showed men on
horses chasing dogs, which in turn pursued a fox, a fearful
russet blur at the bottom right of the canvas. Set into the
base of the frame was a large plaque with two words engraved
on it.

"What do you think of that piece?" asked Mr. Emberton.

"I think it adds to the decor, sir," said Lance. "But

46

honestly, painting's not really my... I don't know so much about fine art. I'm strictly furniture."

Emberton had swivelled in his chair, and now tipped it back to take in the painting's full height. "Are you familiar with this artist?"

"Don't know who it is, sir."

"Harvard Kent. Not widely celebrated, but very dynamic, very forceful. His most famous work is *The Shooter*. But this one, *The Chase*, is quite striking too."

"*The Hunt*," said Lance quickly.

Emberton's gaze latched onto Lance's. "What did you say?"

"Uh... I think..." Sweat was exploding from Lance's forehead. What had just happened? "I think maybe it's called *The Hunt*." How did he know this?

"You're quite right, how silly of me." Emberton chuckled. "I ought not to mix up such details. Precision, you know—it's very important when you run a dictionary. And with the title right there on the frame! But I'm not a young man like you, not anymore. My eyesight is not what it was."

"Oh, I didn't notice that," said Lance. "I guess... I must know the painting from somewhere." But where? His parents had hardly been gallery-goers, and they never kept art books lying around the house.

"Anyway," said Emberton, "I do appreciate your opinion. I imagine you know your way around interiors— you were so convincing as a furniture salesman."

"Thank you." This warmed Lance. He took another sip.

"As you did, I work at my father's place of business. He built this Tower, and it was his father who founded the dictionary. Indeed, interest in language goes back

47

a very long way in my family. It's my inheritance. Never had children myself, I'm afraid, so I won't be passing the torch to a son of my own. I have neglected to prolong the bloodline."

Lance wasn't sure how to react to this bout of sharing. He kept silent.

"But I appreciate your loyalty, all those years of service to your father's cause." The old man smiled, which was not a soothing sight. The contents of his mouth had passed a threshold beyond the reach of dentistry. "I see great things for you at Emberton Tower, Lance Blunt."

Silence took over the office; in the weak light, Lance could see dust furring a corner of the desktop.

"Is something troubling you?" asked Emberton.

Somehow, at some point, Lance was going to have to start asking questions. He had to figure out who had pulled the strings to get him this job, and why. But in order to explain why he had applied for work at Emberton Tower, to divulge the strange invitation he had received during his father's dying days, Lance would have to admit that he could not read or write. And he didn't dare. Here, with the boss himself, the danger was at its peak, but so was the potential: surely this man was likelier than anyone to know the identity of the benefactor—indeed, to *be* the benefactor. Or he might be the worst possible confidant; Lance could be out on the street in seconds if he took a wrong step.

"Lance? I asked you a question."

The silence grew longer as Lance struggled to summon something to say. Before he could shape the right question, though, a rumble sounded beneath his feet. Gently, the floor shook. Pens on Emberton's desk rattled in their holder.

"Earthquake?" Lance said, raising his voice above the roar.

"Nothing to worry about," Emberton said quickly. "But you'd better be off. Pressing matters require my attention."

"What's going on?"

Emberton shook his head. He didn't have to speak: *None of your business* was clear from the forbidding expression on his face. He pointed markedly at Lance's glass; Lance drained its contents.

"I am hopeful for you, Lance," concluded Emberton. "If you do well here, I may reveal more of the work I do in this Tower. But not yet."

"Thank you," said Lance as he set down his glass. The sticky yellow residue of the beverage glimmered at its base.

Floor four was empty. The door to Ms. Shillingsham's room was ajar; no one was within. Lance found a corridor branching off from the main hall and strolled down that. Voices became audible. At the end of the corridor was a doorway, and through that was a boardroom. Bare beige walls, no windows or decorations, only a whiteboard, which was completely blank, not even smudged by old erasings. Its pens lay sealed on their aluminum ridge. The sales and marketing department's eight employees sat around the conference table: a woman wearing a shawl and apparently knitting a second one, wool heaped on the table in front of her; another woman in a shiny, tight silver blazer, hair dyed a frightening metallic red; various folk in drab business dress. Ms. Shillingsham occupied one end of the table and Mr. Furlanetti the other, his doughy back facing Lance.

One of the marketers was in the middle of a passionate speech: "...simply will not do," he blustered, pounding a liver-spotted fist on the table. His white hair, yellowing at the ends like old paper, was slicked back. He wore a tan jacket and a silky orange cravat. "If the filter sits overnight, soggy, all those grounds collecting mould, then the basket gets filthy. Do you hear me? Filthy. I refuse to martyr myself trying to—"

Ms. Shillingsham raised a silencing hand. She had spotted Lance. The faces that turned to him were charged with awe. The knitting needles paused in their clacking.

Lance nodded in everyone's general direction. "Hello."

Ms. Shillingsham found her voice. "What did he want?"

"Mr. Emberton, you mean?"

The marketers recoiled at the sound of the name.

"He just wanted to say hi. You know, welcome me to the team."

Most of the jaws in the room appeared incapable of closing.

"Well..." said Ms. Shillingsham quietly. "That is most... um..." She gestured at a vacant seat.

He sat. "I'm Lance."

"Oh, we know," said the man with the orange cravat.

"Ah," said Lance. "Good," he added, though it did not seem to be quite the right word.

Eyes remained on him. Somewhere, a duct exhaled.

"Meeting," said Mr. Furlanetti into the void.

"Yes, indeed," said Ms. Shillingsham, gathering herself together. "We are having a touch-base. Every few days we get together to air whatever needs airing."

Bodies relaxed into their chairs. Cautiously, the knitting needles eased back into motion.

Ms. Shillingsham inclined her head toward the man in the cravat. "Mr. Hutchman has been suggesting improvements to protocol surrounding the office coffee machine. Would you care to continue, Mr. Hutchman?"

"I believe I've made myself clear," said Mr. Hutchman. "Are you a coffee drinker, Lance?"

"Not so much," said Lance. He'd always found coffee a complicated grocery to buy. The simpler the better: things he could grab off the shelf, take home, and eat straight from the package or boil in water or stick in the stove for twenty minutes as his mother had shown him.

"Well, then," said Mr. Hutchman, "I think I'm done."

"Thank you for your perspective," said Ms. Shillingsham. "I'm sure we can all make an effort to change the filter more promptly. Got that one down, Mr. Furlanetti?"

A burble and an affirmative grunt. Mr. Furlanetti was jotting on a yellow notepad. Pinched in his enormous fingers, the slim pencil resembled an eel in the jaws of a sperm whale.

When the meeting was adjourned, everyone seemed glad to be done—and yet there was no hurry to vacate the room. Marketers dawdled while gathering up their papers and pens; butts were hoisted from chairs at the speed of drying tar; quiet conversations broke out.

"Well." Ms. Shillingsham trained an energetic smile on Lance. "That was productive, I think."

Lance made a noncommittal noise.

"How about I show you to your office." She led him back to the main corridor and all the way to the elevator doors, where a right turn took them into a little stub of a hallway. To their left were the washroom entrances, with an old brass drinking fountain between them. To their right, another door was slightly ajar. Ms. Shillingsham pointed at a cardboard square taped to its surface. "That's just makeshift;

we'll have maintenance do you up a proper name plaque one of these days." She pushed open the door and fumbled for the light switch, averting her face from the dusty air. "It hasn't been cleaned out yet," she said, "but it should serve you well. It was Jeanine's office."

"Jeanine?"

Ms. Shillingsham's hand found the switch, and lights came on inside the room. She stepped back and stood shoulder to shoulder with Lance, peering in. She didn't seem to want to step inside.

The room was a standard office—desk, chair, computer, shelves with an array of books. Already the dust was resettling, and daylight—weak and fog-addled, but daylight nonetheless—seeped through the grungy window. In one corner, a small potted tree was shedding its leaves.

"Jeanine worked for us," said Ms. Shillingsham.

"And?"

"She doesn't, anymore."

"Oh."

"So I'll leave you to settle in for now. I'm at the end of the hall if you need anything." She was already backing away.

"Sure thing," said Lance. "No worries."

He stepped into the room and sized it up. Small, sure; and it would need a pass with a duster. But it was his—his very own office. He sat in the chair, a standard-issue ergonomic. It wheezed, which suggested it was adjustable. After some fumbling and one sudden plunge, Lance worked out how to achieve the optimum seat height. He pushed back from the desk to test the wheels. They rolled, if a bit reluctantly. He tried a three-hundred-sixty-degree spin. It worked. Bare walls rotated through his field of vision.

A photo was on the desk, trapped in a gaudy fake-gold

frame. It showed a man and a woman and a big, long-haired dog, posed in the manner of a studio photo. The woman had to be Jeanine: sixty-something, with tidy makeup and a well-preserved, attractive face. A kind face. Most notable was her hair, a lustrous blond cascade—dyed, Lance assumed— which added a great deal of youth to her appearance.

It felt weird to scrutinize a photo belonging to this woman who for whatever reason no longer worked for Emberton Publishing. But it would also feel wrong to toss the picture out. He laid the frame face-down on the desktop.

He took a closer look at the computer. The apex of his social exclusion. Sure, you could use it to watch movies, listen to music, add up numbers—things Lance knew how to do on other machines. But you had to type and read to make it happen. The computer worked in mysterious, invisible ways, and you had to converse with it. In text.

This one had all manner of extra keys crammed onto its keyboard, far more than the alphabet and numbers. It had a mouse on a pad, and even the pad was frightening: in what must have been some sort of tribute to lexicography, it had a bunch of letters printed on it, different sizes and fonts, swirling on a dark background like the noodles in alphabet soup (not Lance's favourite childhood food).

Something yellow was attached to one corner of the flat-screen monitor. A Post-it note. Lance plucked it free. It bore writing. First an *L*, just *L*, followed by a comma. Below that was bunch of writing. Lance knew enough about writing to understand that notes were addressed this way—the recipient's name, or just an initial, plus a comma. And he had a pretty good hunch that *Jeanine* did not begin with *L*. Which made it likely that someone had left this here as a note for him. Which meant he had some deciphering to do.

The lobby was quiet. Someone sat by the fireplace, poring over a book. A few smokers hurried to the exit, patting pockets and fumbling for lighters. Lance sidled up to the security desk. "Excuse me."

"One... moment..." The guard was staring at a screen and his fingers clattered over a keyboard. "...please." He flicked a switch and nodded at Lance. "Sorry about that. How can I be of assistance... Mr. Blunt, right?"

"You have a great memory."

"I try to stay on top of things. What's up?"

"I'm hoping you can give me a hand." Lance allowed his shoulders to sag, his gut to go pudgy—he gave his best help-less look. "So I'm trying to suss out how things work around here—you seem like the guy to come to for help." Lance gestured at the extensive control panel.

The guard nodded sagely.

This might be the worst person Lance could approach, with his surveillance screens and his capacity for remembering names. But Lance didn't dare approach someone in his department; any one of them might have written the note.

"What it is..." Lance rummaged in his pockets. He put on a goofy, incompetent *give me a sec here, I'm such a lug* face—the same expression he'd used with customers at Blunt Furnishings when it was time to pass the baton to his father so that the paperwork could begin. *A goof like me! Me and paperwork's like oil and water.*

"Aha!" He retrieved the crumpled Post-it. "Someone stuck this on my computer." He smoothed it out on the desktop.

The guard bent to study it, his face hidden by the cap's peak. Lance took the opportunity to scan the lobby, check that no fellow marketers were afoot.

The guard smiled. *No worries,* said the smile, *problem solved.* He pointed to a corner of the lobby from which a passageway extended. Above it was a hand-painted sign, old and chipped, containing a single word, a long one. "Cafeteria's that way," said the guard.

"Oh, good. Thanks."

"Glad to be of assistance." The guard started touching things on his control panel, his peak-hidden face glancing from side to side. The message was clear: *We're done.*

But Lance needed more. He lingered until the guard looked up with a scowl.

"Well, see, I'm hoping you can help me understand this a bit more."

The guard looked irritably at the note. "Well, I don't have any idea who Elena is, if that's what you're wondering."

Elena. The etymologist. Lance took a second to find his voice. "But, um, you have such a good memory for names. Elena... she's not that easy to forget."

"Sure, I know people who work here, but not every cute girl in the city."

Lance let this go. No point questioning the guard's memory for names—a talent he obviously held dear. "Okay, then, hmm. I wonder what Elena wants."

"Beyond the obvious, you mean?" The guard smirked. "What do you think I do here, pal? Does the sign on my desk say *Relationship Counsellor*?" He pointed to a brass plaque.

Lance laughed feebly.

"Or maybe it says *Psychic*? *Secrets of the Heart Revealed*?"

Lance tried but failed to reboot the laughter.

"Well? Does it?"

"Of course not," mumbled Lance. "I just—"

"Well? What does the sign on my desk say?" The guard's patience was evaporating. This banter could not last.

"*Security,*" Lance said, giving the plaque a passing glance.

"Well, actually, it says *Protection Services,*" said the guard, apparently proud of the distinction. "Anyway, you get my point. I can't tell you anything more than what this note says. It's not exactly written in code, and if it is I can't crack it for you. Now, if you'll excuse me, I've got plenty of—"

Lance interrupted with what he knew was his final stab. "But when you say 'the obvious'—what exactly do you mean?"

Okay, bro, said the guard's face, *now you're being a downright jerk. Enough with this dumbass game.* But he didn't leave it at that. Fortunately for Lance, the guy was clearly enamoured of his own voice, and one more time he let it ring out: "The obvious, meaning..." He checked the creased yellow scrap. "Meaning that on Monday, at noon, in the cafeteria, this Elena wants you to meet up with her. Beyond that, Mr. Blunt, I don't know any more than you." The guard jabbed the Post-it with a fingertip and slid it toward Lance. "Congratulations, pal. Seems you got yourself a date."

Chapter 4

Lance expected further instruction. He antici-pated some on-the-job training, Ms. Shillingsham standing over his shoulder, Mr. Furlanetti burbling in the corner. He braced for the hard sweats he'd break into when someone pointed to a list of written instructions or handed him a binderful of departmental guidelines. Pronouncements had been made that he would be given HR material, orientation packages, to-do lists. But his first week passed, and nothing like that happened. Once or twice, Ms. Shillingsham showed up with files she wanted him to go through.

"Go through?"

"Yes," she repeated, "go through. If you don't mind."

"And then?"

"And then nothing. Just go through them, please."

And so he flipped through the pages, understanding nothing of what they said, and piled them on a corner of his desk. He worried about follow-up, questions he might have to field about the files' contents. But those questions never came. So Lance sat in his office and tried not to pry into the personal effects of Jeanine. He watched the mist move outside his window.

And he attended meetings. Every day that first week, for big reasons or small, the sales and marketing department gathered in that windowless room, sat around that conference table, the knitting woman knitting, Mr. Hutchman exclaiming vehemently, everyone weighing in on topics of unimaginable tedium: Whether it was okay to sign letters to clients using unconventional colours of ink. What flavours of tea should be stocked in the kitchenette. Whether subsequent meetings should begin two minutes before the hour, to encourage punctuality.

During these torturous confabs, when Lance feared the boredom might literally corrode portions of his brain, he distracted himself with thoughts of his upcoming appointment with Elena Wright. He visited and revisited the few images of her he had—the flash of her green eyes, the haphazard fall of her hair, the hints of a figure under her workaday clothes. The look that had come over her face when he asked her to tell him the roots of a word. It was a look he wanted to revive.

On Friday Ms. Shillingsham showed up at his door wielding a fat leather-bound book. "Your complimentary copy."

He waited, expecting her to carry it across the room to him, but she stood paralyzed at the threshold. So he rose, came to the door, and accepted the book.

She turned to go, but Lance's voice halted her: "Um, is there like a mailing address for Jeanine or something?"

Ms. Shillingsham's shoulders clenched. Rather than turning to face Lance, she directed her answer out into the hallway. "No," she said. "We have no way of contacting Jeanine."

"Because, uh, there's this photo? On the desk? Must be hers."

Ms. Shillingsham turned now. She ran one fingertip beneath her eye. "I think you'll find," she said quietly, "that your office has a waste bin..." She pointed at a pair of plastic buckets in one corner, next to the shedding tree. "...a recycling bin... all the usual receptacles."

"Oh, sure, I'll just throw it out. If you think that's okay."

"I think that will be fine."

Lance went to his desk and laid the dictionary on the lacquered pine surface. He ran his fingers over the embossed cover. It was different from the copy in the Blunt household—the leather was thicker, bumpier, more like the skin of a reptile. The pages had golden edges and thumb tabs so you could easily find a certain letter. He lifted the thick cover. Its inside was marbled, like the interior of an oyster shell. He opened deeper, found a page in the middle. He stared into the dense blocks of words. On these two pages alone, such a wealth of information! So much vocabulary, meaning, power! The columns of text were solid and imposing, pillars of a mighty temple. He imagined a life in which he could look past their shapes, see them as more than unyielding blocks of matter. He imagined he could see the words.

It was as if some kind of veil, the thinnest skin of fabric, lay over his vision, blurring each word. Through a gap in the veil, he might discern a letter, no problem: here an *e*, there a *w*. But the next letter was hazy until he focused on it. He could not take in a sequence of letters as a single unit; he could not make that magical leap in understanding, where a stack of bricks at once cohered into a tower. Numbers were never a problem; a clock face contained no mystery. The symbols of math and traffic signage had always been legible. It was words that were denied him. His whole life, all twenty-five years of it, this was how it had been.

After Blunt Furnishings was bought out, and Lance's mother was killed by her cancer—*lost the battle,* as his dad said, although it didn't seem like much of a battle when the cancer was so fast and decisive; more like a running up of the white flag and lying down in the trench to die—after all these sudden and cataclysmic changes in the Blunt family, Lance's dad sold the house and moved them into a two-bedroom apartment *away from all these memories, Lance—we don't need to wallow in the pain, to remember every day how she's gone.* Between distressing bouts of coughing—it was in the lungs that his own cancer had started, those years of smoking claiming their toll—Lance's father concerned himself with how Lance was going to get by, *how you'll find your own two feet.* There was still plenty of money left from the sale of the store and then the house, but medical bills had taken their chunk. The money would not last forever.

One afternoon, returning from a failed visit to a work-today, paid-today office, Lance came home to dim light filtering through the gauzy curtains and his father's voice coming at him scratchy and weak: "A postcard came for you, son."

"Me? Are you sure?"

"On the big table."

When they moved from the house, the enormous dining room table was the only piece of furniture Lance's father didn't sell off. It was sturdy oak Arts and Crafts number, originally purchased to be sold at Blunt Furnishings but instead claimed by Blunt Sr. himself. Where it had been scuffed and seared, he had lovingly refinished it. It was laden with memories—all those meals, birthdays, squabbles, etymologies, wisecracks, shootings of the shit. Lance's mother had kept it adorned with an arrangement of candles or flowers, placed in the centre, on top of the macramé runner she had made. The three places had been carefully set with old silverware, an heirloom from her own mother. The fourth, uninhabited spot would be heaped with supplies for whatever project she had on the go: knitwear she'd donate to the Salvation Army when it was done; Christmas tree decorations cobbled together from household detritus; in earlier years, before Lance's literacy was given up for lost, some teaching aid she'd read about in a how-to book—a stack of colourful flashcards, a vocabulary board game.

But now the macramé runner was long gone and the teaching aids were tossed, except for one flashcard, depicting *lion* and *brave*, that Lance had stowed in his bedroom. Meals were downed in front of the TV, and the table had become a repository for all the crap that Lance's dad couldn't find a place for. This included a small mountain of mail, most of it unopened.

At its peak was a single sheet of cardboard with a photo of the downtown skyline. Lance flipped it over, recognized his name—or at least its first and final letters, the *L* and *e*. The letters were faint and jagged. An unsteady hand had written them. "What does it say?" he asked.

"It's about a job opportunity."

"You're serious?"

"Someone who knows your work at the store."

"What's the job?"

A pause. "Sales and marketing department."

"Whose?"

"Emberton Tower. Where they make the dictionary."

"This doesn't sound right, Dad."

"I know." His father stirred in his bed and his cough resounded, the sound of a spent ignition turning over and over, for a motor that was never going to start. "Bring it here, would you?"

Lance shuffled into the bedroom. His socks picked up bits of carpet lint. When they first moved in, his dad had hired a cleaning lady once a week. But that early extravagance fell away as the savings dwindled, and now she only came every couple of months.

His father took the card in his ashen hand. His expression said, *What other options do you have?* He used his index finger to find the last part of the message and read out loud: "Lance may face a particular difficulty. Its resolution waits for him in Emberton Tower."

Lance snorted. "Sounds like a fortune cookie." But his derision was a bluff—the words had set his heart pounding. *Particular difficulty.* Was it possible somebody out there knew about his problem? And—more stunning yet—could it be true that somewhere in Emberton Tower, that fortress of language, the solution awaited him? It was too crazy to believe. It was too crazy to ignore.

And here he was. Employed at the Tower, installed in his own office. And no solution in sight.

He found a gap on the bookshelf, a vacancy between two of Jeanine's old tomes, and pushed them farther apart to make room for the Emberton. Something lay curled in the gap; with one finger, he pulled it free, leaving a tiny trail in the thick dust. It was a long, blond hair. Jeanine's.

Toward one end—the root—the blond faded into an ash grey.

Without knowing exactly why, Lance shuddered. He let the hair drop to the floor, but it didn't land right away—it twirled lazily in its descent, momentarily latching itself to Lance's trousers at the shin, before he brushed it free and it settled on the grey carpet.

Lance slotted the dictionary into place.

Friday ended, a weekend of excruciating anticipation passed—all he could think of was the crisp yellow Post-it and the request it reportedly bore—and Monday morning arrived. At eleven, Lance was hauled into a touch-base meeting that exceeded the human capacity for endurance. An hour was devoted to deciding whether they should ask maintenance to fix the water fountain, which had been busted for weeks. Consensus was reached, and something was decided, sort of: the marketers agreed that the maintenance department was not going to react well to a glut of requests, and that they should "pick their spots" and wait until they had a more pressing request, so that it might be answered unbegrudgingly. Eye contact was established between the marketers; nervous nods were exchanged.

Just as his watch's minute hand was creeping toward twelve, where its hour hand already firmly resided, Ms. Shillingsham turned to him. "How about some input from you, Lance?"

"Look, I'm really sorry, but I have to get downstairs. I went ahead and booked a lunch meeting with a client."

It took several moments for the room to process this. Lance could hear each tick his watch made, could almost feel its vibration on his wrist.

Ms. Shillingsham was the first to shake off her shock. "You're cultivating clients already?"

"Yeah." Lance wasn't sure why he'd lied, but this did feel like a more impressive excuse than *I'm supposed to grab lunch with this woman and, well, she's pretty damn alluring, and there's no way I can be up here with you talking about water fountains when she's down there waiting for me, and who knows how long she'll wait, and even now I can see her there, in whatever sort of place that cafeteria even is—I'm imagining it maybe with candles on the table and a bottle of wine.* It seemed a better idea to go with *client.*

"Who is it?"

"Just a contact I... Someone I knew in, um, retail. I thought I should check and see that they stock our dictionary for their shop. Of books. Bookshop, that is."

Various strangled noises from the marketers.

"A bookseller!" thundered Ms. Shillingsham. "Is it one of the big players? We've been having problems in our contract with Folios, it would be lovely if you had an inside edge...?"

"No, just... um, a small shop. Just this one person runs it."

"An independent? I wasn't aware there were any left."

"Yeah, and anyway, I have to be at the cafeteria at twelve, so..."

"The cafeteria?" shrieked Mr. Hutchman. "Good God, man, whyever there? Do you *want* to blow the sale?"

"I haven't been down there in years," the knitting woman said.

"And after just a week on the job," continued Mr. Hutchman, fondling his cravat, "our young friend braves its offerings."

"Go easy, now," said Ms. Shillingsham. "He's learning

the ropes. For future reference, Lance, the cafeteria doesn't serve the sort of cuisine that will impress clients."

"It stinks," Mr. Hutchman affirmed.

"Going forward," continued Ms. Shillingsham, "I would recommend that meetings be arranged for another venue."

"Okay," said Lance. "Good to know."

"Anyway," said Ms. Shillingsham, "you can contribute your thoughts on this discussion another time. A meeting with a flesh-and-blood client is nothing to take lightly! Off with you."

He stopped at the water fountain that had provoked the marathon discussion. He turned the tap; nothing happened. But then a splutter from deep in the machine's guts, and a fountain of water burst forth. Lance let it run a bit before he put tentative lips to the gush. It tasted corrupt somehow. He spat it from his mouth. A string of something dark was in his saliva as it swirled down the drain.

Lance descended to a lobby swarming with lexicographers— most made a beeline for the exits; those who'd sneaked out early returned bearing bags of fast food. The revolving door hummed. Through the blur of passing bodies, he could see the glow of the fireplace. On the mantelpiece sat a row of leather-bound Embertons. The security guard was busy talking to someone at his desk. Lance passed under the hand-painted sign, travelled down a short hallway, and stepped into a large room.

Back when the cafeteria was designed—probably half a century ago, judging by the decor—the planners must have been optimistic about how many Emberton employees would choose to eat here. The dining area, carpeted with a lurid square of something like Astroturf, was large enough for a couple dozen circular tables ringed with eight chairs each. But a grand total of seven lonely souls had chosen this as the venue for today's lunch. Each sat alone, far from the others.

The decor was faux tropical. Descending from the rafters, orange lights on stalks cast a very poor approximation of sunlight. An escarpment of plastic rock jutted from one wall, and a waterfall plunged into a pool where goldfish darted, aimless and sad. A palm tree adorned one corner of the pond. Its trunk had a run, like a stocking. Past this jungle diorama was the room's only window, a large square pane showing fog beyond.

Under dusty sneeze guards, food awaited selection. Sandwiches wrapped in saran. Shuddering squares of jelly. A giant bald man spooned soup into bowls—way more bowls than this near-empty joint could possibly sell in an afternoon. But the man kept ladling.

Lance had been startled by the warnings of his colleagues, but he was hungry. Setting his fears aside, he selected a sandwich. It maybe had meat: between the thin slabs of bread was a mess of yellow sauce and off-white chunks. Something was written on a label stuck onto the saran wrap, but of course that was no help. He checked out the selection of hot dogs—chubby, sweaty thumbs jabbed on rotating spindles inside a heated glass box. Beneath them, on an expanse of tinfoil, grease droppings pooled. Lance turned from that display and instead augmented his sandwich with a brownie.

The cash register was unmanned. Lance cleared his throat. The giant remained fixated on his ladling.

"Heavens to Betsy!" A woman on crutches had emerged

from the kitchen. She made her way toward Lance, one bandaged foot lifted from the tiled floor. Behind her, a large door swung, revealing intermittent glimpses of cooking equipment streaked with grease.

With a final lurch, the woman reached the till and laid her crutches against the countertop. Huffing, sweaty, she glared at Lance and pointed to a silver service bell sitting off to the side. "You coulda rung! Jeez!"

"Sorry," Lance said, "I didn't see it."

"Heavens to Betsy." She jabbed the till. Money changed hands. She retrieved her crutches and hobbled back toward the kitchen, turning to splutter, "Next time, ring the bell!"

Lance sat at an unoccupied table. Still no sign of Elena. Maybe her department liked to hold long meetings too. He unwrapped his sandwich and lifted one limp half. The taste was okay, but the texture was terrifying. Slick and soft, slightly oozing to the bite. Lance willed it down his throat.

Once it was safely down, Lance returned his attention to the room's entrance. And there she was: Elena Wright, pausing at the entrance and looking over her shoulder before heading for the service area. Suddenly aware that he probably should have waited for her before starting his meal, Lance folded the sopping saran wrap back over the bitten part of his sandwich. He watched Elena select a drink from the milk fridge, the sides of her cardigan falling forward; watched the tilt of her head as she talked with the lady at the till, a conversation that was clearly going better than Lance's had. Bearing a tray, Elena wove among the tables to reach Lance.

Her lunch was a carton of chocolate milk and a salad of spinach leaves with a few halved cherry tomatoes bleeding onto the greens. "Thanks for coming," she said, setting it down. "I don't think I was spotted."

The few other diners focused on their lunches or paperbacks or crosswords. One fellow stared deep into a ceramic mug, as if he had downloaded movies into it.

She opened the plastic shell containing her salad and cast a pitying glance at Lance's ample meal. "I should have warned you: the eating part was a decoy. This is the perfect spot for a private meeting, because everyone stays away. It's not so ideal for an actual lunch." She took in the room, its few and far-flung patrons. "Okay. To the matter at hand. I need your help."

"With etymology?"

"God, no. The less etymology I have to deal with, the better." She made a *work, yuck, let's talk about something else* face. Lance was disappointed. He thought back to his father, forefinger planted on the dictionary page, declaring the origin of a word. "*Manure,*" he'd cry, "comes from the Old French for *manoeuvre*. And all this time I thought it came from a cow!" Lance would listen, puzzle over how the word's evolution would have played out over the centuries. Language would appear in his mind's eye as a tangled garden—the visible flower was the word used today, but it was only the tip; beneath was the long stem, leaves sprouting in all directions, and below that the reaching roots and somewhere, deep in the soil, the single seed, the origin.

"No," said Elena, "I need your help with something else entirely. But tell me: your visit to the top floor. What was that about?" She speared a bit of salad and brought it cautiously to her lips.

"Mr. Emberton wanted to say hi."

She raised an eyebrow. "He's not the sort of man who

goes around saying hi. Most people who work here have never even seen him."

"He wanted me to feel welcome. We had a drink. Shot the breeze."

She whistled. "That's... Wow. You've got his attention. No mean feat."

"Sure, I guess. He knows who I am."

"I have a feeling we could help each other." She leaned closer. "I want to find out what Emberton is really about."

"The man?"

"Everything. The company. The Tower."

"Well, uh, it's a dictionary, isn't it?"

She slapped her palm on the table. "Lance, look around! This is not a normal dictionary. A dictionary doesn't need to occupy a whole Tower, with full-time staff for every little detail."

"Why not? I mean, it's a big deal. It's the most important book, right? It tells you about all the words that make all the other books."

"It's the least important book! It's nothing but a... I don't know, a snapshot. A cross-section. A bunch of words in current usage. It doesn't tell a story, doesn't do anything. It's no more a book than a dishwasher manual's a book. They're both useful, but..." She appeared suddenly embarrassed by the passion of her rant, the crescendo of her voice. Colour had come into her cheeks. One of her hands had curled into a loose fist.

Lance didn't mind. "Go on," he said.

Her voice was subdued now. "My point is that this whole enormous endeavour of making the Emberton Dictionary is a ruse. Something more than lexicography is going on in this Tower."

Lance took a bite of his brownie, which crumbled dramatically. "So what is it?"

From a pocket inside her cardigan she produced a piece of paper. "Check this out." After lowering her head to check the surface of the table for cleanliness, she laid the document flat and smoothed it. "On loan from the company archives. Well, unofficial loan. I smuggled it out. But here, take a look. Tell me what you see."

What Lance saw was a typeset page from the dictionary: those grand columns of text, each entry headed with a single word in bold, a bunch of inscrutable print jammed in beneath it. But splashed over this orderly typography was a bright mess of scribbled notes in various shades of ink—red, black, magenta, lime, jay blue.

"Notice anything odd?" Elena asked.

Lance's pulse was heavy in his ears. Surely there was something obvious, something she expected him to read in that mass of jottings. And he was going to fail to do so. He could discern one thing, though: each colour of ink had a different look to its letters. The magenta was tight, ferocious; the lime-green lines looped in wide, relaxed curves. "Well, obviously," he tried, "a bunch of people have written all over it. That's odd."

"This is how they used to hash out content," she said. "A proof was passed from editor to editor. Everyone weighed in." She tapped the page with her fingertip. "But take a closer look."

Lance did, but now he wasn't searching anymore. He knew he was doomed to miss what she was going to point out. "Well," he said in a low voice, "it's weird they used different colours."

"Not really," said Elena. "It helped distinguish each editor's input. But look at what they actually wrote."

The hum of distant refrigerators intensified. The page had blurred. God, not again. After all these years, you'd think he'd be used to this. But he still had to well up every time.

"You all right?" Elena was frowning at him, but on her face he saw no trace of disdain, nothing mocking or unkind. She could see he was in distress and she was concerned. Her eyebrows made the most extraordinary shape as she frowned, like those holes they put in violins. She was more enchanting than ever, even through the blur of his emerging tears.

But he could not take the risk. He could not confide in her.

"Okay," she said, "here." Her voice had a hint of impatience now, and with a sinking heart Lance was taken back to first grade, to his teacher, Miss Wilkins, who wore shapeless flowing skirts and on the first day had yanked the desks from their traditional rows and arranged them in one big circle, "for community." When someone lagged in a subject, she assigned a smart student to help, and they would perform a little tutoring session in one corner of the circle (because in fact the circle was more like a jagged square) while the rest of the class, the average middle, plodded through the lesson at the regular pace. And so Lance had been stuck in the corner with Hailee Carter, her chestnut hair adorned with a tidy pink barrette. And Lance had been flooded with gratitude for Hailee when she sat beside him with a cheerful let's-get-it-done energy and led him phonetically through a string of words. And then, as it became evident she'd never be able to help him, never dispel the fog, impatience edged into her voice, tinged with disbelief—how hard it was to break through to this oaf, how clearly she was wasting her time!

And here, a subtle echo of Hailee's impatience. Elena slid the paper so that, rather than facing him exclusively, it was balanced between them. She pointed at a word entry. "'*Tetraplicity*,'" she read. "'The state of having four parts.'" She pointed to the red scribble beside it. "'Omit. Barbaric coinage, sure to go extinct.'"

"Barbaric coinage?"

Elena laughed softly. "A bit of bombast from that editor. He—or she, there were a few women editors back then—didn't like to see Latin and Greek jammed together. Maybe *quadraplicity* would have met with his approval."

"Huh," said Lance. "My dad used to say the same thing."

"He used the word *tetraplicity*?"

"No, I mean, he didn't like it if the dictionary included words with roots from different languages, all mixed up. *Tangled roots*, he'd call it."

"What kind of work did he do?"

"Sold furniture."

"Really. A furniture seller after my own heart."

I hope he won't be the only one, Lance almost said out loud.

"But language does what it does. It's inexorable; no one can impose their pet peeves on it. By the time these editors were scrawling on this proof, *television* had already been coined, along with other mixed-root words. Life went on. Earth was not shattered." Elena's finger slid along the page. Another comment, in blue. "'Keep this,'" she read. "'Appeared twice in newspapers this week, in context of Bennett-Stevens policy rift. May have staying power.'"

"So the editors disagreed."

"Yep. Par for the course. But now check this out." Her fingertip found a new word. "*Tetracylia*," she read. "A healthy balance of the humours." She pointed to the single scrawl beside it: faint and jagged, plain black. "Withhold," she read.

"That's it?"

"That's all it says. As you can see, no one wrote anything further. No one argued, no one talked back. Pretty unusual for these editors not to have any opinions at all."

"Tell me about it. I've met a couple of them."

"I'm hoping," Elena said, "you can help me discover what happened to these words marked *withhold*. The other ones, the *omit* ones, they're just like any other word that gets rejected from a dictionary. You can find them in old source texts, and in later ones too—sometimes the editors were wrong, a word did become prominent after all. But the withhold words... those vanish. It's like they never existed. You can sift through old texts, you can search the Emberton archives to see what the sources were—but you won't find anything." She straightened and surveyed the cavernous room. "Something impossible happened to those words: they were exterminated. Wiped from human history."

"Why?"

"That's what I want to find out. But I've gone as far as I can by myself. I need a partner. Someone with different connections, different access. Someone who hasn't already outstayed his welcome." She bit her lower lip and looked anxiously at Lance, sizing him up. "So my question is, are you with me?"

Lance nodded, too breathless to speak.

"Wonderful." She smiled, but it was fleeting—a frown promptly replaced it. "We have to be discreet, though. We can't discuss this over phone or email; those can be monitored. What I need you to do," she said, lowering her voice further, "is carve out some time when you can get away and meet me at the archives, on the eleventh floor. How about tomorrow morning? Eleven?"

Obviously, his answer was going to be yes. But Elena's constant checking over her shoulder, the secret meeting in a derelict cafeteria, the insistence that they not email each other or use the phone... Lance wanted to spend time with a happier, less paranoid Elena. There was a particular image he held in her mind, of her face doused with eagerness, possibility, her green eyes wide, her mouth parting to answer a question—up in her office, during his tour, when he asked her to provide him an etymology. That was the Elena he longed to see more of.

"Tell you what," he said. "I would love to help you. But there's something I need from you first."

Apparently this was a terrifying thing to have said. Colour fled from her face.

But Lance pressed on. "Before we go to the archives, we'll meet here—"

She cut him short with a vigorous shaking of her head. Her eyes were downcast. "We can't meet in the same place twice," she said. "Not if we can help it. We can't let them see a pattern."

"'Them' who?"

"Security guards. Whoever else watches the surveillance footage; I don't know. We have to be careful. Stay under the radar."

"Okay. So how about we meet somewhere else at eleven. We sneak out of the Tower and hook up at a café. Grab a coffee."

"I can't."

Lance was botching this. Inexperience left him ill-equipped for setting up a date.

"Literally," she was saying. "I literally can't."

"All I want," he said, trying in vain to keep the exasperation from his voice, "is for you to teach me an etymology. Tell me the story of one word. And then I'll do whatever you want me to."

Her shoulders, which Lance noticed had gone rigid during the last exchange, relaxed. Colour returned in ragged patches to her cheeks. "One word."

"Yeah. I love etymology. I'd like to hear it straight from the source."

She laughed. "The source."

"An expert. Someone who knows what she's talking about."

"And that's the price? Of getting you to help?"

"That's my fee. One word."

She toyed with her plastic fork. Lance watched the hesitant motion of her small fingers. No jewellery. Unpolished nails, a bit jagged around the fringes. Chewed.

"Fine," she said. "One word. Meet me tomorrow at eleven o'clock on the third floor. There's a place there we can talk."

"Third floor." This was Lance's equivalent of taking notes. Repeat what the other person said, inscribe it on his brain.

"Yes. You want to turn left after you get off the elevator. Immediately. Don't go straight ahead, whatever you do."

"Turn left when I get off." He paused, mentally inscribing. Then: "And don't go straight ahead? Why not?"

"Straight ahead is the infirmary. You do not want to go into the infirmary."

"Third floor. Turn left." Then, for good measure: "I do not want to go into the infirmary."

"Follow the corridor all the way. There's a garden there, tucked away. Nice and private." She was back to her furtive mode. She turned one way in her seat and then the other, taking in the room. The giant stood at his post, ladling. The cashier's crutches leaned against the till as she tinkered with the sandwich display. All the other customers were gone. "We shouldn't leave together," said Elena. "I'll go first. You wait five minutes, just to be safe."

"Got it."

"And Lance?"

"Yep?"

"Thank you." She touched his forearm. Then she was up and away, bag over her shoulder, weaving among the chairs. Watching her go, Lance pushed his tray to one side, with its meal he would never finish.

Tomorrow, eleven, third floor. Turn left. He had this.

Chapter 5

Tomorrow arrived. The morning oozed by—Lance frequently caught himself staring at his watch, trying to mentally nudge it forward. A full two hours expired, and somehow, by some miracle of the highest order, Lance was not summoned to a meeting. No excuses needed; no partial truths or out-and-out lies. He was free to slip into the elevator at five to eleven for the short ride down.

On the third storey, the elevator doors opened to a square of frosted glass bearing a large red cross. Through that translucent surface, Lance could see a huddle of shapes, like miniature Stonehenge boulders. Then one of the shapes moved. They were people.

As he turned left and started down the corridor, his motion caused the square of glass to part, its two halves sliding open. Beyond, he could see a stretch of white tiled wall. The doors slid shut, and the cross was once again complete.

The corridor went several paces before turning ninety degrees right; he was making his way around the outside of the infirmary, which was windowless. Another turn brought a sudden incursion of daylight through floor-to-ceiling windows. Grass grew from the floor and flowers proliferated neatly in their beds. A gnarled apple tree stood near the windows, pruned to fit the room. And there, nestled between two thick roots, a book spread on the grass in front of her, sat Elena.

She wore a white blouse and a tan corduroy skirt. She didn't look up as Lance approached; she closed her book and slid it into the purse sitting beside her on the grass. "You made it."

"Here I am." Lance sat beside her. On the nearest flowerbed, blossoms—dusky red, purple, ash white—sprang from limp stems bent low to the dirt. Unflowering vines tangled along the surface of the soil. "That smell," said Lance.

"Sweet."

"Too sweet. It can't be just these flowers, can it?"

"Chemicals of some kind," said Elena. "Fertilizer."

Lance craned to take in the branches above them. "How do you even get a tree in here? Don't the roots have to go deep?"

Elena shrugged. "I guess you can breed them not to."

The light changed as clouds slithered over the sun. When the shade reached the flowerbed, the blossoms lost their colour. Grey reigned.

"So," he said. "My word."

"Pick one."

Lance hadn't anticipated this. His brain jammed. The motor overheated; the gears fused. Not a word came to him. He looked at this green stuff, which consisted of blades and sprang from dirt and was all around them and beneath them where they sat. It had a name. What was its name?

Elena was watching, waiting.

Lance was willing his brain to ease back into motion.

The greyness outside intensified. More than clouds, now: that pervasive mist was back.

Elena shifted her position.

This distracted Lance, drew his attention long enough to ease his brain and let the word pop free. "Grass!" he shouted, much more loudly and suddenly than he would have liked.

Elena didn't flinch from this barked word. Her response was immediate, delivered in a fast monotone: "*Grass*. From the Proto Indo European *ghros*, for 'grow' or 'become green.'"

"That's it?"

"What, you wanted something more?"

"There's got to be some origin better than that. A really good one. Like, with a story behind it."

"I can't think of one."

"There's got to be..." He waved at the tree, the flowerbed. "Somewhere in this whole room there's got to be a word with a story."

She too looked around. Her eyes fastened on the glass walls, the world outside. Lance looked there too. Through thickening mist, the nearest building showed itself only in haphazard swaths. When Elena turned back, her eyes were alight. "Okay. Here's one. *Hazy*."

"*Hazy*."

"Yes. Indistinct, vague, unfocused, unclear."

"Perfect. How did we get the word *hazy*?"

"Okay. You know John Cabot?"

"Does he work here?"

"Cabot was an English explorer in the fourteen hundreds. First European after the Vikings to set foot in Newfoundland."

79

"Right, of course. That guy."

"So when he was over here, he kidnapped a Beothuk man."

"Beothuk?"

"The Beothuk were a people native to Newfoundland. Wiped out, eventually—the last of them died in the nineteenth century. Almost their entire language went with them."

"Brutal."

"It is. But if I told you that one of their words lived on, and actually crept into the language of the colonizers... that would be something, right? Some small compensation?"

"No. It totally wouldn't."

"You're right." She plucked a blade of grass, looked at it for a moment, flung it away. "It wouldn't. The story wouldn't fix anything."

At first Lance thought she was gathering her thoughts, marshalling her memory of how *hazy* entered the language. But the silence stretched longer than seemed right. "And...?" he prodded.

"You still want your etymology? Even though it's useless?"

Lance felt he should be apologizing, but he wasn't sure exactly what for. Through a furious blush, he stammered, "Yes, yeah, totally. Please. I want to hear it."

Seeing his confusion, she laid a hand on his arm. "Sorry, don't worry. I do want to keep going. Where were we?"

"John Cabot just kidnapped a guy."

"Yes. Right. So he captured this Beothuk man and hauled him aboard his ship. He was going to take him back to England and parade him before the royal court. But on the voyage back, the ship was beset by fog. The Beothuk prisoner became very agitated, and started yelling: '*Heze! Heze!*'"

"This is a Native word?"

"It's Beothuk for *omen,* but its etymology goes back to Europe." Elena had a distant look on her face now, as if she were trying to recall a dream. The tip of her ring finger rested on her lips. "Long before Cabot, Vikings came over. They traded with the natives, but sometimes those encounters went bad. There were slaughters. The Vikings had a variety of battle cries. One of them was *hurrâ*, a hunting shout derived from Middle High German, meaning 'hurry, go!' Hunters in Europe would shout it when they spotted their prey. The Vikings started to use it when they spied the village they were going to plunder, or the locals they were going to disembowel. Another, friendlier, derivation is *hurray*."

"*Hurray*," said Lance. "That comes from chopping up villagers?"

"It does. And that Viking word must have left its mark on the Beothuk. They associated it with a terrible fate about to strike. It seeped into the language as *heze*, and by the time Cabot arrived it was well-established. Altered phonetically, but the same word.

"The Beothuk believed that doing something truly terrible, a real atrocity, could prompt the vengeance of the gods. Sometimes the vengeful god would arrive in the form of a thick fog. The fog would approach and engulf the scene of the crime, and under its cover justice would be done. So here's this ship, completely fogged in. The crew could not see each other; the watchman in his crow's nest could not even see his own hand. Over and above the crew's cries to one another, the only sound was the repeated shrieking of '*Heze! Heze!*' And then the clanking of chains, and then a loud splash.

"When the fog rose, the Beothuk man was gone. His chains lay loose at the base of the post they'd tied him to. Beside them lay a crew member, dead—the cruellest one, the one who'd made it his personal mission to torment and harm the prisoner. His skin was eaten away, like he'd been doused in acid.

"From then on, whenever a heavy fog descended, the crew would start to mumble the word below decks. '*Heze,*' they'd say. 'This means trouble.' From the pinpoint of that single ship, the word bled out into the seafaring world. Over the years the connotation of menace fell away, and *hazy* meant, simply, 'foggy.'"

They were quiet for a moment.

"All that, in one word?" said Lance.

"Yes."

"Incredible," said Lance.

"Yes, that would be one way to describe it." She plucked a blade of grass and inspected it. "Okay, then. I've paid your fee, right? We're ready for the archives?"

Lance was not ready to stop listening to her voice. He was not ready to have her rise from this peaceful place and lead him to a room stuffed with papers and written words. He wanted to sink deeper into this grass, recline with her, let her talk as long as she wanted, let the sky outside the glass walls darken until they were together under the stars. But a deal was a deal. He'd been lucky to convince her to talk to him this long.

"The archives," he said. "Let's do it."

In front of them was a vast metal wall. Its smooth, implacable face was broken only by a door like that of a bank vault, complete with a large spoked handle like the steering wheel of an old ship. Mounted on the wall was a number pad. Elena punched it. The door moaned. Its handle clanked through two rotations. Thuds resounded as bolts slid into position. Then the whole monstrous contraption swung open.

Lance had never had occasion to visit a morgue, but he had seen enough TV to know this room resembled one. It was cold and dim. Large metal drawers were set into cabinets. A polished steel counter ran from wall to wall.

Elena dinged the service bell. A man transpired from the gloom. Like a tombstone, his face was flat, grey, and engraved with lines. All his clothes were black. His feet, shod in patent leather, were neatly aligned and pressed together. "Miss Wright," he said. "I see you've brought a guest."

Elena smiled and dropped her eyes. A flirtatious gesture. Lance felt a jealous pang. "Yes," she said, "and I'm really sorry, but I forgot to file the paperwork in time. He's helping me on a project—do you mind if we let him in this one time, even though he's not authorized?"

The archivist plucked a clipboard from the metal countertop.

"No need," said Elena, "for noting it down, is there? We're in a bit of a hurry."

The archivist's face twisted into a smile. A fit of giggles descending on a sea cucumber would have been less incongruous. "Just this once," he said. He pressed a button and a gateway swung open, letting Elena and Lance pass through the counter and into the gloom.

"Thank you," called Elena over her shoulder. They

passed dozens of metal drawers. Whenever they turned a corner, an automated bank of lights flicked to life, illuminating their path. Overhead, lamps dangled from white stalks, which rose into a tangle of hissing pipes and ducts. As he passed beneath them, Lance's head was caressed by little gusts. "The climate is strictly controlled," Elena said. "Have to keep the temperature and humidity just right, or the old documents will decay."

They stopped at an intersection; corridors lined with cabinets branched away straight ahead and to either side. Elena whispered, and Lance had to lean closer to hear. "All these drawers," she said, "are filled with files. And the files are bursting with documents. Taken together—if you can find the time to go through them, and I have plenty of time on my hands—they tell the story of Emberton. Most of it, anyway." She pointed to the left. A bank of lights illuminated about twelve feet of the corridor, but beyond that it was lost in shadow. "Further down there is a metal gate. The punch code won't open it. I managed to coax the archivist to tell me what's in there. It's the history of the Emberton family. Before they started this dictionary. Back through the generations. Only one person gets to see it."

"Who's that?"

She looked at him.

"Oh, of course. Stupid question."

"But I've read a great deal of what I can access. The story of the most venerable dictionary in the nation. The story of how it was built."

The lights overhead switched off: Lance and Elena had been motionless for too long. All Lance could hear, beyond the constant fussing of the ceiling, was his and Elena's breathing. His eyes began to adjust, and now he could see her silhouette, her head close to his. Her arms rose over her head and, like a flamenco dancer, she clapped twice in quick succession. The lights snapped on.

Her face, looking past him down the aisle, in the direction of the forbidden section, was rapturous. "I love to read. I read a ton. Anything I can get my hands on. But this... I've spent so many hours here. It's better than any library. If you want some intriguing reading material, this is the place to come."

"But you were saying before—you don't care for the dictionary all that much."

"The book itself, no. But this is different. The book is just a list of words. All the paperwork in here... this is a *story*." Her rapturous look faded, and she focused on Lance with a businesslike expression. "But the story has gaps. And I'm trying to fill them."

She opened a drawer, riffled through some files, and pulled out a sheaf of papers. She led Lance to a table, where she spread them out. "For show," she whispered. "So we appear to be at work on something. Now I'm going to go back to the front desk, keep the archivist occupied for a few minutes. I need you to go around that corner..." She pointed past the edge of a stack of cabinets. "Go to the drawer marked *Draft One Circulation, Edition Two*. Open it—carefully, one smooth motion so it doesn't make noise—and find the file labelled *Final Comments, Signature Fifty-Two*. Got that?"

"*Draft One Circulation, Edition Two*," repeated Lance. "*Final Comments, Signature Fifty-Two*."

"Slip the whole file inside your shirt or something. When we leave together, I'll distract the archivist again so he doesn't notice you're hiding something. Okay?" She tilted her head. "Something the matter?"

The words would not come. Not quickly, anyway. He had to frame them, find the right sequence, the right method of telling this woman—who surrounded herself with books, who lived in a different mental realm entirely—the whole truth.

"What is it?"

"Nothing." He couldn't do it. "All good."

She glided away, back through the maze of cabinets, bulbs flicking to life to light her way.

Lance went around the corner and confronted a wall of drawers. The ceiling huffed and sighed. His mouth was parched. Quietly as he could, he started opening drawers at random, peering at their contents. He might find a page that looked like the one she'd shown him in the cafeteria; or maybe he'd win the lottery and chance upon the one thing she was looking for. But all he saw were typed forms, brittle carbon paper sheets, sheaves of graph paper crammed with numbers. Nothing resembling the page Elena had laid out so lovingly on the cafeteria table. He started to flip through files in a panic, sweat breaking out on his face. Like a drunk, he fumbled on with only the merest awareness of what he was doing.

"Lance? Lance?" It was a half-whisper. She had returned, and was wondering why he was not back at the table, the file safely shoved under his shirt. He turned to her like a child caught in a forbidden act. His face swam in sweat. A half-dozen drawers stood open.

"I couldn't find it," he said.

She pointed to a drawer that Lance had not yet opened. "Right there."

She made no move to open it, so Lance slid it open himself.

"Final Comments, Signature Fifty-Two," she whispered.

He made a feeble show of flipping through the files.

"Hurry," she urged.

Metal glared all around him, a small, shiny realm, the darkness of the unlit passageways pressing against its borders. "I have something to confess," he whispered.

She was waiting, but his voice would not come out. A click, a drooping noise, and the ceiling went silent. Not only Elena but the room too was waiting, holding its breath. The documents in their files, the thousands of pages of history—they'd grown ears and pricked them up for this one occasion. Everything in this room was eager and ready to hear Lance Blunt humiliate himself.

"Elena, I don't know how to read."

Lance watched her eyes and facial muscles, the slope of her shoulders. The truth was, Lance *could* read. He could read a pair of eyes, the clenching at the corners of them. The muscles in a shoulder as it slouched forward or drew back. The motion of hands. The subtle inflections in a voice, and the inflections under those—the truth that the performance was hiding. He knew how to translate arms crossed on a chest, or a palm laid open on a tabletop. Understood the message in a bowed head or a crossed leg. People spoke a million ways, and Lance could read what they said—until they picked up a pen, or set their hands hovering over a keyboard. The only thing Lance failed to read was text.

And as he watched her face, the series of reactions—incomprehension; comprehension; surprise; alarm; wonder—he knew he'd found an ally. Someone who would not impulsively judge. As he observed the softening in her shoulders, the thoughtful tilt of her head, he saw that she might even *admire* him. For his fearless disclosure? (Not fearless, in fact, but forced.) For his landing this job, given his handicap? (Hardly admirable; it was a fluke for which he could not be credited.) But this moment, which he had so dreaded, was upon him, and it might not prove so disastrous after all.

"Oh," she said. But here was the beauty of the things he could read! Forget "oh," forget the sound her mouth had manufactured. That was nothing; that was the little black blip on a movie screen where the film got scratched. No meaning in the word. The meaning was in her tone, the trombone swoop of that one short word, and then the thing her face muscles did as she spoke it. With keen sympathy, Elena was taking the first few steps toward figuring Lance out. Which was to say, knowing Lance. Knowing him beyond what he lacked.

There were questions moving under her voice, of course—How did he function? How had he landed here, at Emberton Tower, of all places?—but she kept them at bay. He read the steadiness of her muscles as she willed the questions to subside.

She laid a gentle hand on his forearm. "All right," she said. She turned to the open drawer, her long fingers dancing over the tops of the files before plucking one folder free. She raised it triumphantly.

"Everything okay?" The archivist had approached with remarkable stealth. He stood framed by the morgue-like drawers, hands still invisible behind his back, eyes sliding from Elena to the various open drawers, and then, finding at last the culprit, to Lance.

Elena winced and laid the file on the table. "Had a bit of trouble," she said, her voice weak, "finding what we wanted."

"Evidently," said the archivist.

Lance didn't know what else to do: scuttling, he made his way one by one to the open drawers and slid them shut. The archivist watched; Elena stood frozen at the table, her hand resting on the coveted file.

"Many drawers," said the archivist.

"We had trouble," said Elena again.

"*I* had trouble," said Lance. It was intolerable that Elena, of all people, should shoulder the blame for his defect.

"Yes," said the archivist.

Lance noticed how each word the archivist spoke suggested a hundred others. It was like a stone dropped in a well: by the sound it made when it landed, it implied all the space and depth around it. This *yes* also said: *Your trouble will not be tolerated here. You should go. You should never have come.*

Elena was hearing it too. Her face had crumpled with disappointment. "I think," she said, her voice reduced to little more than a whimper, "I've got everything I needed. I'll just..." She didn't need to finish. As she hoisted the file, the rest of her sentence was clear: *...put this file back, and we'll go.*

The archivist kept pace behind them. Lance sensed rather than heard his footfalls, heavy and regular like the ticking of a grandfather clock. With each of those footfalls they got closer to the entrance, the desk, the elevator, Elena's disappointment dragging her shoulders into a defeated slouch, Lance's failure a familiar and loathsome odour rising from his skin. As they left the archives—for the last time, Lance was sure—the door was heaved shut behind them, and its inner bolts clanged thunderously shut.

"I'll see you back to your floor?" offered Lance.

"No. No, we have to separate. We can't raise suspicions."

Elena eyed the arrow above the elevator door. "I'll get in first. You wait for the next one."

"Are we going to try again?"

She shrugged. "I'll see if he'll let me back."

"And then we can…" Lance gave up on the question; it was too obvious how inappropriate it was to say *we*.

"I don't… I mean, how can you help? Everything I'm doing, everything I'm digging up…" The elevator door opened behind her. She stepped toward the empty car. "I don't think you can help me, Lance. I'm really sorry."

He couldn't stop himself. He gripped her shoulder, harder than he'd meant to, so she couldn't step forward. "We need to…" He let go of her and considered the best approach. "I screwed that up, and I'm so sorry. I should have told you about the reading thing, but… I… We need to talk. Somewhere… somewhere else. Like, safer. No one to overhear us."

"Somewhere else?"

"I mean we should go out. To talk. Somewhere that's not here."

He may as well have told her he needed to borrow a kidney. Her eyes widened and her head shook rapidly. "I told you before. I really can't."

"I'm not some idiot. It's…"

"I know you're not, Lance. I know it must be so hard."

"Just… you know, like briefly? A coffee or something?"

Her eyes were yet wider. "I told you, Lance. I literally can't." Then, as she stepped back and the doors closed on her: "Sorry."

Chapter 6

The days on floor four were long. The walls made their inscrutable noises. Sometimes the Tower trembled. From time to time Lance thought of a reason to visit Elena, some observation he'd made that he thought might interest her. Each time, he quailed; there were so many reasons not to travel to the ninth floor and seek her out. There was the fact that he hadn't discovered anything truly interesting about the Tower; what she wanted to learn was historical, buried in documents and blocks of print and therefore barred to Lance. There was the fact that she had explicitly forbidden visits and phone calls and (not that this made any difference) emails. But above all, there was the crushing humiliation. It was still raw, suppurating, and the prospect of seeing her face again—sympathetic though it had been; kindly as she had treated him—was too painful. He lacked not only an excuse to contact her; he lacked the courage.

So he sat through meetings and stewed in his shame while the marketers prattled on. He sat in his office as the light changed outside; he studied the grain of his desktop's glazed pine. He had yet to be given a single assignment that taxed him. He had yet to be caught out on his inability to read. Ms. Shillingsham brought files to "go through"; he put them in a drawer, where their stack inched slowly higher. He knew he should be grateful to have a job at all, let alone this one. But he was no closer to finding the help he'd been promised—however vaguely—he would find here.

Lance may face a particular difficulty. Its resolution waits for him in Emberton Tower. But so far, nothing. No suggestion at all that help was on the way.

On Monday of week three, as he stood over his potted tree (it now boasted a single surviving leaf) and pondered how to resuscitate it (he suspected the paper cups of water he'd carried in from the men's room had in fact been poisoning it), he became gradually aware of a strange noise. Something like the bubbles you hear working away at the edge of a fish tank. But slower, sludgy. Mr. Furlanetti was entering the room, belly-first. "Email," he said. "Set you up."

"Oh, yeah. Of course." This was supposed to have happened when he first arrived, but no one in the sales and marketing department, let alone Mr. Furlanetti, was a dervish of productivity.

He pointed at Lance's chair. "Up."

Lance rose. Mr. Furlanetti slouched across the office, settled into the vacated seat, and started prodding the computer keyboard. Lance had seen a variety of approaches to typing, from the assured clatter of veteran receptionists to the savage henpeck his father had employed, but he'd never seen anything this painfully slow. Mr. Furlanetti's doughy forefinger depressed one key, then hovered uncertainly while the rest of him gurgled and frowned, until finally the finger descended to press the next letter.

Mr. Furlanetti pulled a notepad and pen from his breast pocket. Pressing the pen hard into the paper, he wrote with giant, clumsy strokes. This process followed the same slow pace as his typing, and the tip of his tongue, slightly grey, protruded from between his lips. "Address, password," he said, planting a finger on the pad. He clambered from the chair. "Give it a try."

"A try?" Lance perched on the edge of his chair and eyed the notepad.

"Type them in. Check they work."

"Well, see, I'm kind of busy right now. I was about to—"

A meaty hand clamped on Lance's shoulder. "It will take ten seconds."

"But I'm really—"

"Ten seconds." The hand was not letting up.

Two things were written on the notepad. The first, Lance noticed, included the symbol @, which he knew was used in email addresses. Below that was a longer string of numbers and letters, presumably the password.

"Click there." Mr. Furlanetti pointed to an envelope icon.

"Sure thing." Theoretically, Lance knew how to operate a mouse, but he had never given it a try. He gripped it and dragged it toward him, painfully aware that a seasoned mouse user—that is to say, any normal person—would have quick, slick moves.

With the speed of a geriatric tortoise, the arrow made its way to the envelope. It arrived. Lance hit one of the buttons at the front of the mouse. Nothing happened. A long, quiet burble behind him. He tried not to trouble himself with what might be happening in Mr. Furlanetti's innards. He pressed the other button. A box popped up on the screen.

"Address, then password," said Mr. Furlanetti. Curiosity had crept into his tone.

Lance pretended to have a sudden itch on the back of his neck.

"Having trouble?" Mr. Furlanetti planted both hands on the edge of Lance's desk; the front of his belly spilled over the wooden surface. "Young guy like you? Trouble with computers?" The curiosity had given way to something like delight.

Lance looked at the scribbled line containing @.

"Read it okay?" inquired Mr. Furlanetti.

"All good."

The address began with *L*. Probably it included some portion of Lance's name, which, if he concentrated hard, he could spell out letter by letter. But he couldn't be sure. He'd have to look at each letter Mr. Furlanetti had printed, find the corresponding key on the keyboard, press it, look back up at the notepaper, repeat the process. He would have to do this without losing his place.

While he strategized, he scanned the keyboard for *L*.

"Don't like the address?" Mr. Furlanetti said with mock concern. "Want something better? Something more... *hip*?"

There was *L*. Lance depressed the key. "No," he said. "Thanks."

The second letter in his address was not *A*. Not *B* for Blunt. It was... Come on. He knew the damn letter, it was... Beside him, the burbling recommenced.

Sweat again. His cheap, crappy collar abraded his neck.

Mr. Furlanetti's fingers had begun to drum on the desktop. Lance tried to concentrate on the keyboard, but now he noticed that his companion too had started to sweat—a gooey sheen plastered his forehead.

"Yeah," said Lance, "the address is great. I just..."

"Yes?" Mr. Furlanetti's burbling grew more frantic. Body odour began to waft over Lance.

"Have to..." *M*. That was the next letter. Where the hell was it on the keyboard? Lance struck *H* by mistake, and had to break off the search for *M* and scan instead for some sort of... what did they call it... *backspace*.

A forceful expulsion of air from Furlanetti's nostrils. He was trembling now. "Look," he said. "Don't have all day."

"Sorry. Where's the backspace on this thing?"

A doughy finger jabbed at the keyboard, but missed the destination key and struck something else; suddenly the email program vanished altogether. "Damn," Mr. Furlanetti muttered, all ten fingers now colonizing the keyboard, scrabbling around to rectify his mistake. The email window bobbed back onto the screen.

"Thanks," said Lance. He tried to sound convincing, but forging cash would have been easier than faking gratitude at this point. The *L* was still onscreen, the cursor blinking to its right. He resumed his search for *M*.

"Look," erupted Mr. Furlanetti. "This... not..." A cataclysmic series of gurgles shook him from within. His skin had gone chalky. His cheeks puffed out, his eyes widened, and he pitched to the floor, convulsing.

Lance grabbed immediately for the phone on his desk. Here was one thing he'd been trained to do from childhood, hit those three crucial numbers. He jabbed 9 then 1 then 1 again, simultaneously crying toward his open door: "Help! Anyone out there?" He knelt, the curly phone cord half wrapping round him, and fumbled to loosen the knot of Mr. Furlanetti's tie.

A voice in his ear: "Emberton security."

"Oh, shit, I uh… I need 911. I dialled 911."

"What seems to be the problem, sir?"

"No, I need…"

Mr. Furlanetti was still writhing, his breath coming in quick, gurgly gasps. Lance rose and turned, the phone cord wrapping tighter around him, and hung up and dialled 911 again.

"Emberton security."

"Dammit, I'm trying to get 911."

"You again? Just please explain what the emergency is."

"I need 911. An ambulance. A man's in trouble."

"Could you state the nature of the trouble?"

"Can you please get me 911?"

"Sir, please calm down and state the nature of the medical emergency."

"For Christ's sake, the man needs an ambulance. He's… I don't know… it's some kind of seizure."

"Hold on."

Silence on the line. Mr. Furlanetti's breath returned to normal. His eyes bulged less severely.

The voice was back: "I've dispatched first aid to your floor. Fourth, correct?"

"Yes, that's right, but why—" Lance broke off as Mr. Furlanetti heaved to his feet, pushing Lance away, and ran heavily from the office. "Wait!" called Lance. He dropped the phone to give chase, but he was too tangled in the cord.

As he tried to unwind it, he could make out the voice on the line: "Sir?… Sir?"

Lance grabbed the mouthpiece. "He's gone. He got up and left."

"Good. Emergency averted. I'll repeal the first aid responders."

"Why won't you call me an ambulance? He still needs... I don't know. He needs to be checked out."

"Sir, Emberton Tower is equipped to handle these emergencies."

"Can't I dial through to 911?"

"We route such calls through security. I am equipped and empowered to assess the severity of the problem and react accordingly."

"Is this even legal?"

"We have everything under control. Thank you for your concern." The line went dead.

Lance set aside his fury. For now he'd better find Mr. Furlanetti and see if he was okay. But the more he tried to disentangle himself from the phone cord, the more enmeshed he got. As he was about to yank the phone free and take it with him into the hallway, he noticed movement out of the corner of his eye. A hand gripped the door jamb. Its nails were painted maroon.

"Hello?" called Lance.

Ms. Shillingsham pulled herself into view. "Good morning!" She frowned. "You appear to be tangled in your phone."

"Mr. Furlanetti just fell down in here."

"My word! Is he all right?"

"He was shaking and having trouble breathing. Then he got up and ran off."

"Oh, thank heavens. So he's all right." Her cheeriness had a brittle edge.

"Well, no, I don't think so. He seemed pretty sick. I tried to call 911."

Ms. Shillingsham's face darkened. "Lance, 911 is a number to be dialled only in case of emergency."

"It was an emergency! He was having a seizure or something."

"Well, I imagine your attempt to contact emergency services was not successful, was it?"

"No."

"See, Lance, here at Emberton Tower we sometimes undergo unique stresses. It can be difficult, in the anxiety of the moment, to distinguish a true emergency from a... from an *idiosyncrasy*. Outgoing 911 calls are routed to security, who are equipped to make a calm, level-headed assessment of the situation and react accordingly. Do you have a cellphone?"

"No."

"If you did, you'd have found that it didn't function inside the Tower. Signals are suppressed. We can't have people going off the rails and summoning the authorities at a moment's notice, can we?"

"That's the whole point of 911. A moment's notice."

Ms. Shillingsham made a shooing gesture and giggled. "Oh, Lance. Brimming with vim, aren't you? No harm in that—this department could use a dose of passion. Now, look. Don't worry yourself with Mr. Furlanetti's little disturbances. Something far more serious is afoot." A theatrical grimace. "Quarterly numbers are in."

"Oh. Is that bad news?"

"Always is, Lance. Always is. I'll need you in the board-room in five."

"I don't know."

"Excuse me?"

"I don't know about having a meeting right now. I

think I should go outside, find a pay phone. Call a proper ambulance."

"Lance, this is tiresome. I've explained to you that the Tower has personnel who are perfectly qualified. If they've declined to send help, that means help is not needed. I am calling an urgent departmental meeting, and I require that you be there. Furthermore, I require that Mr. Furlanetti be there. And there he will be. Looking the picture of perfect health, I'm sure. All your doubts will be put to rest, and you can turn your energies—your *considerable* energies—toward helping us solve the sales crisis. Come, now. No more nonsense. It's time to meet."

But Mr. Furlanetti was not there. The other marketers took turns glancing nervously at the empty seat.

Ms. Shillingsham was installed in her place at the head of the table, and her hands were smoothing the stacks of papers laid in front of her. "Mr. Furlanetti is aware of the gravity of the situation. I expect he will be here very soon."

The silence in the room was punctured by the occasional cough or cleared throat. Lance was reminded of the viewing room at his father's funeral, occupied by himself, a few people who'd worked for the furniture store, a trio of aging and ailing aunts, a dearth of conversation.

Ms. Shillingsham stood. She did so with enough force that her chair rolled away from her on its wheels, thudding gently against the wall. "I will have to look for him," she announced. "Please excuse me for a moment. And please do not leave the table while I'm gone."

"I'll help."

Ms. Shillingsham froze.

"Let me help. You might need backup."

"Why on earth would I..." She looked around at the rest of the marketers, who were murmuring at Lance's apparent breach of etiquette.

"Because I'm concerned about him, Ms. Shillingsham. And if anything is wrong, you'll be glad you took me. I'm a handy guy in a crisis."

"Very well," she said darkly. "This may be valuable for both of us."

They stalked the halls of floor four. Lance struggled to keep up with Ms. Shillingsham as she swept from one room to the next, checking under every desk and behind every door.

"Why," said Lance, "is it so important? Can't we start without him?"

Ms. Shillingsham recoiled from the suggestion as if it had come with a puff of mace. "Our meetings," she said, "must be properly attended. That is paramount. We meet. It is what we do. We meet; we discuss matters. All of us, together."

She bustled ahead into another room. Lance hurried after her, only to find her standing in the middle of a disused office, tottering on her heels. She pointed at the wall.

At first Lance thought Mr. Furlanetti was dead or unconscious. He lay on his back on the dusty carpet, near the window. His face was obscured by the radiator. Then, stepping closer and getting better vantage, Lance could see Mr. Furlanetti's mouth clamped over a tube extending from the radiator. His stomach was rising and falling, his Adam's apple sliding back and forth.

"Mr. Furlanetti!" barked Ms. Shillingsham.

He convulsed and sat up. The radiator hissed where his

mouth had been, hot air warping the view of the wall behind it.

"There's a meeting!" said Ms. Shillingsham. "I expected you to be on time for the meeting!"

Mr. Furlanetti scrambled to his feet. His face was blotched red. "Sorry." The word was painfully slow, borne on a creeping tide of gurgles. "I thought." His eyes were shiny and bloodshot. "Thought was later." One tongue of his shirt had spilled over the front of his trousers; he tucked it in. "Okay," he said. "Ready. Good." And he marched out of the office.

Ms. Shillingsham knelt beside the radiator, placing one palm above the tube, which still issued wrinkled air. She held her hand to her face, sniffed it. Then she screwed the radiator closed. "I guess we can get back to our meeting," was her only comment.

Lance stopped her in the hall. She glared icily at the hand he'd laid on her elbow; he withdrew it. "What was going on?" he said. "What was he doing?"

"It appears that he was inhaling fumes from the radiator."

"What fumes? What's going on?"

"Radiators," said Ms. Shillingsham, "emit heated air. That's all I know."

"He was completely changed. It's like…"

"He was inhaling hot air, Lance. That's all we know."

"But he couldn't talk. Something in the building's air supply? Something that…"

Ms. Shillingsham was biting her lower lip, hard. She released it to say: "The building's air supply, Lance, is not a concern of the sales and marketing department. We breathe it; we do not control it." More gnawing at the lip. "But you,

Lance, have found favour with our owner. If you have questions that exceed my pay grade, perhaps you should reserve them for him."

With that, she strode back to the boardroom.

Doom prevailed. Sales were plummeting. No one wanted to buy dictionaries anymore. And by the time the print edition was ready for the warehouse pallet, whole new categories of slang and jargon had arisen, dominated, and died. The book was redundant before it was even in stores. On the highest floors of Emberton Tower, discussions had begun about the possibility of moving the dictionary entirely online. But those plans were in their infancy and likely never to come to fruition—or so the sales executives hoped. Lance could hear, below their words, a submerged fear. They didn't have the first clue how they'd market a database; they knew how to sell a book. Or, at least, they were comfortable pretending they knew how to sell a book. They needed to find new ideas, fresh perspectives. "We need," said Ms. Shillingsham, "to think outside the... er... what is it again? Outside the pot?"

"The square," offered the knitting woman.

"Uh, no," snorted Mr. Hutchman. "You're thinking of *be there or be square.*"

"Anyway," said Ms. Shillingsham, "we need to find and embrace a new approach."

"Why not leave it up to the newcomer?" Mr. Hutchman waved a spotty hand Lance's way. "That's what he's here for, right? Revitalize us codgers? Show us how it's done in this brave new world?"

"No," said Ms. Shillingsham, "I think the opposite is true. I think we need to call upon our experience—"

"Experience *failing*," muttered Mr. Hutchman.

"Our years of *experience*," continued Ms. Shillingsham, "as *professionals* in the area of *sales and marketing,* which after all is what every last one of us is ostensibly here to do, and rather than sloughing our duties onto our greenest member, we will allow *him* to learn from *us.* Got it?" She stood. Her voice was heavy with a menace Lance had not heard before. "I believe it behooves us, every once in a while, to behave like a legitimate department. Am I understood?"

Not a knitting needle clacked. Ms. Shillingsham surveyed the table one last time, gathered her things, and stormed from the boardroom.

Faces regarded other faces. Mr. Furlanetti burbled.

Lance looked at the man who minutes ago had been splayed on a dirty carpet, the better to get his mouth around a radiator tube. Carpet fibres clung to Mr. Furlanetti's pinstriped jacket. The same jacket, Lance now noticed, that he'd been wearing every day for the past week.

"What are..." Mr. Furlanetti's mouth opened and closed with a moist sound, as if he were working on a large wad of gum. "What are you..." He smacked his hand on the table, worked his jaw more furiously, and the whole question popped out: "What are you looking at?" Jowls quivering, he tossed out an extra, contemptuous "...kid?"

The other execs were still in their seats. Like spectators at a slow-motion tennis match, they eased their gazes from Lance to Mr. Furlanetti and then slowly back. Their faces were alight with curiosity, with eagerness to see a quarrel, to see any kind of ripple on the bland surface of the departmental day-to-day. But Lance saw no concern whatsoever for the well-being of their vice-president, no fear of what deeper troubles his outburst might betray.

"Come on!" cried Lance. "Are none of you... I mean, no offence, Mr. Furlanetti, I respect that you're my vice-boss or whatever—"

"Boss," snarled Furlanetti. "There is no vice."

"Well, okay, my vice-*president*—"

"Above you." Mr. Furlanetti's out-thrust finger trembled badly. "I rank above you. Boss."

"And I respect that. But something's wrong here. You need help."

"Someone," Mr. Furlanetti said, his mouth lined with fine froth, "needs..." Burbles overtook him.

"Sorry," said Lance, "I can't stand by and watch this." He was thinking of his own father during those early, undiagnosed years of illness. His father, racked by spasmodic coughing fits that took him out of commission for minutes at a time. His father's spit in the toilet bowl, its grisly palette. His father refusing time and again to seek help, sticking to some stupid macho code, gruffly belittling Lance (*Where'll you be without me, son? They stick me in hospital, keep me away from you, how will you even survive?*), until that one morning he couldn't get out of bed and the phlegm spattered on the sheets beneath his chin was more blood than mucus. Lance tried to take matters into his own hands. He walked into one medical clinic, where he was told *This is not a walk-in, can't you read the sign?* At another place, he set aside his shame and explained that he couldn't read any signs, couldn't fill out any forms, but could someone please come look at his father? After grovelling his way through a handful of medical establishments, he'd secured a house call, had a doctor in to peer through rimless specs at his dad's crimson spit, and a few tests later, they learned it was too late, the game was over. Metastasis.

Lance was thinking of the awful futility of pride that refused help, of his own agony over whether he should have helped his father sooner, whether that would have made a difference.

"Needs to m—... needs to m—" Mr. Furlanetti was gagging on the *m*; it emerged from his mouth like a puked-up bowling ball. "Mind his own business," he finished, gasping with the effort. He blinked several times. Then he wiped the corner of his mouth, transferring the grey froth to his sleeve.

"Yeah, see, I respect your seniority and everything," said Lance, "but no. I'm sorry. If this Tower won't let me get you any proper help, I'm going to leave and do it myself. So if you all don't mind, I'm headed for the nearest pay phone."

A murmur shot through the room. It looked like one of the marketers might speak up, might protest—Mr. Hutchman was stroking his cravat, which today was teal, with increasing fervour, as if to prime his voice—but they couldn't spit anything out, and Lance stood and looked at Mr. Furlanetti, at his now-bulging raisin eyes and the slow, beseeching shake of his head, and excused himself from the boardroom.

The lobby security desk was vacant—otherwise, Lance would have given the guard a piece of his mind. In addition to summoning an ambulance, Lance figured he might talk to the cops, tell them about the blocked 911 call.

He continued to the door. The floor rumbled up through his soles, a comforting thrum, the rhythm of the press room. He'd never actually used a pay phone—never had occasion. But how hard could it be? It was just another phone, right? He could do this.

But did he really want to? Mr. Furlanetti had made it to the meeting in the end—he was back to normal, by his own admittedly dodgy standards. And what would it involve, contacting the authorities? Sure, the pay phone might not be an obstacle. But what then? Would Lance have to make his way to some station? Would they give him paperwork? Who knew what humiliations lay ahead? And after all, why not have faith in the systems at Emberton Tower? It was a fully functional business, run by professional adults. Surely there were reasons, sensible reasons, for the way things were done. Who was he to run off in a tizzy and rile his bosses? He'd barely been here three weeks.

"Excuse me." Someone wanted to get out; Lance shuffled aside to let her by.

She had blond hair, up in a bun. This put Lance in mind of an alternative to leaving in search of a phone. Elena could provide a good perspective. She knew the Tower's quirks—and if she didn't know about this one, she'd be glad to hear about it. Had she not asked Lance to keep his eyes peeled for strange goings-on? Maybe he could be of some use to her after all.

That decided it. Lance's fear of facing Elena was gone. He would return to floor nine.

It was lively today; etymologists moved in and out of offices and clustered in the hallway to chat. Somewhere, a photocopier was working with a gentle, locomotive rhythm. Lance started forward.

"Can I help you?" A young man had detached himself from a conversation. He watched Lance warily through fashionable specs.

"Hi," said Lance. He used his put-a-male-at-ease voice,

his *I'm not as brainy as you, and I sure could use your help.* "I'm looking for Elena?"

The young man squinted through his specs. "Sorry, who?"

"Elena. Works here. This is etymology, right?"

"Yeah, this is the floor. But there's no Elena."

Lance waited for further explanation.

"No Elena works here."

Now Lance was just confused. "Well, there must be some mistake. She's an etymologist. Elena Wright. Her office is... I'll just..." He started walking again; something in the body language of this group of etymologists unnerved him, and he wanted to get out of their orbit. They shuffled after him.

"Seriously," said the young man, "there's no Elena. I think you should—"

Lance's cry of triumph cut him short. "Here!" The familiar poster was there on the wall, inside the office he'd arrived at. The rest of the room conformed to his memory of Elena's office: books piled over every available surface; desk crammed with papers; a charming mess. But with one key difference: the woman at the desk—who wore a bright, capacious floral print blouse, whose hair was a cascade of copper-toned curls—was decidedly not Elena. "What are you doing here?" asked Lance, unable to corral his rude tone. "Isn't this Elena's office?"

"Elena?" said the woman. "I'm afraid I don't know any Elena."

"This is her office! What are you... That's her poster, her desk..." Lance trailed off, noticing the expression with which the etymologists regarded him. They had concerns about his mental stability. "Okay," he said, changing gears. "The mistake, I guess, is..." He swallowed. "Mine."

That was his exit line. The etymologists wanted him gone, and he had nothing more to do here. But for a few seconds he didn't stir. The poster was transfixing him. Groves, brooks, meadows, sheep, the great sweltering orange sun—all were painted accurately enough. But something wasn't right. Something was missing, but what? The little grazing sheep were delightful. The grass was lustrous, the big sun warm and beguiling. Its light bathed everything. Absolutely everything.

Lack of shadow. That was the problem. In that omnipresent glow, not one figure cast a shadow.

The young man took gentle hold of Lance's bicep. His face was doing its best impression of sternness, but fear simmered beneath. "Come on, now," he said, his voice imploring rather than tough. "Time to leave."

Lance shook his arm free. "You don't have to touch me."

"Time to ship out, man," said the young man. "There is no Elena."

The countertop in the fourth floor men's room looked like badlands viewed from space. Dark brown lines—the borders of old stains—wended over the surface like topographical boundaries. A green line of mould spread from the edge of a sink, branched into tributaries, cut its path through the brown-fringed canyons. Here and there, tiny craters were punched into the surface, visible when Lance bowed to splash his face with cold water.

He watched himself in the mirror as he swabbed his brow with a paper towel. The etymologists thought he was crazy. Was he? Had he hallucinated this girl who had once asked for his company, who had needed him for something?

He crushed the towel in a fist and shoved it into the waste bin. The metal push door squeaked shut. Of course he wasn't crazy. Some sort of miscommunication had occurred, and he was going to find Elena.

He would check the garden. Then the cafeteria. If she wasn't there, he would inquire of the staff—not the most helpful pair, but who knew what they might divulge. He'd work his way through the building. He was a salesman. He could talk his way into Fort Knox, couldn't he? He'd move up and down this Tower, asking discreet questions, until something gave. Elena had to turn up.

A gurgle from one of the stalls. Mr. Furlanetti? Tilting his head, Lance discerned no shoes planted on the floor. He pushed the door open. The toilet gurgled again and bubbled in its bowl. The caulking around its base was studded with black mould. Lance pulled the door shut, leaving the toilet to its private disturbance, and backed away.

Chapter 7

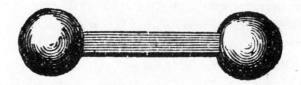

On the third floor, the frosted glass doors were firmly closed, the red cross undivided. He could see, beyond, a congress of hazy silhouettes. Taking care not to trigger the sliding door, he edged along the corridor and found his way to the garden. It was not sunny today; the lawn looked drab. The tree seemed to strain against its confines. Its boughs were knobbly and crabbed and hooked like arthritic fingers. The fruit it bore looked thin, colourless, pocked with holes made by worms. The flowerbeds were a mess of unruly colour, sloppily flung together. The place had looked a lot better in bright light.

Or it looked a lot better with Elena in it.

A slurping sound caught Lance's ear; it seemed to be coming from behind a shrub. Lance crossed the grass and peered into the thorny tangle of brambles up against an interior wall. In the wall was a vent, its stripes of rusted metal angled downward so that any outflow would head for the ground. It was steaming faintly, and Lance was struck at once by that sickly sweet smell he'd noticed in the garden before. *Fertilizer,* Elena had proposed. And now, something more than odour came out of the vent. Something like gruel. Coloured beige and grey with splotches of red, it plopped onto the soil and sat there in a steaming, sweet-smelling mound.

"Who's there?"

A man approached with a bucket and a rake. He was haggard-faced, balding, dressed in green medical scrubs.

"Hi," said Lance. "Just enjoying the..." He gestured lamely at the surrounding grimness.

"You're in my way," the man said, shouldering past. He laid his bucket on the grass and removed a scoop, which he used to heap the gruel into the pail.

"Fertilizer?" Lance hazarded.

"Something like that," said the man.

"Why does it come from the wall?"

An appraising glance. "Curiosity, huh? Don't see much of it on this floor."

"I'm just wondering. Seems a bit odd, you know?"

"Odd?" The man gave a gruff laugh. And that was that. He was off to his work, emptying the bucket's contents, gob after gob, onto various patches of soil and raking it in. Lance tried a few more questions but got no response. His query about Elena, whether the gardener had seen her, drew only a raised eyebrow.

Waiting for the elevator, Lance contemplated the frosted glass doors and wondered if he should take a look in there. *You do not want to go into the infirmary,* Elena had said. And it was true: he really didn't. No way he'd find her there; she was too determined to avoid the place. He'd check it out only as a last resort, if all other corners of the Tower turned up empty. Even just standing outside of it was making him edgy. He was relieved when the elevator arrived.

As he stepped quickly in and pressed 1 for the cafeteria, a low moan came from behind the frosted glass.

The cafeteria was even emptier than before. The sole customer nibbled on a hot dog. The woman on crutches was behind the cash register, slamming coffee filter baskets into their slots on an industrial-size brewer. Lance rang the service bell.

She spun furiously. "Didn't hafta ring," she bellowed, hobbling toward him. "I'm right here. Ain't blind." She leaned her crutches against the countertop. "What'll it be, then?"

"Do you remember when I was in here before? I had a sandwich. I sat with a young lady over thereabouts."

"Why should I remember you? Sun shines outta your ass?"

"No, I mean, you don't have that many customers, so I thought—"

"What does *that* mean?"

"Not a ton of people come through here, so I thought you'd—"

"What are you insinuating?"

"I'm not insinuating. I'm just saying."

"Whatever, hotshot. I don't remember you." She raised one crutch and shook it in Lance's direction. "But I sure as hell will now. Coming in here, disparaging the customer count."

"I bet you'd remember her. Blond hair, green eyes. It looked like you and her had a nice, pleasant interaction at the till."

"Don't remember nothing." The woman was already crutching her way back into the kitchen. "When I'm back here," she threw over her shoulder, "*that's* when you ring."

The giant was at his post, ladling soup, concentrating as deeply as ever. Maybe it was a meditative exercise. Lance was pretty sure it wouldn't be worth talking to him. He dinged the bell once and headed for the exit.

That low customer count was the reason Elena had chosen the cafeteria in the first place. Quiet; less of a chance she'd be observed. Lance approached the security desk. It was occupied this time.

"Seems I see a lot of you," said the guard.

"Yeah, so?"

"My line of work, it's not always the best sign when you see the same person over and over." He jabbed absently at his panel. "I guess they don't give you much to do up in sales and marketing?"

"I'm efficient."

"You got a question for me or what? I'm sort of busy with protection services."

"Just wanted some advice. I need to review some notes for a presentation. But my floor's pretty noisy. Anywhere quiet I could go, do my work with no one around to bug me?"

The guard jerked his thumb toward the cafeteria. "One of the quietest spots in the building."

"Yeah, see, I kind of used that one up. Hoping for something new."

"Try the recreation facility. The gym. No one uses that either. It's on the fifth floor."

But the facility was not a gym. It had a few gestures in the direction of fitness. A badminton net drooped over a patch of hardwood; a dozen antique barbells sat on a rack. More prominently on offer was a non-athletic means of recreation: along one wall was a bar, complete with stools and beer taps. The mirrored back wall was grimy, and the bottles did not manage to twinkle through their layer of dust. But it was still, recognizably, a bar.

Lance walked the perimeter of the room. He pressed a tentative toe against the badminton court. The wood sagged softly at his pressure, rotten beneath its laminated surface. He lifted a barbell. It was extraordinarily heavy, and he immediately dropped it back onto the rack. Dust puffed up at its landing.

A sandpit occupied the farthest corner. It was the size of a boxing ring. A concrete curb bordered it. The sand was coarse and light grey, sprinkled with glinting black flecks.

"Blood sport." A stooped woman was emerging from a door in the wall behind the bar. She was squeezed into a shiny pink halter top, exposing deeply wrinkled arms and shoulders. "Back in the early days, they used that pit for blood sport. They'd wrestle, fight with weapons... those were wilder days."

"When was that?"

"Back before my time. They got bored building this big dictionary, the men did, so they'd come in here and lay down money and bash each other bloody. Strange hobby." She grunted in appreciation of the strangeness. "So what brings you in here? We don't have many regulars anymore. People want the newfangled gizmos, treadmills and the like. As if life isn't a treadmill already, eh?"

"I guess so," said Lance.

"The folks who show up these days are looking for an after-work drink." She stage-winked. "Sometimes a mid-work drink, too, know what I mean? Sometimes even an early bird special." She laughed uproariously. Lance worried it might tax her unduly, but she recovered. "There's a TV behind the bar. I can call up the sports channels, all that. But I keep it off when no one's around. Don't like all the clamour."

Something stirred in the air, a cross breeze. Lance noticed a faint disturbance on the surface of the sandpit. The light grey grains tumbled over one another; the black flecks rolled in place like sea lions sunning on a rock. Lance bent and picked one up. It had a sharp point. Isolated from the sand and held in the light, it was more dark green than black.

"Glass," said the woman, coming to Lance's side. "From broken bottles. Customers used to smash their empties and sprinkle the glass into the sand."

"Why?"

"It was a blood sport, like I said. More glass, more blood." She kicked at the edge of the sand, revealing a new layer to the concrete border: a low gutter running along its length. "The blood flowed along this thing." She pointed to a corner where the open mouth of a pipe was set into the floor. "It went there to drain." She laughed again, but with less enthusiasm. "Wouldn't want to have all that gore lying about, would we?"

"Where did it go?"

"How should I know? Somewhere. Away."

Lance examined the pipe, which was slightly rusted— or stained—at the lip. The list of things to tell Elena was lengthening. "So is there a young woman who comes in here, ever? Real pretty, blond hair, green eyes?"

"Nope. The ones I get in here ain't pretty, ain't young, and ain't female. None of them."

"Well, thanks for your time."

"Oh, I got plenty of it."

"Well," said Lance, feeling that something encouraging needed to be said, "I hope to, um, be back someday. For a drink."

"No need to fib to me, dear. When you feel the old thirst, take yourself someplace nicer. Meantime, I hope you find your girl."

"Thanks," said Lance. "So do I."

He tried the archives, banging a futile fist on the vast metal door. He may as well have been punching the hull of a submarine. He slunk from floor to floor, poked his head where it wasn't welcome, drew suspicious stares. He dipped into the cellars, surveyed the press room, watched from above as its workers scrambled up ladders and consulted dials and held fresh-printed pages to the light. He let the lullaby rhythm of the machines course through him, drew some comfort from it before snapping himself back to the task at hand. He checked the cafeteria once more; braved the security guard's scowl to see whether anyone occupied the armchairs by the fireplace.

Finally, in defeat, he headed back to his office.

Another week slid by, and Lance completed a circuit daily: the cafeteria, first thing in the morning, and then again at noon; the archive in the mid-afternoon, when his whole department seemed to fall into a meeting-free slumber; the garden at various points throughout the day. He did not see her, nor did he see anyone who could remember seeing her. Maybe the nervous guy on floor nine was right: maybe there was no Elena.

There definitely was a Mr. Furlanetti. He liked to drop in on Lance's office unannounced. "Mind your business," he'd grumble. Or, "Watch your back." Sometimes he would just stand there and watch Lance. Intently. It looked like he was piecing something together. He'd murmur something to himself, his lips making slow movements but producing no discernible words. Then he'd retreat with a cunning smile.

He seemed to be in acceptable health, however, and Lance's idea of calling the authorities rarely came back to mind. The thick air of the Tower, issued in sluggish spurts from radiators and ducts, made his brain sleepy, soporific, uninterested in such altruistic deeds.

But it did not make Mr. Furlanetti's intrusions any easier to take. "Look," Lance sputtered one afternoon. It was an overcast Tuesday, heavy and grey outside. He shut the file folder in his hand and laid it down, hard, on his desktop. "You wanted me to leave you alone. I'm doing that. So how about we make it a mutual thing, and you stop watching me all the time?"

Rather than replying, Mr. Furlanetti pointed to the file folder. "What's that for?"

"What do you mean, what's it *for*?"

"What's it for?"

"Ms. Shillingsham asked me to go through it, is all."

"*Is all*," mimicked Mr. Furlanetti. His speech today was burble-free. Maybe his new zest for persecuting Lance had kept him away from the radiators.

"She asked me to go through it. I'm going through it."

"That's not what I asked."

"Fine," said Lance. "Here's what it's for." He grabbed the file and strode toward the vice-president. He thrust it in the man's face. "See it? You see the label? *That's* what it's for."

Mr. Furlanetti's raisin eyes gleamed.

"No, sorry," said Lance, his voice gone high-pitched, prepubescent. "Sorry, here's what it's for." He took two steps sideways to his recycling bin. "Here's what it's for." He relinquished his grip and the file fell free, opening in mid-air and disgorging its contents. They swirled and fluttered like autumn leaves and fanned over the floor, missing the bin entirely. Lance stooped and, fully aware of the indignity of the act, knelt to gather the sheets.

"My point is," Mr. Furlanetti said, his voice oozing such derision his tongue must surely have been sticky with it, "I want to know what they *say*."

"Nothing," mumbled Lance. "Nothing. That's why I'm chucking them."

"Dunno," said Furlanetti. "I thought they looked import— Oh, hello."

Lance scrambled to his feet. "Ms. Shillingsham!"

She had raised an eyebrow. "Am I interrupting something?"

"Nope," said Lance.

"Nothing," muttered Furlanetti.

"Well, then, I suppose you gents won't mind coming to the boardroom."

"Meeting?" said Mr. Furlanetti.

Her eyebrows performed further antics. "*Major* meeting."

"What's happened?" asked Lance.

"Just be there."

What had happened, it turned out, was that the marketers' standards of dress had begun to decline on Fridays, which, Ms. Shillingsham hastened to point out, were designated semi-casual. "That's *semi,* which I'm sure you literate folk don't need to have explained. It's semi-*casual*, not semi-*dressed*." As far as Lance could tell there was absolutely no variation in the marketers' formality from one day to the next. Mr. Hutchman reliably sported a cravat; the dyed redhead—whose name Lance hadn't learned—always wore something bright and tight but never unprofessional; Mr. Furlanetti, for all Lance knew, hadn't changed his clothes once in the three weeks since Lance had arrived. And yet, allegedly, the standards had slid. And this was a serious problem—a *major* problem, worth its own entire meeting.

"We're a professional sales and marketing office," said Ms. Shillingsham, having worked her speech to its climactic lather. "Not a rooming house." She let the distinction sink in. "We *work* here, right? We *do* things. Am I right?"

Sullen silence greeted this. The knitting woman looked glumly at her shawl-in-progress, possibly assessing whether it was going to be up to dress code par.

"Well, friends," said Ms. Shillingsham with a sudden shift of tone. "I hope you don't think that's why I called this *major* meeting."

Eight pairs of eyes watched her warily.

"Oh, no, don't fret. There is a far more serious item on today's agenda." She was now grinning broadly. She nodded at a bald man wearing a paisley bowtie, a man who Lance was pretty certain hadn't said a single word in any meeting Lance had attended. "Mr. Meeks is celebrating his birthday! Don't worry Philip, I won't reveal which one. But..." She rose from her seat and raised a forefinger to indicate *wait one sec.* She disappeared from the boardroom. The suspense in the room was nonexistent. Everyone knew what was coming next, and so, by osmosis, Lance knew it too. A trundling noise from the hall, and Ms. Shillingsham reappeared with a wheeled tray bearing a bright pink cake.

"Dig in, everybody!" she said, lifting a napkin and fork from the tray and thrusting the tines ceilingward. Then, sorrowfully: "The bakery was out of grownup birthday cakes. But hey, what's wrong with a bit of colour around here anyway?"

Tentatively, like newly captured animals offered their first zoo meal, the marketers edged toward the cake. For a few moments they just looked at it, as if waiting for it to make the first move. Finally, with a decisive burble, Mr. Furlanetti grabbed a fork and napkin and carved himself a jagged piece. One by one, the marketers stepped up to take a slice of the garish pastry and celebrate the birth of Mr. Philip Meeks. Teeth or dentures went to work; napkins sagged under their burdens. The conversation improved in volume and frequency until something audible was being said by one marketer or another at least every half-minute.

Lance was on the fringe of the group, nibbling a tough crust of icing. If there had been a window, he would have gazed out of it, but instead he contented himself with a stretch of beige wall. What *were* these walls made of? Cork? Bristol board? Painted Plexiglas? He was ready to reach out and feel it, get a read on the texture, when something tapped his shoulder. He discovered, to his discomfort, that it was Mr. Hutchman's hand. "I say," the man said in a furtive voice, "I haven't seen you in the kitchenette for a while."

"Don't think I've been," said Lance.

"You missed some interesting chatter this morning," continued Mr. Hutchman. "Not your typical water-cooler chin music."

"You don't say." Lance turned back to the patch of wall, imploring it to catch fire or break out in measles or otherwise distract Mr. Hutchman from continuing.

But the wall did nothing unusual, and there was no silencing Mr. Hutchman. His eyes slid meaningfully in the direction of the woman who would ordinarily be engaged with her knitting needles. But they lay on the table, thrust into their heap of wool, and instead she occupied herself balancing a giant cake chunk on her small plastic fork. "Gina there told us about something that happened on her way in to work. She takes the subway, of course."

"Of course."

"So the automated voice came on announcing her stop. Except it came out as gobbledygook. She thought that perhaps the tape, or whatever they use, was garbled. But then, as she stepped from the— Oh, hello, John. "

Mr. Furlanetti burbled in reply. His cake was gone, leaving a gory smear of icing on the plate. He eyed it mournfully.

"I was telling the kid here about Gina's... Oh..." Mr. Hutchman's eyes narrowed. "You weren't in the kitchenette this morning either, were you, John? Haven't seen you snacking in there so much these days."

A wave of gurgles rose and broke. "Haven't been."

"Indeed. So, anyway, today Gina related the most extraordinary— Well hello, Gina."

Lance realized he was in the midst of something he did not believe he had ever witnessed on floor four before: a conversation interesting enough to draw a crowd. Indeed, a very nervous-looking Ms. Shillingsham was now edging toward the group, and a short man in a sweater vest had materialized at Gina's elbow.

"I was filling these gentlemen in on your interesting commute," said Mr. Hutchman.

"Mm," answered Gina, her eyes darting frantically from Lance to Mr. Furlanetti and back again.

"I guess it's your story. You may as well do the sharing, no?"

She squeaked and frowned into her cake.

"Go on, then, Gina," said Mr. Hutchman. "The boys are all ears."

"Well, uh, I couldn't follow the announcement on the subway car. I was scared, I have to say. You worry about strokes and whatnot. And then it got worse."

That appeared to be the end of the story. Lance looked to Mr. Hutchman, who squinted intently at Gina.

"Yes," Mr. Hutchman said at last, "it got much worse, didn't it?"

That seemed to be the prod that Gina needed. "Yes, well, I stepped from the train. And there in front of me was a big advertisement. I'd seen it a million times, it's for that—you know, what's it called, the reality show. The one about the..."

"Parking enforcement?" suggested Mr. Hutchman.

"No, no, the..."

"The plastic surgery competition?" tried Ms. Shillingsham.

"No. The butchers. Competitive butchering."

"Ah, yes," said Mr. Hutchman. "That one. What do they call it again?"

"No matter," said Ms. Shillingsham sharply. "I hardly think the title is important. Is your story coming to a point, Miss Winters, or shall we move on to another topic now?"

Slowly the anecdote regained its feet. "Yes, well, it was that particular advertisement. And I know what it says—it says, in big red letters, *The Final Cut,*' and then it says, 'Who can wield'—"

"We have *established*," Ms. Shillingsham said, teeth gritted, "which advertisement you mean. I'm sure we don't need to repeat whatever banalities are printed on it."

"The point, I think," said Mr. Hutchman hurriedly, "is that you knew by heart what the ad said?"

"Yes, thank you."

Mr. Furlanetti ran a finger along a streak of pink icing and brought it to his lips.

Ms. Shillingsham's piece of cake was virtually untouched. She placed it on the conference table. "Well," she said, turning back to the circle (which every last marketer had now joined), "that was a good tale. Most amusing. Thank you for your contribution, Gina." She smiled painfully. "It's nice when we can share a laugh over a good little story, isn't it? Very *bonding,* yes?"

"Ah," said Mr. Hutchman, licking his lips, "but I don't believe we've quite come to the end yet, have we, Gina?"

Ms. Shillingsham shot him a stern look, which he appeared to deliberately avoid noticing.

"What was different," continued Mr. Hutchman, "this morning? About the ad?"

"I couldn't read it," Gina moaned. "Couldn't read any of the words. They looked like bundles of letters. An *f* here, an *h* there. Like a bulldozer just shoved them all together. Rubble. No cohesion. No words."

"Meaningless," said Mr. Hutchman.

Mr. Furlanetti rumbled his agreement. "No meaning."

His words hung in the middle of the circle.

"You were a bit early to work this morning, weren't you, Gina?" said Mr. Hutchman.

"Yes."

"You said this was about eight-thirty, am I right?"

"That's right."

"So none of us... I mean, I think we all probably arrived after you did. Because no one else in the kitchenette reported anything like that. How about you, Mr. Furlanetti? When did you arrive today?"

Mr. Furlanetti looked panicked. "Not sure."

"Nine? Earlier?"

"Not sure." He backed away from the conversation. "More cake."

"How about you, Lance?" said Mr. Hutchman.

"Oh, no, I'm full. It was delicious, though."

"This morning, I mean. Did you notice anything like what Gina said?"

Lance chuckled. Every single day, every single piece of writing that crossed his path resembled exactly what Gina had described. As far as he could tell, this morning she'd had a taste of the affliction he'd endured his whole life. "I didn't see anything out of the ordinary."

"I was so worried," Gina said. "About my health, I mean. But then I noticed that the other people getting off the subway with me, they'd all stopped in their tracks. There we were, staring at the poster. Causing all kinds of congestion—other people wanted to get on the train, of course. Although some of the incoming folks had stopped too—the ones who were texting. They were staring all bewildered at their screens. So I worked up my courage, and I said, 'The words. What happened to the words?' And a lady beside me said exactly what I hoped to hear: 'They're all mixed up.' And then the train sounded its chimes and shut its doors and went away, and slowly the words settled back into position. Their meaning melted back into place. And then an announcement came over the loudspeaker—something about don't litter, or don't attack your driver—and the poster made perfect sense again. And we all looked at each other, there on the platform, and there was relief on every face, let me tell you."

"And then?" said Mr. Hutchman.

"That's it. I came to work."

Nobody spoke. No cake was chewed. Ms. Shillingsham appeared to be watching a movie projected on a wall very far away. "I was early too," she said at last. "I was in my office at eight-fifteen."

"Leadership by example," said Mr. Hutchman.

"Not much sleep," Ms. Shillingsham corrected him. "What point is there lounging around in bed if you're not getting any sleep? So I came in early."

"And you didn't have any language problems?"

"None. I was going through files. But I did notice a tremor. The Tower shuddered, as it does from time to time."

Everyone was very still.

"Well, that's enough of such talk," continued Ms. Shillingsham. "Where does it get us?"

"Interesting story, though," said Mr. Hutchman.

"On the contrary," said Ms. Shillingsham, colour emerging on her cheekbones, "it's a rather dull story. Minor earthquakes are not interesting. I doubt this one even makes the news. And as for your experience..." She turned her best haughty expression on Gina. "I can't imagine that a bit of perfectly banal morning bleariness should be of interest to one's professional colleagues."

Gina shrank to the fringes of the conversation circle, nibbling the business end of her fork, which did not contain any cake.

"We are, after all, a sales and marketing department," continued Ms. Shillingsham, enough frost in her voice to line a deep-freeze. "We are not some sort of social club specializing in idle chit-chat and tedious anecdotes. I would not be heartbroken, Miss Winters, if you chose to keep such artless gobs of narrative to yourself in future. I don't think the well-being of the department would suffer for it. Do you believe it would, Gina?"

The reply, already spoken at the quietest possible volume, was obscured by plastic tines.

"Sorry, Miss Winters, I didn't catch that."

"No," whispered Gina.

"Ah, how fortuitous. We're in agreement. Now." Ms. Shillingsham exhaled and took a moment or two to winch her smile back into position. "That delicious cake is not going to simply eat itself. Who's for seconds?"

Chapter 8

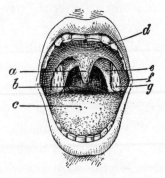

When the meeting was over, Lance made a break for his office. But this time he had a shadow.

He spun round in the hallway. "Something I can help you with?"

"We're not done," said Mr. Furlanetti. He stormed into Lance's office and made for the computer.

"Finishing up that email setup?" asked Lance.

No answer, just those heavy fingers attacking the keyboard like the world's slowest hawks plunging for prey.

The throbbing of the radiator grew louder. Mr. Furlanetti's fingers faltered. His head turned very slowly toward the radiator, then very slowly back toward the computer. A few more keystrokes, and the computer issued a low beep. Mr. Furlanetti stood. Sweat was prominent on his forehead. "Firewall installed," he announced.

"Oh, good. I was getting worried, not having one."

"Really."

"Course I was. Can't get far without a firewall."

Mr. Furlanetti allowed a surge of burbles to subside

before getting out his next question: "Is that why you haven't used it?"

"Haven't what?"

"Used your computer. No record of activity. Online cache empty."

"That's right. I was waiting for that firewall." Lance plucked a book from the shelf and pretended to flip through it.

"Don't believe you."

"Huh? Don't? Why?" Lance wanted this to be a cry of righteous grievance, but it was more like a twerpy squeak.

Mr. Furlanetti waddled toward Lance. It took a while. At last he was near enough to be almost threatening. The sweat was getting really bad on his forehead, sending slow tendrils down his jowls, dampening the edge of his collar. "Did you empty your cache?"

"I don't even know what that— or, I mean, why? Why would I do such a thing?"

"Hide where you've been."

"I've been right here the whole time, man." Lance returned his book to its shelf. He sauntered to his desk, eased into his seat, and idly slid his mouse along its pad.

"I think," said Mr. Furlanetti behind him, "you need a new log-on password."

"Doubt it," replied Lance. A distinct odour was billowing into the space the two men shared. The smell of a body that had been only sporadically washed, and of a suit that had not been changed for a long time.

The pretence with the mouse had run its course. Lance turned his chair away from the desk and tried to stand, but Mr. Furlanetti stopped him by clamping a hand on each armrest. "I'm concerned," he said, his voice fighting through a rising tide of burbles. "Looks like you've been hacked."

"No, of course not. Who would hack me? That's not..." Lance didn't know how a computer-literate person might reply to such an allegation.

"Why is everything empty, then? Recent documents? Recent programs? Cache?"

Lance shrugged miserably.

"Did you never use the computer, or were you hacked?"

"Don't know." Lance sighed. "Hacked, I guess."

Mr. Furlanetti released the armrest and exhaled loudly through his nose. "Good," he said, fumbling in his jacket for a notepad. "So let's give you a new password." He laid the pad on the desk and wrote something in large, looping letters. He showed it to Lance. "Will this be easy to remember?"

Lance nodded. "Of course."

"Why?"

"Because it's... well, it's easy. Just one word."

"English has many words. Why is this one easy?"

"Well, anyway, you can leave it here for me. This paper, I mean."

Mr. Furlanetti laughed uproariously. "Leave it here? Lying around? You call that secure?" He pointed at the paper. "Why is this word easy?"

F. That was the first letter. The rest, of course, was garbled. Blurry, too, as moisture had begun to swim into Lance's right eye.

Fat hands crushed his shoulders. "Read it."

"Hands off!" Lance wriggled his chest, to no effect. He tried to plant his feet on the floor and push the chair free of his desk, but he was not going anywhere.

"What's the problem? Read."

"No. This is..." Another abortive attempt to push free. "Let go of me."

"Read."

"No."

They'd both expended energy doing this. The grip loosened. Lance felt too weak to move. Mr. Furlanetti wheezed behind him.

When the words dropped, phlegmy and slow, from Mr. Furlanetti's lips, they felt inevitable. Lance had seen them coming from fifteen minutes away.

"You can't."

Breathing filled the silence.

"Sure I can." Lance's reply was almost inaudible.

Slowly, almost tenderly, Mr. Furlanetti rotated the chair and regarded Lance face to face. Blood was going mad in Lance's cheeks; his eyes welled; he was as capable of delivering a cool, casual untruth as Mr. Furlanetti was of spontaneously starting to smell good.

"So," said Mr. Furlanetti. "The kid has a little secret."

Lance didn't know what to say. Pathetically, he whimpered: "Don't. Please."

A horrible chortle rattled in Mr. Furlanetti's chest. "Maybe I will. Maybe I won't."

"What do you want?"

Those small eyes studied Lance. They still resembled raisins, but now they were glazed, dipped in something sticky and sweet and poisonous.

"I'll do whatever..." Lance left the sentence unfinished. He couldn't go on. He may as well pack up and leave. Already Elena knew his secret, and had rejected him. This whole thing, this whole voyage to the Tower, setting up camp here, poking around with a desk and a computer, making like some denizen of the workforce, some dude who could read sales reports, who could gulp the dictionary whole, share with strangers its wonders—all this was a sordid charade, and now it was failing. One by one, his colleagues were sniffing him out. He would not last another month at the Tower, would not make enough money to stow a year's rent, wouldn't learn what strange beacon had brought him here. He was alone, as he had always been. As he deserved to be. Time to go.

An uptick in the radiator's glugging. Mr. Furlanetti's pupils slid its way, and so did Lance's. Every damn thing in this building, always clanging or gurgling or wheezing or groaning. A tower that would not stay silent. What was in the radiator, anyway, bubbling with such urgency, tempting Mr. Furlanetti's lips? As he had on his first day, Lance stared at it, as if to penetrate the slits between the rods, gaze into the secret heart of warmth.

You don't have to leave.

The thought rose up from the base of his brain, seeped to the surface like a bubble in thick broth.

You belong here.

Mr. Furlanetti whipped a filthy handkerchief from his pocket and dabbed his brow.

"Laundry," Lance growled. A new confidence was building inside him, and it made him feel mean. "You should do it sometime. It's fun."

"Surprised you know how," answered Mr. Furlanetti. But the menace was gone from his voice, and his attention was drawn to the heater. "So many instructions to read."

"Okay. Listen up." Lance stood as he spoke. Mr. Furlanetti relinquished his grasp on the chair and melted back three steps. "How about you keep this to yourself?"

"How about I don't." Mr. Furlanetti folded the hand-kerchief and put it away.

Lance took a step forward. "You might have forgotten what happened," he said. "On my first day. I received a special invite. You had to come up to floor nine and find me, tell me I was wanted in the penthouse."

Mr. Furlanetti was backing toward the door.

"Say I go up there and see my friend Mr. Emberton. Tell him an amusing story about my vice-president and his relationship with heated air."

Mr. Furlanetti glanced at the radiator and licked his lips.

"Or instead," said Lance, "how about we keep our secrets as they are. Keep things nice and quiet. Business as usual."

Mr. Furlanetti looked like he was working up the froth to deliver a threat, but it was fated to go unsaid. Silent except for a strenuous rumble of the gut, he retreated from the room.

Lance sat. Strength fled from his body; sweat emerged; he was chilled and clammy. It was obviously bad news that Mr. Furlanetti had learned his secret, but he was comforted by the certainty that had come over him when that quiet inner voice had spoken: *You belong here.* No, what truly rattled Lance was something else altogether: the tone of voice he'd taken when he rose from his seat, swaggered forward, and mocked his vice-president.

After all, Lance had heard that tone of voice many a time before. His brief and traumatic school career had been rife with it. It roared at him from other desks in the classroom; it ricocheted at recess from the angular web of the monkey bars; it whispered under the door of the boys' room stalls. It was the voice of normal people, people who fit in, when they had found your weakness and wanted to exploit it, wring you out, see what droplets emerged. As a kid he had sworn he would never act like his tormentors. But moments ago he had aped them exactly.

He swivelled in his seat. Why was everything so quiet?

The radiator. Its gurgling had stopped dead. It was a noiseless hunk of metal. Lance stood, bent over it, cocked an ear. No sound. Its episode was done.

"What's going on?" Lance asked. Somehow, he felt this radiator might know.

Apparently not. No insights arrived. Lance muttered a curse and gave the radiator a heavy kick.

It rocked in place, briefly. But it did not respond.

At day's end, Lance joined the trickle of exiters in the lobby. They moved crisply past him; he dawdled. His hand paused an inch from the pushbar on the revolving door. The glass was clear but for a single palm print, beautifully intact. Over his shoulder he took in the lobby, the fireplace, the austere yellow flame. The rhythm at his feet intensified.

He reached again for the pushbar. Less than a quarter inch of air now separated the metal from his flesh. But he could not bridge that gap. He tried the glass. Same deal: he couldn't quite bring himself to touch it. Beyond, a couple strolled the sidewalk, leaning together to open a large umbrella. A weak rain had started. His extended fingers hovered there, just shy of the bar.

He found himself taking a step back—then another, and then he was edging all the way to the fireplace. He peered through the dull flames and focused on the charred brick wall behind. The rhythm of the light was almost hypnotic, but his focus remained on the unmoving wall. He stretched his hands in front of him, palms out, to receive the fire's warmth. But there was no warmth. If anything, the air was colder the closer his hands got to the hearth.

He felt a bit silly with his hands held uselessly out like this. Time to head. He picked up his briefcase and thrust his free hand into his pocket. It met something brittle. The ruffled edge of Elena's Post-it. He must at some point have transferred it from his top desk drawer, where it had lain like a holy relic, to his coat. He must have resolved to keep it with him wherever he went. But he could not recall making that decision.

A breeze in the fireplace caused a faint moan. The flames stirred.

A thought came to Lance. He set his briefcase back down.

Could he really be sure that he and Mr. Furlanetti had achieved a truce? Since Ms. Shillingsham was in on the radiator business too, maybe the vice-president had no reason to fear Lance. Maybe he would be at Ms. Shillingsham's door first thing tomorrow, raring to spill his news. Lance needed to be at work before Mr. Furlanetti arrived. He had to watch the man's every move, thrust himself into the conversation if and when it happened. Defend himself.

The door hummed through its rotations as another lexicographer left for the day. The street bustled with rush hour, the hubbub of engines and sirens and horns. What was Lance thinking? He had to get home, had to eat, shower, sleep in his bed.

The door's rotation finished. The lobby was empty. The only motion was the flames in the fireplace. Taking a closer look, Lance was surprised to see that the logs were still intact. How long since they'd been put in there? But their bark was uncharred.

The flames swayed in place, dancers with seductive hips.

No, this was too important. He had to guard his position here. He had to be vigilant.

The bank of elevators was at rest. Every single car waited on the ground floor, door ajar. Inviting him in.

Lance examined his office floor. The carpet, with its fibres crushed and clotted by years of furniture and feet, was probably not an ideal bed. A survey of Jeanine's belongings revealed nothing that could be spread as a protective sheet.

Even less beguiling than the bedding: his dinner. He unwrapped the two sandwiches he'd grabbed from the cafeteria—pried begrudgingly from the crutch lady, who was trying to close up; even the endlessly ladling giant had been in end-of-day mode, carefully wiping his pot with a foul cloth. The sandwiches were not only paltry, they were frightening. Clones, both of them, of the monstrosity he'd managed a few bites of during his meeting with Elena. With a fingertip, he lifted a flap of soggy bread. Anonymous meat in its monochrome goo.

Bad idea, this. Outlandish. Time to bail, to smarten up and head home.

The walls clanged. Pipes, doing the secret things they did.

Lance thought of the apartment that waited for him a short subway ride away. Dust clinging to heavy drapes. Chairs, tables, dressers arrayed like dinosaur skeletons in a museum. Battleship-grey filing cabinets; old records of a dead business, a dead family, a lineage that had boiled down to one useless guy. Drawers stuffed with his father's sentimental keepsakes—the cufflinks he'd worn on his wedding day, yellowing letters from his courtship with the future Mrs. Blunt, torn snaps from decades past.

Lance couldn't go back to all that. Not tonight. Tomorrow he could face his apartment, the squalid facts of his life out there. But for now it was easier to sink into his chair, which was borderline comfy and allowed a slight backward tilt. This was nice, this was easy. He could drape his coat over him as a blanket, put his feet on his desk.

But it was far too early to sleep. Lance made motions in the direction of tidying—rearranging his desk drawers, straightening up the contents of the shelves, throwing away the dead leaves heaped at the plant's base. But he couldn't bring himself to toss anything other than leaves. Everything here belonged to someone else.

With no TV, and a computer that was useless to him, Lance lacked for entertainment. Jeanine's books did not look likely to have pictures. Except one: it had a stout spine of laminated beige cardboard. A photo album. He took it down and flipped it open. Several shots of Jeanine's dog, large and friendly, with tan fur flopping over its eyes. The occasional night-out pic—friends at a table, Day-Glo drinks with straws and umbrellas. Jeanine as a bridesmaid. Jeanine on a tropical getaway, posing in front of palm trees. Page by page, she was getting older. Her friends reappeared, often with children. The children grew. Then the man started to appear in the pictures too, a genial, bespectacled guy with thinning hair and a wardrobe that didn't stray from the favoured shade of khaki. Business casual, always.

By this point Lance felt he'd snooped enough. He closed the book and replaced it on the shelf, into the groove it had occupied, a clear stripe in the dust. Who kept something like this at work? Didn't it properly belong at home?

After another sad stab at sandwich consumption, he revisited the men's room. The toilet was gurgling again. The spiderwebbed lines of mould appeared to have multiplied. One floor tile rocked under his weight, the loosened adhesive below it crunching slightly. Lance undid his top buttons and splashed water on his face. He pumped the soap dispenser, but the stuff that dribbled out was slimy and heavy with oil. He decided not to apply it to his face. In lieu of a toothbrush, he used a fingertip to polish the fronts of his teeth. Tomorrow he'd go home and give them a proper brush and floss. Even if nothing happened with Mr. Furlanetti, even if Lance was still wondering where things with the big man stood, he'd leave the Tower tomorrow at five. Hygiene required it.

And so, his minimal toilet done, Lance returned to his office. A couple adjustments, and his chair was ready to cradle him. Without much trouble, barely fazed by the discomfort of reclining in a cheap office piece, Lance slid into sleep.

Without knowing quite how he got there, without having risen from his chair and left his office, Lance was across the hall, in the men's room. He was sitting on a toilet, which rocked slightly when he shifted his weight. He peered at its base, the black mould that infested the caulking. He did not have to crane to look past his bunched pants, the dangling tongue of his belt, his scuffed black work shoes, because these did not exist. He was naked, and glazed with sweat, and shivering. He shifted his weight again and the toilet shifted farther than should be possible. It slid from its proper foundation, and the mould-caked gap widened.

Lance heard his name. Not exactly with his ears; it was more like the one syllable tugged at his chest, as if grappling hooks had his ribs and pulled him forward. He stood, the tiled floor painfully cold beneath his soles. He exited the toilet stall. In the mirror was his reflection, a tiny and pale and naked thing, an almost fetal version of himself, curled tight against the cold. And all around the mirror, the tiles of the wall were trembling. And as the Tower emitted a great groan, many of them fell away and slid to the floor, shattering in dusty bursts. And beneath them was not the bare wall you'd expect under tile, with its swirls of dried glue. Nor the view you'd expect behind that, the plumbing and heating and wiring. Rather than wires or pipes, the wall's innards were bone and cartilage and muscle, pulsing.

And as Lance watched, the flesh writhed and rearranged itself, drew together in some parts and spread apart in others, until two lips had formed—giant, deeply cracked, caked with something gummy that could be moistened plaster. And they split, revealing only darkness behind, and they were going to tell him something. The Tower was going to speak.

"Good morning."

Lance snapped awake. The imagery of his dream was dashed; a view of his office ceiling took its place. His feet were on his desk. His jacket was half-draped over him. Drool bisected his cheek.

"Good morning, Ms. Shillingsham."

"Taking a little nap?"

"That's right." Lance gathered up his coat. "Got here early."

"After the worm, are you?"

"Sorry?"

"Early bird. You must be after the worm."

"Oh. Well, you know. Got files to go through." The mention of breakfasting birds made Lance realize that he was immensely hungry. It felt like his stomach was digesting its own lining.

"Mm." Ms. Shillingsham had not stepped through the doorway. One hand gripped the door jamb, hard. She looked around, taking in the office. "Looks pretty good in here."

"Yeah. Tidied a bit."

"Now. Lance." A deep inhalation. "Something unusual has come up. A group of clients are coming in. Clients!" Ms. Shillingsham clutched a broach at her throat. She was dressed today in a relatively muted beige ensemble. No hat. "They insisted on coming here and speaking to us in person. They want..." She shuddered. "Lance, they want a *pitch.*"

"Clients?"

"Yes. They're from the school board. They are interested in stocking Emberton in their school libraries."

"Well, good!" offered Lance. "I mean, that's what we're here for, right?"

She brightened. "That's certainly what *you've* been here for! You and your lunch meetings."

"Yeah. Those."

"Well, I'll tell you what. Let's take this meeting today, with the school board people, as another opportunity for you. I want you to talk to them. I'll watch, get a sense of your style. See you in action."

"Sounds great. When?"

"Right now. I know it's short notice, but don't worry. I've done your prep for you. I threw together a PowerPoint presentation. This'll take the pressure off a bit, allow you to relax and do your thing. Just say a little bit about each point, let your natural charm show through. No need to worry about the actual content—all you need to do is read the slides."

Strangers in drab suits occupied the boardroom: two men and a women, all grey-haired, all with faces pinched into an expression suggesting they were about to dine on something unpalatable. Ms. Shillingsham produced her brightest smile. "Hello again," she said to the trio. "I'd like you to meet Lance Blunt; he will be leading this presentation."

Lance smiled at the three, who did not reciprocate. He tried his best to rustle up his sales persona. Not only was he still caked with the residue of sleep, but now he had internal troubles too. Before leaving his office he'd bolted the remains of the cafeteria sandwiches. They were committing atrocities of some kind in his belly; he hoped its agonized rumblings were not audible to the clients.

But *something* was rumbling audibly, and it wasn't Lance. It was Mr. Furlanetti, just now entering the boardroom. "I came to watch and learn," he said to Ms. Shillingsham's questioning glance, though his demeanour was hardly that of an eager student in the presence of a master. More like a slavering wolf in the presence of a wounded lamb.

Ms. Shillingsham scuttled around to a seat where a laptop sat open. She typed, and a slide appeared on a screen that had been pulled down in front of the whiteboard. All text, of course. Dim, because the boardroom lights were on full-blare.

"Is it too bright in here?" Ms. Shillingsham asked, squinting back at the others. "Shall I turn off the lights?"

"I can make it out fine," said Lance.

The clients offered no response.

"Okay, then," said Ms. Shillingsham. "Take it away, Lance."

"All right," said Lance, trying to make eye contact with the trio. The attempt was unsuccessful—one looked at the floor, another at the wall, and the third at the PowerPoint screen. "So I'm here to tell you about... uh..."

Ms. Shillingsham cleared her throat and inclined her head in the direction of the screen.

"Well, I guess I don't need to tell you that," said Lance, hitching a thumb back toward the screen with its barely visible letters. "You can see for yourself."

The member of the trio who'd been staring at the screen hunched forward, squinted, and nodded.

"I think," said Lance, "we can break this down pretty easily into a few main points. Next slide, please." Is that what you said with PowerPoint? Lance wasn't sure, but Ms. Shillingsham obediently prodded her laptop, and new blocks of text filled the screen. Bullet points, Lance believed they were called.

Mr. Furlanetti had begun to drool, a dull grey dribble mounting the bulge of his left jowl.

"So..." Lance started. "As you can see..." Dust motes danced in the light. A hand shot up. The woman. "Yes?" said Lance.

"I can't make out point number three."

"Oh," said Lance as calmly as he could, "I wouldn't worry about it. It's hardly—"

"Tell the lady," said Mr. Furlanetti.

"Sorry?" said Lance.

"Tell her what it says. She's the client. Help her."

"John!" said Ms. Shillingsham. The clients' eyes roved from her to Mr. Furlanetti to Lance.

"Sorry," said Lance, "I'm not clear why you're sitting in?"

Mr. Furlanetti opened his mouth. First there was a fanfare of burbles to get through. Then his voice made its debut. "I am here…" He paused, ears pricked.

The handle of the boardroom door was turning.

One by one, picking up on Mr. Furlanetti's reaction, heads turned to the door. Its handle concluded its rotation, and the door eased open.

Mr. Furlanetti closed his mouth. Ms. Shillingsham opened hers and covered it with a shaking hand. Lance's throat made a noise like a watch being wound. The clients, in their confusion, looked from vice-president to president to the doorway, where a very old man was gliding into the room.

"Please continue, Lance," said Mr. Emberton, taking a seat.

Lance did not know where his voice had gone or whether he might be able to retrieve it. His mouth, already dry with nervousness, had become a full-on Sahara.

"I'm sorry to have interrupted," continued Emberton. "Please, continue exactly where you left off."

Somehow Lance's voice croaked back to life. "I was just, um, explaining how… this here…" Lance gestured at the screen. He saw Mr. Furlanetti, his raisin eyes widened to prunes, sneaking to the open door to slip away.

"There was a question," Lance continued, "about point number three here, and I was saying we don't need to worry about it, since it's probably the least important one."

"Then why," asked Emberton, "is it up there?"

"Oh, some reason," mumbled Lance. "Anyway." Desperately, he returned his attention to the trio, who appeared as joyless as ever. "You know what, folks? I have to admit, I'm not much of a PowerPoint guy. I'd rather tell you about the product myself, face-to-face, just you and me and the plain facts."

A warm serenity had come over Emberton's face; apparently he approved.

"Ms. Shillingsham," Lance said brightly, "why don't you turn off that thing, and I'll just tell these good people what our dictionary has to offer."

Ms. Shillingsham bristled. "Turn it off?"

"Yes, if you don't mind." Lance hooked a finger under his collar and tugged it loose. "If that's okay. I think we could all benefit from a nice chat. Low-tech, like."

"Well, I suppose..." Her finger wavered over a button, then plunged, and the screen went dark.

With the bullet points gone, Lance eased into sales mode. He did everything he could to describe the dictionary in glowing terms. He related the anecdote about his father running to the dictionary whenever an unfamiliar word was uttered on TV. That got their attention. They were thawing. His old techniques were working. "On a personal note, another thing I really like about the Emberton Dictionary is the etymology. We have a dedicated staff of etymologists, really good professional ones, who find out where the words come from, go back into the mists of time, and find the stories that shaped each word. You can't understand the present if you don't know the past. The dictionary is richer for it." He threw in his father's joke about manure—*I thought it came from a cow*—which earned mild titters. Then he eased out of his coat, laid it on the table, and lowered his voice. "This is why the Emberton is invaluable in an education type of scenario like yours. It's perfect for eager young minds, hungry for knowledge, hungry to get the full story."

It went on like this for a while longer. But, with a loosening of the knot in his chest, Lance knew that it no longer mattered precisely what he said: he had them. The school board reps were in the palm of his hand, swept up in his enthusiasm, and they were going to place an order for hundreds of Emberton dictionaries.

"Well," said Lance, "I guess that's about all I have to say. But I genuinely believe our product is the best fit for your needs. I hope you feel the same."

"We have a concern," said the woman.

"Of course. Any questions, concerns, go ahead. I'm happy to help."

"We recognize the quality and authority of the dictionary, of course. But you haven't yet published an edition specifically for schools."

"We haven't?"

"No. Do you plan to?"

Lance had no idea. His three weeks on the job had not indoctrinated him into such knowledge. His hours spent in meetings had not exactly been a fount of useful data. About the only thing he could tell these clients with any certainty was that the water fountain on the fourth floor would not be repaired anytime soon.

"No." It was Emberton who spoke, injecting the word with surprising force. Ms. Shillingsham flinched at the sound. "We have no such plans."

The school board woman looked from Lance to Emberton and back.

"No," echoed Lance. "No plans."

"Well, then," said the woman, "what about the next edition? Will it be suitable for all ages?"

"Oh, I get it," said Lance. "You're worried about, like, dirty words?"

"Mature terminology," Ms. Shillingsham cut in, correctively.

"That's our concern, yes," said the woman. "Will edits be made with younger readers in mind?"

Lance looked at Ms. Shillingsham, who was looking at Mr. Emberton.

"No," said the old man, more vehemently than before. As one, the clients faced him. "My dictionary will include whatever words I wish it to include." He smiled at the trio, or perhaps he was baring his teeth. "Every last fucking word."

Abruptly, the trio stood. "Thank you," said the woman. "This has been edifying. But we will continue our search for a family-friendly product." They hurried out, pursued by Ms. Shillingsham, who tossed polite phrases at their retreating backs.

Emberton rested his palms on the tabletop. "Good show, Lance."

"Thank you."

"It's regrettable I had to undermine your sale. You had them hanging on your every word. I appreciate your ditching that PowerPoint nonsense. It was not going to grab them."

"No, I didn't think so." Lance waved dismissively at Ms. Shillingsham's laptop. "Technology. Overrated."

"And you very deftly steered past your own area of weakness."

"Sorry?"

"You avoided some embarrassment. Surrounding the fact that you couldn't read the screen anyway."

Lance tried to laugh, but it sounded more like a gerbil drowning in soft butter. "Well, sir, you're right. It was very dim. These fluorescent lights, they're pretty, um, you know. Bright."

"That's not what I mean, Lance. I'm talking about your special problem. Your *particular difficulty*?"

A noise escaped Lance's lips. He didn't know exactly what sort of noise this was, but it suggested that the drowned gerbil had come back to life and was enduring unspeakable abuses.

"Don't worry, Lance. I am here to help. There is something I wish you to see. I will expect you at my office in ten minutes." And Emberton glided to the door, leaving Lance alone in the silent room.

Chapter 9

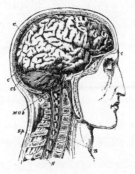

Lance stepped from the elevator onto floor twelve, his brain so addled that he did not see the trio of editors huddled in the hallway until he almost collided with them.

Mr. Tradd was one of the three. "Your stance," he was saying, "is demented!" His voice rose a notch. "We are the keepers of the gates! You propose we fling them wide, invite the vandals in, let them batter the temple, ravage the library!"

"Oh, Lord," groaned Mr. Allsop.

Lance tried to edge around the group without being noticed.

"If cretins out there corrupt the word," continued Mr. Tradd, "we must rectify their idiocy, not cast it in bronze."

"The bronze *age*, I'd say," muttered Mr. Allsop. "That's where you propose to retain us."

Lance was past the group. He was about to pick up the pace when Mr. Tradd's piercing voice stopped him short: "Ah! Here's a young fellow from the fourth floor. One of our marketers. What was it again? Blurt? Bluster?"

Lance turned to face the man. "Blunt."

"Ah, even better. That's where everything is headed,

isn't it? All the fine points dulled away, precision instruments worn blunt. I have seen the future, and it is illiterate."

The word stung, as ever. Lance had rarely heard it used in a tone that was not disgusted or pitying or aghast. "Okay, great," he said. "Thank you for that. I'm just heading up to see—"

But Mr. Tradd seized him by the shoulders and wheeled him to face the other two.

"Young man," continued Mr. Tradd, "do me a good turn, would you? Can you answer some questions?"

"Oh, no," groaned Mr. Allsop.

"You don't have to listen to this," said the third editor, a woman in a gingham skirt and matching blazer. "You're free to go."

But he couldn't: the wiry Mr. Tradd had him in a firm grip.

"Imagine," continued Mr. Tradd, "you're a city engineer. You program traffic lights."

"Fine," muttered Lance.

"It is brought to your attention that one particular intersection has a problem. Drivers regularly run the red. There's not much cross-traffic, they don't see any harm. But you do! You know perfectly well that, one day out of a hundred, a truck will come thundering along the perpendicular route, an eighteen-wheel juggernaut!"

Sweat had sprung out all over Mr. Tradd's face. A scent of damp wool rose from his tweed blazer. He released Lance's shoulders, but Lance—like the other editors—was under the spell of the tirade and did not make a move.

"So, young man," continued Mr. Tradd, taking big gulps of air between words. "Your colleagues in the civic engineering department have a modest proposal." His voice galloped forth on a steed of rage. "They propose," he roared, "to make the light green all the time! People want to run the red? So be it! Go with the flow! Let the light shine green *in both directions at once!*"

A break for face-wiping, performed with the coarse tweed of Mr. Tradd's left sleeve, leaving angry red marks.

"Never mind the collision," he said. "Never mind the day of judgement when the barrelling rig arrives. If people want to cross at the wrong time, let them! If they wish to drive *in exact opposition to the correct flow,* so be it! Amen!" Both arms were flung wide now. "Amen, brothers and sisters! Let the chariots crash! Let the metal crumple, the infants in their car seats perish! Why have red lights at all? Why have lights? Where the people choose to drive, there they shall drive! Engineers ought to *record* the flow of traffic, not *control* it! Who do we think we are? It's not our place to guide, instruct, protect. Merely to reflect. If the hoi polloi use *hone in* where *home in*'s wanted? List it! Folk use *infer* to mean *imply*? No problem: simply add a definition!

"So tell me, young man from the fourth floor, how will you respond to your colleagues? Will you support their innovative new plan?"

"Uh..." Lance looked to the other editors for help.

"Don't worry yourself," said the woman. "Our Mr. Tradd is a bit excitable. No need to bother with—"

"*No need!*" mimicked Mr. Tradd. "*No need!* This is a game for PhDs and eggheads. Is that your angle, Miss Easdown? Language does not matter to the common man?"

Something clutched Lance's elbow. It was Mr. Allsop's hand. "I imagine," he said in Lance's ear, "you were hoping to get to the elevator. No doubt you're *late.*" He flung the word aggressively in Mr. Tradd's direction. "For an important appointment *upstairs.*" He was steering Lance to the elevator. "Another editorial spat, I'm afraid. Sorry you got dragged in."

"But tell me!" shouted Mr. Tradd, trotting behind them. "Tell me one more thing!"

Mr. Allsop's face was maroon. "Enough, Edmund! Give it a rest, for Christ's sake. This poor kid's got a—"

"Nauseous!" Mr. Tradd screamed. "I'm nauseous!"

Mr. Allsop took a step toward his colleague, hands held out in the manner of a negotiator talking down a gunman. "I've got antacids in my—"

"I'm talking to the *kid,* Chuck. What does it mean to you, Blunt? If I tell you I'm nauseous, what does it mean?"

"Um, it means you're sick? You need to vomit?"

With an ear-splitting shriek, Mr. Tradd slammed his palms over his ears. He doubled over as if trying to bury his face in his belly. Then, shaking off Mr. Allsop's attempts to restrain him, he unfolded himself to holler: "It means *you're* sick, kid! *You're* sick! *I* make *you* sick! *You're* nauseated by *me!*"

Lance decided now was the time to make for the elevator.

"I make people sick! I'm nauseous! That's what it means!" The words were filling the hallway despite Mr. Allsop's efforts to clap a hand over his colleague's mouth. "A *big* collision's coming! Eighteen wheels of language karma! Buckle up, Blunt!"

The shrieks continued as Lance escaped into the lift.

Before leaving the luxurious elevator and entering the shabby anteroom, Lance composed himself, smoothed his clothes, braced himself for whatever was to come.

A fly—possibly the same one from his first visit—now lay dead on the floor, at the edge of the circle of light cast by the bare bulb. Lance was buzzed in. The secretary smiled benignly and simply waved him through. "No need to sign in, hon."

The office was a little brighter than it had been last time—this morning's clouds were white and confined to the sky, rather than grey and creeping between skyscrapers. The furnishings looked shabbier, the leather spines on the bookshelves cracked and scuffed, the hung paintings dulled with time. Even the imposing *Hunt* looked banal, its colours leached, its figures crude.

Lance sipped gratefully from the glass Emberton handed him. That lacquered-wood taste soothed his throat even as it slightly burned. His head felt warm. Taking another look around, he conceded that his thirst, his irritability after a night in his office, had tainted his vision. This office wasn't so bad.

Emberton laid his own glass on the desktop. "Today's discussion will be entirely confidential."

Lance's throat relaxed as the drink went to work on his nerves. "Sure. No problem."

"I never suggested it would be a problem." Emberton moved to his bookshelf and took down a giant leather-bound book—bigger even than the Emberton. "I hoped to save this for later. I wanted to give you more time to settle in."

"Oh, I feel pretty settled in. I may as well live here."

"But my hand has been forced. Events are accelerating." Emberton laid the big book on his desk and flipped through the pages. He rotated it and gestured Lance closer.

Lance glanced at the text, then instinctively away. There

was no point scrutinizing such things, as if their encoded meaning might suddenly open to him.

"What book is this?" asked Emberton.

"I don't know. Something important?"

Emberton chuckled. "Yes, I suppose it is. Certainly it has been significant in the history of my family." His hand slid along the page, which whispered under his touch. "Centuries ago, in England, my family owned a press. We were among the first publishers in the kingdom. We printed Bibles." His voice hardened. "But there was a scandal. Many of our clients were nobles; they would have us print a small number of copies for use within their families. It wasn't long before the specific requests began. We would be asked to change the words, ever so slightly. Adjust those passages that did not suit the client's theological views. Tweak a Beatitude. Nudge the advice of an Apostle. Many clients showed a particular editorial interest in Christ's remark about the eye of a needle." Emberton's finger froze on the page, then moved horizontally, following a printed line. "And we obliged. For a little extra lucre, we tampered with the Word of God. Until the Church sniffed us out. The scandal ruined us. Drove us into exile on our own estate. And that's when..." He snapped to attention. "But I get ahead of myself. This, Lance, is a Bible. Did you study this book as a young man?"

"No. I didn't study books."

"Did you attend church?"

"My mom went, but my dad let me stay home with him. We'd play cribbage."

"Good. I want these words to be new to you. Have another sip. Go on. Now, look at the page and tell me what you see."

Lance did. He saw line after line of printed words. Numbers hovered in the margins beside the text and also were sprinkled throughout the words, breaking them up. Here and there, an especially large letter was wrapped in illustrated vines.

"You're not telling me what you see, Lance."

"I don't see anything. A lot of letters and numbers."

"What do they say?"

As had happened in the cafeteria with Elena, a tear welled. This kind of humiliation was so familiar, so achingly common through the years. How many teachers had tried in exactly this way to break through to him? How many teachers, striding the aisles between desks, maybe nervously tapping a yardstick on their thigh (Mr. Harker) or leaning back to look at the ceiling as if in anguished prayer (Miss Grant), had insisted that he look again, try again, look at the whole paragraph and not just the sounds, or work through the sounds without worrying about the words, or just stare until his corneas bled, until somehow a sunbeam would crash through the roof, illuminate this shitty page on this shitty elementary textbook with some shit story about a boy and his bouncing ball? It never worked. The ceiling never tore open to admit the shaft of light that would strike the page and drench it in meaning. And the classmates, watching hungrily as if they could eat his misery, gulp it down and smack their lips. Then the first few titters, the smirks behind hands, maybe one from the far corner (Cody Munn) and another from nearby, a girl's voice (Jenny Carson), and then a couple more, until the dam broke and the standing wave of laughter crashed in, everybody racked with giggles then with chuckles then with full-out guffaws, even sometimes the teacher, because who could resist such

153

contagious hilarity? How many times had he suffered through this? And here he was, a grown man, in a downtown office tower, and it was happening again.

While these wretched memories revived themselves, Emberton's hand, shrunken and spotted and yellow under the nails, pointed to a spot on the page. "What," the old man asked gently, "are the first six words?"

Lance looked up at the old man with burning eyes.

"Trust me, Lance. Look where I'm pointing."

Lance did. And everything changed.

"What are the first six words, Lance?"

"'In the beginning was the Word.'"

The old hand moved aside to reveal the letters it had blocked. "And what does it say next?"

"'And the Word was with God, and the Word was God.'" The letters were no longer a tangle of lines and squiggles, wires dumped haphazard in a trash bin. They were a pattern, a system, lines guiding his eye, taking it through words, which were built into sentences, which offered up their meaning effortlessly, as when Lance saw a triangle and thought *triangle,* or spied a chair and his mind said *chair.* It was that easy.

"Keep going, Lance."

"'The same was in the... was in the be...' I can't. It's gotten hard again."

"Take another sip of your drink."

He did. "'The same was in the beginning with God.'" Lance peered into his glass. Suspended in the bottom of the amber liquid was a dark blot. "This?"

"Yes."

"What is it?"

"It is the essence of language, Lance. The essence of a

great power which, for all these years, you have been denied. And only I can give it to you."

Lance looked around the office in wonder. Everything was still the same, exactly as it had been last time: the same bombé cabinets; the same expensive de Sedes; the same vast mahogany desk. There was the wall-sized painting, its pursuing hounds, its hunted fox. And there, on the brass plate beneath, its title: *The Hunt*. He held up his glass. "How did you make this?"

"That, young man, is a family secret. Centuries in the making. After the scandal, my ancestors abandoned publishing. They had come to understand the power of language, and they turned their genius to harnessing that power. Physically extracting it from the word. For generations they toiled at it."

Ever so slightly, the fluid in Lance's glass shone.

"Lance, if you prove yourself loyal to me, you can enjoy an unlimited supply. I can show you its source—I can show you how it is created. Here, in the Tower, this fluid is born. But the secret is a heavy thing to divulge. There is something you must do so I can be sure I can trust you."

Lance couldn't bring himself to speak.

"A spy is at work in the Tower. Someone is digging around, nosing into my family history, rooting around the secret places of the Tower. Security have been unable to catch him."

Lance almost blurted the correction aloud. The spy was not a he.

"But I have indications," continued Emberton, "that this traitor may on occasion cross paths with you. So I'll need you to be observant, and when the time is right, to act without hesitation. Your task is to identify the spy. Use your abilities—you can get along with people, talk your way into their confidence, sell yourself as a friend who can be trusted. You must prod and probe until you find out who it is. And then you will identify him to me. Can you do this, Lance?"

This drink would transform his existence. Satisfy a lifetime's craving. He would do almost anything for a steady supply—but he was not going to betray Elena. Sure, he barely knew her; sure, his affliction was a closer and more constant companion than she might ever be. But snitching on her, even if it just meant a bit of trouble with her boss, and even if she was in the wrong... there was no way he could do it.

"I'll try," he said quietly.

"Good. Very good, my boy." Emberton rose. "Drink up," he said. "I will see you again when you have identified my spy."

Lance gulped down the rest of the fluid in his glass. It was more than he'd thought—a big swig. He almost choked on it, but forced it down, felt it slide over his throat and nestle in his belly, warming him from the inside out. His salvation. Part of him now.

Lance nodded at Emberton's secretary as he passed back through the anteroom, trying not to betray how dazed he felt. She tilted her beehive respectfully toward him. He noticed now that a small plaque was on her desk. *Miss Fairburn,* it said. Then, *Receptionist.* He could read this.

Tacked on the wall behind her was a poster: a schooner silhouetted against a sunset, all its masts and rigging outlined in brilliant detail. But it was the words Lance savoured, golden letters splayed against the dark sea. *Smooth Sailing,* they read.

"Things feel different, hon?" said Miss Fairburn,

bringing Lance's attention back to her calm face. "Things making a little more sense now?"

"Something like that," he mumbled.

"He has that effect," she said with a smile. "He's a great man. He's more than just a lexicographer."

Something more than lexicography is going on in this Tower. Elena had said that.

"It's been my honour to serve him half a century," said Miss Fairburn. "Half a century now."

"That's a long time," said Lance.

"I'll tell you one thing about Mr. Emberton." She pushed her glasses farther up her nose. "He places great value in loyalty."

"Good," said Lance. "That's good."

She peered at him through her cat-eye frames. "Need something, hon?"

"It was you," said Lance. "Wasn't it?"

"Not clear on your meaning there."

"You left a message on my answering machine. Weeks ago now. Telling me to come here for a job. First a postcard came, but I didn't answer it. And then there was a phone call. It was you."

"Yes, it was."

"Why? How did you... how did *he* know about me?"

"I do as I'm told, hon. That's all there is to it." She fussed with the clipboard and its pen on a string. "Loyalty, Mr. Blunt. It's got me where I am." Her voice changed— slowed, went raspier. She was imitating Mr. Emberton, quoting his words, without quite knowing it. "Loyalty will take you far, if you cultivate it."

"Thank you," said Lance. "For calling me. I don't know where I'd be otherwise."

A maternal smile. "Off you go, hon."

Waiting for the elevator, Lance found himself swatting at something that buzzed around his head. A new fly had claimed the space and patrolled it in slow, droning circles—either that, or the fly on the floor had been resurrected. At this point, Lance was ready to believe anything. *I once was blind, and now I see.* The problem in his brain could be fixed. The lifelong trouble could be allayed. And maybe—why not?—the dead could struggle back to life and circle again around a sputtering light.

Back in his office, he took Elena's Post-it from his pocket, laid it on his desk, and flattened it. There it was, plain as day, her message to him: *Can you meet me in the cafeteria? Monday, noon? Need your help. — Elena (from etymology).*

Lance found he was shivering. This was a kind of ecstasy. A thought had formed in the mind housed in that small and beguiling body. An entreaty, a question that she wanted him to understand. So she had laid it out on crushed pulp, with whatever dyes constituted ink, and had encoded it. And now he could look at those small, anxious pen strokes, and he could know what she was thinking, what she wanted, a little slice of the thoughts and needs that stirred within her.

This was what people did every day, by the billion. It was so simple. And yet it was miraculous.

Hunger for written language raged in his brain, his eyes, his chest. He wanted to drink it in, gorge himself. He pulled one of Jeanine's books off the shelf. It had a red, waffle-textured cover. No picture on the front, only crisp silver letters. *Fundamentals of—*

"Hello, Lance."

Lance almost dropped the book. He had not noticed the

visitors at his doorway. "Ms. Shillingsham," he said. "What can I do for you?"

"What are you up to, Lance?" She was frowning intently at *Fundamentals of*.

"I'm just..." Lance suppressed a whim to shout the rest of his sentence, to let it clang off the walls and ceiling of this drab little office. He savoured the magnitude of what he was about to say. He looked down at the cover. *Fundamentals of Closing the Sale*. A hysterical burst of laughter tripped from his lips. "Just doing some reading."

"Really." She turned her frown on the figure behind her. "He's reading."

Like a hippo squeezing past a giraffe, Mr. Furlanetti made his way around Ms. Shillingsham and charged into the room, finger pointed at the heavy book. "Nonsense!" he shouted. "Liar!"

"What's this about?" Lance looked from the blustering big man to the frowning skeletal woman.

"Bring it over, Mr. Furlanetti," she said, and he snatched the tome from Lance's grip and stormed back to the doorway. "Please come here, Lance," said Ms. Shillingsham. She had the book open and was examining a page.

"What is this?" demanded Lance.

Ms. Shillingsham had finished studying the page. She rotated the book so it was facing him. "From the top of the page, please."

"I don't understand."

"Mr. Furlanetti has made some curious allegations about you. I'd like to put them to rest. For his peace of mind, if nothing else."

A chortle from Mr. Furlanetti. "Peace of mind!"

Ms. Shillingsham cast the man a pitying look. "Let's get this done, please, Lance. From the top of the page."

Lance looked at the page. The taste of the drink was a distant memory. The text wavered as if it were printed on a wind-puffed sail. Was the drink's effect waning? He took a breath, and plunged.

As before, it came to him. No struggle, no effort, no deciphering each letter. The words were words, blocks of meaning that zapped along his optic nerve and straight into his brain. "'Selling isn't something done *to* our customers,'" he read. "'It's something done *for* them.'"

Ms. Shillingsham turned the book around again and reread the top of the page. She looked at Mr. Furlanetti.

"What... you..." Mr. Furlanetti tore the book from her hand. "What kind of..." His features stretched like bread dough, jowls tugging, brow expanding into an enormous incredulity. "More!" he yelled, shoving the book back to Lance. "Keep going."

"'A good salesperson does not convince people to buy what they don't need. A good salesperson helps people identify their needs.'"

The book was torn again from Lance's grasp and ferociously scanned by Furlanetti. Helplessly, he lowered the page and looked pitifully at Lance. "Why would you... Why would you pretend..." His mouth kept opening and closing, but the questions had run dry. His raisin eyes rolled from Ms. Shillingsham to Lance and back. "He told me he... or I mean suggested... I could have sworn..."

He dropped the book. It thudded to the floor and was trampled as he stalked to Jeanine's bookshelf and yanked another volume free. It was the Emberton Dictionary. He flipped madly, pausing to scan the occasional passage before renewing his chase. He settled on a page and showed it to Lance. "That word. There."

At first the letters threatened to blur beyond legibility, but Lance was able to make it out: "'*Hazy,*'" he read. He checked the window, and indeed the air beyond was smudgy with fog. Somehow it was no surprise that here, in this room in Emberton Tower, with the radiator clanking and stirring to life, and the ceiling muttering in its private conduits, Mr. Furlanetti's random flipping would have guided him to this word. In this Tower, Lance was certain, nothing that happened to him was random. No accidents, no coincidence. *You belong here.*

"Definition," Mr. Furlanetti roared.

"'Misty,'" Lance answered calmly, "'Vague. Uncer—.'" His eyes, already confident in their ability to absorb the text, to digest without effort its content and pronunciation, had skipped ahead to the end of the entry, to the etymology: *17th century. Origin unknown.*

Mr. Furlanetti yanked the dictionary back from Lance's grasp and resumed flipping through it. The radiator's latest blast of heat was expanding through the room, and Mr. Furlanetti's forehead looked shinier than ever.

Origin unknown. Had Elena, or some other etymologist, made new discoveries *after* this edition was printed? No. Surely that wasn't how the profession worked—sudden, dramatic breakthroughs that revealed, in one swoop, rich backstories. Elena had simply invented an etymology for *hazy.* Not lied, exactly, Lance realized. She'd given him a story. Invited him into her imagination.

Where was she? More than ever, Lance had to know. He had so much to tell her.

The dictionary was shoved back into his hands. "There."
Mr. Furlanetti jabbed a grubby finger at another entry.

"'*Serpentine*,'" read Lance. "'Of or resembling a snake.'
Did you want me to read the second and third definitions
too?"

Mr. Furlanetti slid the dictionary back into place.
He stood for several seconds staring at its spine. Ms.
Shillingsham looked at him with tender concern. "John, I
think you've been under a lot of strain."

Covering his mouth and burbling heavily from the gut,
Mr. Furlanetti rushed past her into the corridor.

"He's not well," said Ms. Shillingsham, to herself as
much as to Lance. When she looked up at him, her eyes
were imploring. "He was making some silly fuss about you
being—well, I realize how ridiculous this will sound. He
seemed to think that you were unable to read. That you
couldn't follow the PowerPoint this morning." She shook
her head, her upper teeth clamped hard on her lower lip.
"Please don't mention this to the others. He's been under
enormous stress."

"Sure." Lance found it hard to feel much pity right
now. The man had come within a hair's breadth of exposing
Lance. Even now, the drink was running out: glancing at
the cover where it was splayed on the floor, Lance could still
read *of* and *Sale*, but *Fundamentals* was a rubble of letters. Had
Mr. Furlanetti sprung his trap an hour later, Lance would
have been busted. This might be irrelevant now, seeing
as Mr. Emberton himself knew the secret. But the intention was there: Mr. Furlanetti had tried to get Lance fired.
Banished from the Tower. Severed from his destiny.

You belong here. Damn right, he did. More than that
burbling buffoon. As before, when Mr. Furlanetti had

uncovered Lance's handicap, rage took hold, and with it an alien confidence and an itch for revenge. He tried to simulate a concerned face. "Poor guy," he said. "I can only imagine."

Ms. Shillingsham reached out a hand. It appeared that she wanted to touch Lance, but they were standing a bit too far apart—and, as ever, she seemed incapable of stepping inside the office. So, after a moment's awkward stretching, her arm simply drew back in. "Thank you," she said. "Your discretion is much appreciated."

"But tell me," said Lance, stepping closer. "What is wrong with him?"

She pursed her lips and shook her head.

Now Lance reached out and found her forearm. He was close enough. "I don't want to tell the others a thing," he said. "But I feel I need to know. For my own peace of mind."

Her lips unpursed. Lance took a step back and almost stumbled as his foot crunched the spine of the book. He gave it a quick glance. No more *Sale*. Even the two-letter *of* meant nothing to him now.

"He's sick, Lance," she said. "Addicted."

"To what?"

"Something in the Tower's systems. Something in the pipes."

"What is it?"

"I don't know."

"What does it do for him?"

"I don't know. Makes him want more of it."

"And it damages his language, right? Doesn't improve it. Damages it."

"Why would it *improve* anything?"

Lance spoke quickly. "No, I mean, you know, it affects his speech."

"Sure. It always affects their speech."

"*Their?*"

"Oh, dear." She muttered something under her breath. "Others have had the same problem. It's not only John. Others who are... who are no longer with us."

"Jeanine?"

"No. Jeanine was clean."

"What happened to her?"

"This isn't about Jeanine. She didn't have this illness. But Mr. Furlanetti does. And it's very important to him... to *me*... that his illness not advance. If he gets any sicker, they might put him in..." Speech broke down for a while. She seemed to try to speak to Lance with her eyes alone.

"Third floor," he said.

She nodded.

"But that would be good, right? They'd make him better."

She shook her head. "No more questions, Lance. You know too much already. I mean, don't you ever wonder what you're doing here?"

"Working. Going through files."

"I do. Wonder, I mean." She reached out to touch him again. "Please, no offence. But I imagine John's probably told you—it wasn't our idea to hire you. We have a... a policy, you could say. About hiring. We only hire when we lose someone. Jeanine was the last to leave us; Mr. Meeks replaced her. And we only hire... well, I don't mean to sound discriminatory or what have you, but we hire people with plenty of experience of life. *Older* people. You—you're young. Life ahead of you. Plenty to live for. You should be out there, living, working with others your age. Don't you think?"

"Ms. Shillingsham, I believe I'm very fortunate to have this job. I believe I'm very lucky to work in Emberton Tower. I can assure you, I belong here."

"Well," she looked forlornly at the floor. "Anyway, I'm terribly sorry about John and his silly accusation. I wanted to prove him wrong, disabuse him of this crazy notion. He seemed so convinced." She glanced dubiously at the book on the floor.

Lance shrugged and grinned. "Glad I could help."

"And you'll keep this little event from the others?"

"I won't say anything to a single soul on this floor." *Always tell 'em the truth. But never the whole truth.* Of course Lance had no intention of speaking to the other marketers. He was devising a far more satisfying plan. Mr. Furlanetti, with his botched attempt at treachery, had handed Lance a beautiful gift.

Chapter 10

The following morning, in dreadful silence, Lance rode the elevator alone and stepped off on floor twelve. It was mercifully free of editors; he made his way unaccosted to the penthouse elevator.

Miss Fairburn's voice at the intercom: "What is it you want, hon?"

"To see Mr. Emberton. Please."

"I don't believe you have an appointment?"

"No, ma'am."

Something blinked in Lance's periphery. A red light was flashing on the wall beside him.

"This office is by appointment only. Please return to your floor, hon."

"But I have something important to tell Mr. Emberton. Really important."

"What is it?"

"I've identified the spy."

The red light stopped blinking.

Slowly, teasingly, fluid filled the glass. Emberton placed the decanter back on the tray and—with a languor that seemed intentional and cruel—held the glass to the light and rotated it. "So. You have fulfilled the assignment."

"Yes, sir."

"That was very fast work. Can I be sure," inquired Emberton, "your eagerness for this drink hasn't prompted... shall we say, an easy solution?"

"It wasn't actually that fast, sir. I made all these observations a while back... it was last night, thinking things over, that the pieces fell into place. The, uh, scales fell from my eyes. As it were."

In the amber depths of Lance's glass a darker thread stirred, thin and twisting like a string of spat-out blood. "The, uh, suspect has done two different things, on two separate occasions, to make me think it's him. I don't have proof, but I have..."

"Yes?"

"A feeling." Lance took a hefty swig. He could read the spine of a book on the shelf, ten feet away: its large, bronze letters spelled *Orthography*.

"So who's our mole?" Emberton asked.

"The vice-president of my department, sir. Mr. Furlanetti."

Emberton addressed his words to the fluid that swirled in his glass. "And how has he triggered your suspicion?"

Lance told the tale of the radiator incident as truthfully and as accurately as he could. Emberton did not acknowledge the craziness of what Lance was describing; it may as well have been a news report on fluctuations in the price of wheat.

"Is that all?" Emberton asked when the testimony was finished.

To avoid answering, Lance tipped his glass. It was empty.

"Nothing more?" pressed Emberton.

"Well… isn't it weird? He was, like, *sucking* on a radiator hose."

"You will learn, in time, that people behave strangely in the Tower. I'm surprised you haven't already made that general observation."

"Oh." So this wouldn't do it. Lance needed more. And although he didn't want to lie about Mr. Furlanetti's behaviour—he would have preferred to let facts do the incriminating—he couldn't leave things there. He'd come for a result, and he was going to achieve it. "I guess there's one other thing. He told me he was going to the archives."

Emberton was perfectly still, but something had shifted. Lance had his full attention.

"Yeah, I forgot all about it until now. I saw him in the elevator, he hit eleven instead of four. Just to make small talk, I asked him where he was headed. He told me the archives, to look something up."

"The archives!"

"That's what he said. Then he basically covered up his mouth, like he couldn't believe he'd told me. Started to backtrack. He was still babbling when I got off at my floor."

Emberton stood slowly and, in silence, made his way around his desk. He turned to the large painting, *The Hunt,* and spoke with his back to Lance. "The archives are rather important to me, Lance. They hold the past, and the past has enormous value. Origins. Tradition. It is alarming to think of someone plunging in there unauthorized. I will look into this."

"Good. It alarms me too, sir."

"You will need to stay late this evening. Once your floor has emptied, I will come to you."

"Sorry, what?"

"Surely you have not forgotten my promise. I will show you where this fluid is made. Lead you into the Tower's secret places. You will wait for me in your office."

Five o'clock arrived, but the sales and marketing team took a long time to vacate floor four. Lance listened as footsteps approached the elevator doors and shuffled forward upon the ding of arrival.

Beyond Lance's crooked blinds, the pervasive mist thickened. He yanked the cord and they rose, still crooked. The tail lights of vehicles and the glow of traffic lights twinkled through the mist. The gridwork of another tower's windows faced him, also obscured.

"We're ready."

Lance had been leaning toward the window, straining to see detail on the street, and at Emberton's words he started and his forehead thunked into the glass. It throbbed as he turned to face his employer. He nodded. "Let's go."

Rather than turning left toward the elevators, Emberton led Lance in the other direction, past the washrooms, and held open the door at the end of the short hall. "There are still a lot of people around," he explained, "and I will not share an elevator with them." The stairs were barely lit—each flight was handled by a single bulb. The isolated pools of light revealed dingy white steps, coal-black railings with chipped paint, walls consisting of large stone slabs. Leading the descent, Emberton flung his sentences over his shoulder like a fugitive shooting at pursuing cops.

"You have something of a way with words, haven't you?"

"Sure, I guess."

"The ability to persuade. That's a powerful thing."

"Thanks?" Lance's hand slid down the railing. He could feel the imperfections in the paint, the cold metal where it had chipped away, a slight sting when its hard, broken edge resumed.

"You've always been able to wield the power of language in person, face to face. But this other skill, this process of capturing the words." Emberton stopped walking and leaned on the railing. "Preserving them on paper, retrieving them later—this power eludes you. Always has." He craned down the steps, which grew dimmer as they receded from view. "Do you ever wonder why, Lance?"

"I don't know, sir. Something wrong in my... I don't know. No one could ever pinpoint it. Something wrong with me."

"And all your life, you felt this invisible wall, you on the one side, functioning people on the other. Everybody knew the secret of writing. Everyone belonged to the club. But not Lance Blunt."

"That's correct." Lance's voice kept steady, but only with effort.

"I know it may be hard for you to imagine," said Emberton, "but I too have suffered as you have." He produced from his pocket a slim silver flask, which he unscrewed and handed to Lance. "Fortification."

Lance took a sip. That familiar woody taste with its smoky undertone. He waited for the burning to subside. His senses awakened. The texture of the stone walls was more vivid, the random pocks and stray cracks.

"Language is power, Lance. And written language locks that power inside symbols, inside lines and loops and curves. The Emberton project, the project of my forefathers, was to get that power back out."

Emberton resumed the descent. A dull roar grew louder—they were nearing the press room. Evidently the shifts there extended beyond the confines of nine to five. One more flight and they drew even with that strangely comforting clamour. Emberton stopped and turned. Pockets of shadow marked his eyes and mouth, but his hair caught the light. A single strand stood straight up like a thread of white flame. "I take it you've seen the press room. Was it familiar? Like a place you've visited in a dream, perhaps?"

Lance wasn't sure if he should affirm this or not. He settled for a neutral, slightly perplexed expression.

"Well, I can assure you, it was not a dream."

Lance wanted to ask for elaboration, but Emberton raised a hand to discourage response.

The bottom stairwell opened onto a narrow hallway chiselled from rock, like an old mineshaft. An antique elevator was set into one wall, its black grille like the mask on a suit of armour. Ahead was a door of wooden planks black with rot, girdled by wide bands of metal. Emberton drew a key ring from his pocket, selected a key, and slid it into place. The door creaked open, revealing another rocky tunnel, this one lit by the sickly yellow flames of wall-mounted torches. Twenty feet along, the path vanished around a curve.

"How do these lights work?" Lance asked. Whatever shone from them was not normal flame. It was thicker, more like liquid, and did not appear to be consuming any kind of wick; nor did it flicker or gutter. Each lamp shone steadily.

"Wait," said Emberton. They trudged along until they reached a torch that was sputtering. Emberton unholstered his flask, screwed off the top, and carefully poured a trickle into the flame. It flared to life with a savage hiss, then settled into a strong, steady glow.

"The same stuff we're drinking?"

"It's an enduring source of power."

"Where does it come from?"

"You are about to find out."

They came to a vast door. It had the heavy, age-blackened look of a cast iron frying pan. The torchlight caused the shadows on its surface to shiver, revealing shapes stamped onto it. They appeared to be letters, but as the eye followed them, attempted to identify them, they evaded identification, bled into the neighbouring shape, refused to yield any sense. Emberton selected a second key, and the door swung open with a bellow of grinding metal.

They entered a narrow room. No torches here, just a dim, shifting, yellowish glow. On the floor was a heap of withered scraps of paper, like raked leaves, shifting and rustling with the motion of the door.

Lance picked one up and found he was able to read it. *Grount,* it said in faint black ink, the letters jagged. *Adjective. Caked in earth. Also (metaphorically) shamed.* He let it fall back to the pile, where it nestled in among its fellow scraps.

Ahead, the walls closed in and the ceiling lowered. They looked like they were made of soft clay rather than rock, and they showed a viscous sheen, as if the room were sweaty. Some kind of glow was cast onto the moist surface of the ceiling.

"Welcome to the heart of my project," said Emberton.

As Lance's eyes adjusted, he discerned a brass vat, maybe

eight feet high, dominating the far corner. Its great belly was studded with rivets and one large spigot. Metal steps mounted its side.

"Here," continued Emberton, "I extract the power of language. Please, draw another scrap from the pile."

Lance did. "*Paline,*" he read. But the rest of the words were beyond his reach.

Emberton handed over the flask, and Lance sucked gratefully from it.

There were the words, plain as day. "*Paline,*" Lance read out loud. "Adjective. Wan, sickly."

"Ah, yes," said Emberton, as if recalling a happy event from childhood. "Fell out of usage in the mid-nineteenth century."

He led Lance into the room's depths. The light on the moist ceiling surged and waned, patches of brightness swirling lazily. Emberton pointed his cane at a patch of wall that was rutted and wet, like football field mud. "Here," he said quietly, "is where the Tower receives and distills the power of words." Something like tenderness infused his voice. "Lance, place your hand on the wall, right there. Gentle, mind you. It's fragile."

Lance reached out, guided by the pointing cane. His hand brushed the surface, which was wet and slick.

"Press into it."

He laid his palm on the surface and pushed. It soothed him; the soft wall was like a balm. But a second later he yelped and drew back his hand.

"You felt something?" Emberton inquired.

"It... it *pulsed.*"

"This is what my family toiled for centuries to create. On our ancestral lands, we tinkered and laboured and came

173

up with prototypes. But only here, in my father's hands, was the secret perfected. Here, he built a structure that is sensitive to language, can absorb the word, reduce it to its primal power."

"I don't see any structure, sir. Per se."

Emberton threw his arms up. "Everywhere, Lance."

"Sorry?"

"Everywhere, all around us. The Tower. That is the structure." He approached the wall, his palm spread wide, reaching for the clay but not quite touching it. "And this is where it happens. Watch."

He produced and unfolded a jackknife, raised his left index finger, and pressed its tip into the blade. He lifted his finger and showed it to Lance: from a crevice between wrinkles, a bead of blood welled up and broke, sending a rivulet down his wrist, where it soaked into his white cuff. He jabbed the finger into the wet wall and drew a straight line, then swirled it into a loop, forming a primitive *P*. Then the *a,l,i,n,e.* *Paline* showed on the wall as a series of gouges darkened by the old man's blood. Next he stooped close to the wall and, in a low, husky voice, spoke to it: "Paline."

The clay began to move. Squelching faintly, it closed itself over the crude letters until they vanished.

"It has swallowed the word," Emberton said. He used the hushed voice of someone observing wary wildlife. "Now it will digest it." He pointed at the ceiling. For a couple of seconds, nothing happened. And then the walls writhed, as if a muscle had tensed under their surface. On the patch of ceiling directly above the vat, golden beads of condensation formed. Like oil through a strainer, they began to fall. Emberton led Lance up the metal steps scaling the side of the vat. The drops were landing in a puddle of golden fluid. This was the source of the light that gilded the ceiling. It swirled gently. Something cloudy billowed in its depths, then dispersed, then billowed again, subtle and slow.

"This is it," said Emberton. "The fluid of which you and I have drunk. Language, its very heart, distilled."

It occurred to Lance that, some number of storeys above him, the city was going about its business. It was rigged with traffic lights, a system of streetcars, a functional airport. Its people did sensible work. There were briefcases up there, thousands of them. Buildings with clean and glassy facades. Periodically the streets were swept. And Lance was down here, seeing this.

"Are you all right, sir?"

Emberton's mouth moved, but no words came out at first. He had turned pale. "Yes," he said. "Recovering from the cut."

"How often do you do this?"

"I've done it many times." He held up his finger. It had ceased bleeding. "My hands have learned, over many years, to heal quickly." Lance wondered how many of the lines on that hand were wrinkles and how many were scars.

"Why is..." Unable to finish his question, Lance simply pointed at Emberton's cuff. The bloodstain was fringed with a tide line of gold.

Emberton gave a hoarse laugh. "As a young boy, I was worse than you are—not only with reading and writing but with all of language. Speech, comprehension..." The ancient mouth twisted with disgust. "I was no better than an animal. A gibbering fool."

"Why?"

"Patience, Lance. We will speak of our damage later. I've brought you down here to show you its remedy." He looked again at the vat. "To cure myself, I drank a great deal of this fluid over the years. It saturated my blood."

"So what is all this for? I mean, besides helping us read and lighting the torches and all that. Do you sell it?"

"It's power. You don't need a purpose for amassing power, Lance. It is its own purpose. It is not a means. It is the end." He scanned the illuminated ceiling. "But in its pursuit I have sacrificed much." Emberton touched Lance's arm. "Immersed in my work," he said, "I let my virile years go by. I never started a family." His arm withdrew. "The project must go on. You see, the fluid that you drink—its power comes only from the Tower. If language is not fed to this wall, if the diet of words dries up, the power is lost. Once, when I fell ill, I went several weeks without feeding it. I emerged from my bedroom fully reverted to my childhood state—illiterate, speechless, a troglodyte hauled into sunlight. It was only when the Tower was fed again that the fluid—yes, even the fluid already in my blood—regained its power. My blood binds me to this room."

"Is that why they used to wrestle on chunks of glass? Up on floor five?"

"Ah, yes, the blood sport. Those were different days. Bosses had more power. It was easy to stoke an angry workforce. My father drove his men until they were half-mad with suppressed rage, then he let them have at each other in the sand."

"And the blood? It drained somewhere?"

"Yes, but not here. No, it had a different destination." He unholstered his flask and passed it to Lance. The swig perked Lance up. Around him, the room brightened. Benevolent good cheer welled within him. He was witnessing an extraordinary endeavour—a miracle. If he ever found Elena, she would thrill to him when he broke this news.

As if he had put on badly needed prescription glasses, Lance could see the room better now. He studied the texture of the walls—dozens upon dozens of gouges; it looked as if the space had been hollowed out with trowels— and the smooth face of the vat, puckered where the spigot sprouted from it. His sense of smell was better too. He could detect the fluid's faint odour as it ripened in that massive tank—that tang of lacquered wood. And his hearing was boosted. Somewhere around the back of the vat, something was pattering softly to the ground.

Lance walked a quarter of the way around it, feeling the heat shimmering off the metal. "A crack!" Fluid was escaping through a hairline fracture, each bead swelling until it detached and fell. Lance drew close enough to hear the slight hiss it made with each drop.

"You know the maxim," said Emberton. He'd stolen softly behind Lance, and spoke directly into his ear. "The pen is mightier than the sword."

Another drop hit the ground. Enough fluid had pooled that its surface tension broke, and a tiny rivulet began, following along the slope of the floor, headed for the shadows in the corner.

"Metal is no match for the power of language. From time to time the substance overwhelms the casing and leaks. I can repair the tank, but the substance will always find a way out."

"Where does it go?"

"It drains."

"Drains where?"

"Away."

Lance took a step forward for a better look. Sure enough, the fluid was streaming through a crack in the rock at the wall's base. Beside that, an iron door, about five feet high, was set into the wall.

"And the words you feed it... they're all old?" Pieces were starting to click together. "Like, gone from the language?"

"They have to be. If the word is freely used up there in the world, its power cannot be contained on a single slip of paper. My family learned to cull words that had vanished, fallen into disuse, and died. If they are not in the dictionary, nobody remembers them. So we withheld them from the dictionary. But they do hold residual power. Once, they lived. People employed lungs, palates, tongues, and uttered these words into the air. Their power is diminished, yes, but not destroyed. Those are the words we withhold."

"That's it!" Lance shouted without thinking, and now he realized his mistake and watched, a helpless spectator, as the rest of his thought tumbled freely from his lips. "That's why it says *withhold* instead of *omit*!"

"What are you talking about, Lance?" In the shifting light, Emberton's expression was impossible to read.

Lance shrugged in a desperate bid to seem nonchalant. "Nothing. Nothing at all. You were just saying that the words were withheld. Now I understand what you mean."

"I said nothing about *omit*."

"No, no, nothing about that. I kind of, um, extrapolated?"

Emberton's hand shot up, forefinger raised, silencing Lance. "Listen."

Lance cocked his head. Something burbled—a faint, muted sound, almost underfoot. His eye traced the border of floor and wall. An inch-high fountain of grey fluid erupted from a fracture in the rock, spilling to the floor in convulsive gushes.

"What's *that*?" Lance gasped.

"That, young man, is what your vice-president guzzles."

"And it hurts him. Hurts his language."

"Yes. It is the obverse of the fluid we brew here. The fluid gives; the obverse takes away. I know this all too well—I too was corrupted by this filth."

"You?"

"My mother died bearing me, and my father was too absorbed in his work to pay me much mind. I was free to roam the apartment—we lived in the penthouse, in a small flat tucked behind that painting you so cleverly identified, *The Hunt*. I live there still today. But sometimes my father was careless, and I was able to escape. No Miss Fairburn to intercept me. I got down to the lower floors, and I found this vile stuff leaking from a cracked pipe. And I drank. And returned, and drank again. I was so young, the damage was immense. My father prescribed a cure: he started feeding me the restorative fluid. But that—" His cane extended, the hand that bore it shaking, and pointed its tip at the bubbling grey geyser. "That is what scoured my brain of language."

"Where does it come from?"

"When the fluid leaks from this tank, it finds its way down, flows ever deeper, into the roots of the earth. There, it pools, stagnates, broods over itself, becomes corrosive. And then, restless for new feed, it seeps back up. It has wormed its way into the Tower's pipes and ducts."

"It seems..." Lance cut himself short. Why reveal too much to the old man? *Familiar* was the word he didn't say.

"Take a closer look."

Lance took two steps forward, bending down to see the floor better. What happened next was too sudden to register properly. Something butted him, hard, between the shoulder blades. He was driven into the stone wall, head-first. He slumped, twisting, with his back sliding down the wall. His skull throbbed. His leg was pinned beneath him. Heat flared into it where it touched the ground—he'd fallen on top of the small grey geyser. It pulsed against his flesh, and it seared.

He tried to get up, but the old man jabbed the tip of his cane into his chest, pinning him in place with remarkable strength. "You have lied to me, haven't you." The cane pressed harder against Lance's sternum, its pressure causing almost as much pain as the geyser against his leg. "You have seen the archival documents. You have been consorting with the true enemy, and you have misled me by falsely accusing your superior. So tell me, Lance, who is the traitor in my Tower?"

"I haven't found anyone, sir. I don't know anything." Lance tried again to raise himself, but instantly the cane's end was at his throat, pushing it back toward the wall. His skull ground on the rough rock.

"Your scapegoat, Mr. Furlanetti, suffered for your deception today. I tried to wring out of him a confession that I could not extract. Now I know why. Speak, Lance. I want the whole truth."

"That's all I know, sir."

"Very well." The cane retracted, and Emberton moved swiftly away. At the doorway he stopped. "You have chosen to defy me, Lance. A grave decision indeed—but not irre-versible. I will give you some time alone. You may change your mind." He glided from the room and dragged the heavy door shut behind him. Then came the jangle of keys on their ring, and finally the thud of the deadbolt sliding into place.

Chapter 11

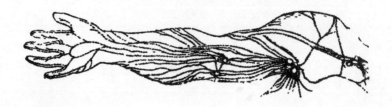

Lance ran his hand along the door's edge. It joined smoothly and impregnably with its metal frame, which was immovably fixed to the rock. No chance of busting out. He limped the room's length to the vat. His leg still burned from its exposure to the grey fluid, and he wondered how Mr. Furlanetti could bear to have it pass his lips, but the pain subsided with each step. He hauled himself up the steps mounted on the vat and looked down into the pool.

The golden fluid bore filaments of froth where it swirled against itself. Dead words, their essence squeezed out, their power taken. It didn't make much sense. Language had power because it was alive, because people used and understood it. Whatever Emberton was wringing out of these old words, it wasn't the essence of language. It was something else.

The gentle movement of the fluid was hypnotic. Ancient words seemed to whisper along the surface of the tank. He thought he heard *paline*. He thought he heard *grount*. He thought he heard his name. Language was pressing against his eardrums, the walls of his brain. It was overwhelming, and brightness was everywhere. Then its shade turned, and it was a billowing darkness. All his senses filled with it, and his environment was bullied away. He was peripherally aware that he was tumbling, bits of him smacking the metal steps, and then vaguely cognizant that he'd landed on the ground. But that was all the awareness he had left. Bathed in the warmth and glow of the vat, he slid from consciousness.

Slabs of Lance's past floated in his awareness, continents drifting on a vast black ocean.

His earliest childhood: long afternoons roaming the furniture store, crawling under beds, nestling with his toys into deep armchairs, looking up from his play when a customer peered in. The memories here were dim and fragmented, the continent's landscape jagged and shrouded in mist.

Then the trauma of school: teachers and peers and shame and scorn. Lance had been a friendly kid, optimistic, eager to meet these fellow creatures and make friends and join the world. And he did make friends—until they discovered that he had this handicap, this unique stigma. Then the friendship was withdrawn. Easier for them to join in the classroom laughter, watch a peer's spectacular failure, giggle behind their hands. The backdrop of chalkboards, windows with blinds pulled against the view, seats fused to their desks by metal tubes.

The agony of watching his mother try to teach him at home; the parade of tutors who'd smile when they met him, then grimace against the challenge, and finally quit in exasperation. His slow apprenticeship to his father's trade. The dawning certainty that he could only ever be his father's assistant, sell furniture in the safe haven of the store, under his parents' protection. He was not fit to fight for himself. He grew, and the sofas and beds and tables no longer loomed so large; they shrank to finite objects, accruing dust in their crevices, balding slightly where hundreds of customers had sat, tested, decided not to buy. The flow of the public, the chatter of commerce, everywhere the hiero-glyphs of banners and signage and order forms.

And the final days: the sale of the store, the illness of each parent, and the messages that would draw Lance to the Tower.

At first, after that strange postcard arrived, Lance procrastinated. Doubts arose. Plainly the message was some kind of mistake. A few days later, his dad brought it up again, asked where things stood. Lance lied, said he had something set up for next week. When the date in question arrived, Lance lied again and said it had been postponed.

"Don't give up," said his father, each word a painful effort. "It's your best shot." But other things were consuming him now—namely the cancer, spreading greedily. When Blunt Sr. was admitted to hospital, Lance spent almost all his time at the bedside. One day, in a brief reprieve from his torpor, Lance's father pushed aside the oxygen mask and said, "Son? That interview? Emberton? How'd it...?"

"They let me put it off," Lance mumbled. "On account of I'm here with you."

"It's going to happen, right? You'll go?"

"Of course, Dad. Obviously."

"Lance, don't be afraid. I've got a..." He was stalled by a nasty burst of coughing. "A feeling you'll be fine." A worried look overwhelmed the drawn, stubbly face. Blunt Sr. opened his mouth, then closed it again.

"What, Dad?"

He shook his head. Whatever he'd contemplated saying, he'd thought better of it. "Make sure you go" were his only words.

And his last. With that, Lance's father slid into sleep and did not wake up.

Lance returned home from the funeral and tore off the tie—his father's—that he had taken from the master bedroom closet and knotted incorrectly. He noticed the winking red eye on the answering machine, an antique thing that used an actual microcassette to log the messages. Lance had never learned how to work it, and the instruction manual—which Lance could identify only by the picture of the machine on the cover—would be of no use. The only way someone could get a message through to him would be if he was there to hear it in real time.

The phone rang. Lance let it.

The machine beeped. A woman's voice. Crackly; seasoned. "Hello, there, I'm calling from Emberton Tower. This message is for Lance Blunt. We wanted to let you know the position is still open, should you wish to apply. Have a good day, now."

The machine gave another beep; the wheels on the microcassette stopped rolling. Lance could see that the tape was nearly done. Once it filled up, the phone might ring forever if he didn't pick it up. Except that it so rarely rang.

He stood beside the old table, the heap of mail he couldn't read. A glass vase, empty of flowers, stood in the centre. His father's Barcalounger held its post in front of the TV. By Lance's calculations, he could last here a year on the money his father had left. Beyond that, he had no way of making rent.

He picked up the postcard. His father had underlined the phone number in red. Lance carried the card to the phone, dialled the numbers in sequence.

"Emberton Tower."

"Hi," said Lance. He should have planned this. Should have prepared his words before he dialled.

"Emberton Tower," repeated the voice.

Too late for planning. The decision was made. He was going to do this, futile though it seemed. What choice did he have? "Yes, hello," said Lance. "Marketing department, please."

Lance made his painful way to his feet. He was still in the cellar. Still locked in—he checked the door.

He went to the patch of wall where *paline* had vanished. *It's fragile,* Emberton had said. Trying to forget that the old man had jammed a bleeding hand in there, Lance planted his palm on the wall. As before, it pulsed, but this time he braved it, did not withdraw his hand. Instead, he pushed it farther in. With a faint squelch, the clay admitted him, bulging to form ridges between his splayed fingers. He pushed deeper. And there, a few inches beneath the surface, he could feel something slippery, a different texture from the clay. He felt around to get a sense of its shape. It was the mouth of a pipe or a tube. Its skin felt like a tarp on which rain had pooled and stagnated, acquiring sludge. It gave a faint throb.

A noise from the room's entrance: the deadbolt had been disengaged. His hand still deep in the wall, Lance watched the door. It swung open. He squinted into the light that broke in. A silhouette blotted it.

"Be very careful." The silhouette moved deeper into

the room and was engulfed in shadow. "One careless movement, one rough twitch of your hands, and you could tear it. Undo generations of toil." The silhouette moved closer. "It would take decades to nurse it, heal it, grow it back. And the drink would be powerless. Wherever the fluid resides— your stomach, my veins, the torches that line the corridor... if this dies, the fluid's power dies with it. You will never read again."

Lance felt another quiver in the tube. The clay swelled and subsided, the flesh of a breathing thing. He withdrew his hand. It gleamed with slime.

Emberton stepped forward into the vat's weak light. "I know who my spy is, Lance."

Lance couldn't muster a reply.

"The archivist is a good servant. He is devoted to preservation, accuracy, faithful rendering. It was easy to extract the truth from him." Voice damp with provocation, Emberton added: "Notwithstanding his own fondness for the girl."

Lance held his hand out to the side and shook it hard, but the slime clung. He could tell that Emberton wanted him to answer, or cry out in shock, fury, fear, but he would not. He would not volunteer a word.

"You lied to me, Lance. Deliberately."

Lance ran his hand down his pant leg, scraping slime from his palm. He stopped before reaching the tender patch of leg that the grey fluid had seared.

"I value loyalty."

"I know." Lance had not meant to speak. He redoubled his effort to keep his mouth shut. His palm still shone.

A change came over Emberton. His chest had been thrust forward; his eyes had blazed from his wrinkled face. But now he shrank back to his usual posture, and the folds of skin conspired to hood his eyes once more. "You did it to protect her."

Lance did not answer.

"That is honourable too, in its way. It is loyalty." He took his flask from his belt and pondered it, then appeared to think better of drinking and replaced it in its pouch. "I remember this Elena Wright. She was employed here, for a while."

"Was?"

"Until a few years ago. And I will allow that she's pretty, if your tastes run to the unconventional." He scrutinized Lance, watching for a reaction. "A pretty spy." Something about his tone, the derision that oozed from each word, aroused the reaction he'd been looking for.

Lance stepped forward. "She's not a spy. She's an etymologist." He found he was shaking. He couldn't get the bearings of this sudden influx of anger, didn't know whether he could control it. "She's only... she just wants to learn. Wants the truth."

"Ah, good. Thank you, my boy."

"Good?"

"You have confirmed she is the culprit. Frankly, I did not quite trust the archivist's account. He appeared to be hiding something. But you have confirmed for me that he was telling the truth. I suppose he was only trying to conceal his own ardour."

Lance stepped forward again. It was meant to be an intimidating motion, meant to make his height advantage more obvious, but instead it settled his weight on his hurt leg, and he sank, pathetically, almost to his knees. "What will you do to her?" he was able to gasp.

Emberton laughed coldly. "Ensure she doesn't meddle any further."

Lance's brain was working at a furious rate. So Elena did not work here anymore... but she kept coming back. And now Emberton was going to bar her from the Tower. How was Lance going to find her again? It was hard enough locating her in this one building; if she vanished into the city...

"But that's not your concern, Lance. She deserves what she has coming. Your conscience should concern itself with your blameless vice-president." Emberton contemplated the handle of his cane. "Ah, well, one can't undo what's done."

Lance was aghast. "You fired him? Sir, that's not—"

This time Emberton's laugh was infused with genuine amusement. "Foolish boy! No, I did not fire him. I tried to extract the truth, and my techniques were not passive. He is now recovering. In the infirmary."

You do not want to go into the infirmary. With a brutal clanging together of components, the picture clarified for Lance. His lie had sent an innocent man to that place, and now Elena might be headed there too. He had to warn her away.

Emberton moved to the furrowed wall. He touched his forehead to it and stroked it gently. "Go," he said. "I'm finished with you, for now."

Lance took a step toward the door. He stumbled on the sore leg, but regained his stride.

"Hurting?" asked Emberton. "Should we have it looked at?"

"No," said Lance. "Totally fine."

"Anytime you need medical attention," said Emberton, his tone mocking, "you come to me." Something glittered at the old man's belt. His silver flask. If the drink enabled Lance to read, then surely it would help him warn Elena the same way she'd first reached out to him. Surely it empowered him to write.

"Just one thing?" Lance asked quietly.

"You want a drink, don't you."

"Yes, please."

A knowing smile. "It calls to you, doesn't it. An appetite you can't shake."

"Yes. Just a drink, then I'll be off."

"As if it knows your name."

"Please."

"All right." Emberton stepped away from the wall and gave the flask to Lance.

He took a long sip, bottoms up, his throat palpitating. "Thank you." He handed it back. "I'm gone."

Beyond Lance's office windows, the city was shrouded in darkness. His watch showed eleven. Had he really been underground for only a few hours? It had felt like far longer. Who knew—it was possible he'd spent the night and the subsequent day.

No matter. The important thing was that he not waste any time.

He rummaged through drawers for supplies he had never had occasion to use. He found a pad of four-by-six-inch Post-its, a blue ballpoint pen, and a roll of Scotch tape for extra sticking power. He laid the pad, its pristine yellow expanse, on the desktop. The drink was strong in him; he checked Jeanine's bookshelf and found that he could read the spines. *Day By Day: 365 Doses of Inspiration. Fundamentals of Closing the Sale. Fifteen Secrets to Personal Success.* He was set.

The lurid colour of the Post-its seemed to expand, to blur beyond their crisp borders.

He could do this. First time for everything.

E. Easy enough. The rest? He pulled her own, original Post-it from his pocket to make sure he'd get the spelling right: *l, e, n, a.*

There it was. Fat-lined and blue on the yellow page. A name. Hers.

H. He hesitated, his brain trying to go brick by brick, trying to assemble this thing by the letter. But then the mental fussing stopped. The knot behind his eyes dissolved. *Just go with it,* he told himself. And did.

He knows.

A sentence. The letters were erratic, off-kilter—long lines at crazy angles, components that didn't quite join up where they should. But he'd written it. A simple sentence. It was like the language had gathered in his veins, siphoned into the slim plastic ballpoint, and simply flowed out of him.

You are in danger, he continued.

He wanted to go on. He missed her—had so much to tell her!—and this was like talking to her. Even if his plan failed, even if she didn't stumble upon the note in her mysterious movements through the Tower, for the moment it felt like she was beside him, listening. The same way he'd gathered her thoughts into his mind when he read her note for the first time, now she could take his thoughts into hers. He wished this first correspondence could be less grim—something like *I'm mad for you and your absence has been murdering me* might be more appropriate—but he had to stick to the plan.

He peeled off the top Post-it and stuck it on the desktop, gently, so as not to use up too much of the adhesive. He copied his note onto the second sheet, then onto the third. One for the trunk of the tree in the garden; one for the archives' bank vault door; one for the office on floor nine, whoever it really was. Yes, other people were likely to find them before Elena—the archivist, that rat, would probably give the copy on his door to Emberton—but any gamble was worth it. She had to be warned.

The copies done, he looked at them in their neat yellow row. He would head out to distribute them in a second. But for now he could not relinquish this glory, this *writing*. The drink would wear off soon, and he had plenty more to say.

He found a sheet of lined paper. He closed his eyes and let the words queue behind his shut lids, a convoy of meaning, a parade of thoughts and emotions he'd never been able to express without speech. And when they were ready, he opened his eyes and he wrote.

I've learned so much about what goes on. And it is worse than we knew. And I fear I have done a terrible thing to someone innocent.

I care about you. It kind of batters me, bruises me inside, that you may be in danger and I can't get you out. That I'm responsible for any of this.

The words came. That's all there was to it: they arrived on the paper. He knew, from his school days, from watching the struggles of his classmates, that some aspects of writing confounded everyone—even the kids who were good writers struggled with punctuation and spelling. Lance did not know whether these elements were coming out right, but somehow he had a sense that they were. No obstacles presented themselves; no brambles of confusion or doubt. The drink took his thoughts and translated them perfectly into the written word.

I have to find a way to make up for what I've done. I think I need to—

"There you are."

Lance must have jumped a full six inches from his seat. He jammed the sheet of paper into his pocket.

Ms. Shillingsham was a mess. Her face was white, its thinness accentuated by the streaks of mascara on her cheeks. Her fingers gripped his door jamb as usual; their nails—unpainted, tonight—were chipped. Her clothes were plain black and dangled off her, untailored, like rags.

"Come in," said Lance.

She took a deep, trembling breath, and did.

"You'll have seen," she said, "the other offices."

Lance shook his head. "I came straight here. A few minutes ago."

Two further steps into the room. Her eye slid along his desk, the bare walls that he had never got around to postering, the shelves of Jeanine's belongings. "I've evacuated the floor. Everyone's gone home. There is no department anymore."

"Why?"

"It's getting worse."

"What's getting worse?"

She held out her palms to show helplessness. "You remember Philip's birthday party. The difficulties Gina described."

"Problems with language."

"It's getting worse. More and more people. Always in the vicinity of the Tower. But never *inside* the Tower. And always after a tremor."

"What is going on?"

"I don't know, Lance. But it starts here. A shudder that we feel in these floors, and then words are siphoned from the world outside. From a bigger area each time. It's bad, Lance. There was a car accident this morning..." She trailed off. "Where were you today? All day you were missing."

So he had been a full day underground. "Bit of a long story," he said.

"This morning, Mr. Hutchman got hurt. He was driving to work, and suddenly the road signs didn't make any sense. The letters were *smeared*, he said. Tugged off their signs, like they were being sucked away. And drivers got confused, and there was a crash. He called from the hospital. They'd put him in a cast and were going to release him. I told him, don't come to work. Whatever you do, do not come into the Tower with an injury. They'll put you..." She buried her face in her elbow and sobbed—three loud, dry, scraping heaves that almost compelled Lance to cover his ears. "He said that at the crash site the emergency crews were going mad. Their radios were garbled, they couldn't communicate with HQ, couldn't read their GPS. And Lance, I was here the whole time. Here, inside the Tower. And I didn't have any of these problems. But I felt the tremor."

"You were here early again."

"I've been coming earlier and earlier. I'm so worried about..." She tried to regain composure. "Point being, Lance, something terrible is happening, and it originates in the Tower. So I decided enough was enough. What we've had to endure here on floor four is a horror on its own. But if the rest of the world..."

"What horror? What've you had to endure?"

"No point in secrecy now, is there?" She seemed to listen to an answer issued from some corner of her own head. "The oath is worthless now," she muttered, as if repeating what someone else had said. She nodded once, decisively. "We old marketers, Lance... our bodies function as fodder. For the Tower. There's no need for a sales and marketing department. The dictionary is prestigious; it sells itself. This department is merely a means of collecting and retaining flesh. From time to time, its members somehow compromise themselves, and they get sent down to the third floor, and bits of their bodies are given away. For what purpose, I can't say. That knowledge is hidden from me. But when one of my people goes to the infirmary, I know I've seen the last of her. She has served her ultimate purpose. Her body is the Tower's now."

He is now recovering, Mr. Emberton had said of the marketing vice-president, *in the infirmary.* Recovering for what purpose? Was he never coming out?

"Before I was made president, I was told all this, and I was offered a choice: I could accept the job, or I could die along with my new knowledge. No one can learn the secret and live. So I reacted out of fear. Nothing more noble than that. But I rationalized. I could change things, I told myself, by working from within."

She had turned her back on Lance and was speaking into the shelf of Jeanine's books. She spread her long arms, resting a hand on each end of the shelf, and let her head fall forward. "The longer you stay complicit, the easier it gets. I became comfortable with my simple, useless job—shepherding a flock that I knew was destined for the abattoir. But now... its malevolence is not confined to us. Whatever our bodies feed, it's starting to damage people out there."

She turned from the shelf, folded her hands in front of her. "So I told them to clear out, and they're all gone. Except one." Through emerging tears, she continued: "Mr. Furlanetti. John. I haven't been able to find him. I suspect he's been staying in the Tower for some weeks, even overnight, to be close to the radiators. He must be somewhere in this building right now, indulging his... *appetite.*"

"No. He's not doing that."

Her eyes widened. "You've seen him?"

"I know where he is."

"Well? Where?"

Lance's hand closed over the lined page in his pocket. Its crumpling was the only sound in the room.

"Lance?"

He had to inhale, and when he did his breath wobbled. "I've done something bad, Ms. Shillingsham. Really bad."

"Lance, I presided over this atrocity. I let it continue. Whatever you may have done, my conscience is heavier."

"I told a... I lied about Mr. Furlanetti. Upstairs, I mean. In the penthouse. I told a lie, and now he's... He's on the third floor now."

She sank against the bookshelf, gripping it for support. "So. They got him."

"It's my fault, Ms. Shillingsham."

Slowly, she regained her feet, let go of the shelf. She lifted her head, assumed her full height. "No, Lance. The fault is mine."

"I lied."

"If I had acted correctly, Lance, if I had not let cowardice rule me, Mr. Furlanetti would not be there." Her voice was strong, clear. The voice she used to regain control of a meeting. The voice of a boss. "Here is our plan."

Thank God she was taking charge. He needed to be told what to do.

"I must get him out of the infirmary. It may be too late, and I may not emerge alive. But I have to do what I can. And I want you to leave the Tower and summon the authorities. Bring the police, bring the medics, anyone who'll come. Tell them there have been murders at the Tower, and people here are still in danger. Go, Lance. We must move quickly."

And he did. Urgency, together with relief at having precise orders to carry out, propelled him swiftly to the elevator. It was only as his descent began that he realized he had left the Post-its on his desk.

The lobby was empty, the protection services desk unmanned. The fireplace moaned as air passed through its shaft. It seemed to summon him. Lance found himself walking, almost involuntarily, between the big wing-back chairs. He noted the parched, cracking texture of the leather cushions; their dry rot was pretty advanced, probably irreparable. Squinting at the fireplace, Lance saw that it did not contain real flame, just the same yellow simulacrum he'd seen in the cellar's wall-mounted torches. Emberton's fluid, burning away, uselessly. This material that was supposed to be so powerful, so precious, wasted in a sham fireplace. It didn't even consume the wood, which sat in an untroubled stack.

Lance's palm slammed against the corner of the mantel and then retracted, stung by the impact. He gripped his hand and massaged it. The old man seemed to have no clue what to *do* with this power he'd concocted, no idea what it was *for*.

What was it Emberton had said? *You don't need a purpose for amassing power, Lance. It is its own purpose.* And Ms. Shillingsham, describing what the grey stuff did for Mr. Furlanetti: *Makes him want more of it.* All these pointless cycles, things existing only to exist, only to perpetuate themselves. Lance was reminded of dreams he'd had as a kid, suffering flu or fever, where cars zoomed backward round a track and he couldn't will them to reverse their course, to move forward as they were intended to. Endless loops, destitute of purpose.

Why did Emberton need flesh? Blood—Emberton's own—was part of the process down there, the feeding of words to the Tower. But the meat of aging marketers? Where did that fit in?

Watching the flame, its sinuous undulations, he thought back to the long descent into the Tower's gut. He remembered the fluid leaking away beneath the vat. The small iron door set into the wall.

A roar moved the marble floor. Enough contemplating, enough wasting time. Ms. Shillingsham had a plan; she was going to fix this thing; all Lance had to do was obey. He made for the revolving door. His extended fingers paused, as before, just short of the bar. He could not touch it.

"Can't leave?"

He knew that voice. He looked up, stunned. In the glass, Elena was reflected behind him.

Chapter 12

He spun. He revelled in the sight of her, really her, close enough almost to touch, in a skirt and emerald leggings that matched her eyes. There were forty thousand things he needed to tell her, and they jostled and elbowed at his mouth's bottleneck, and none of them came out.

"Don't worry," she said. "It happens to some of us, after a while."

"What happens?" He couldn't produce more than a hoarse whisper.

Her smile was oddly radiant. "If it doesn't want us to leave, we find we are unable to. Literally."

"If what doesn't?"

"The Tower, of course."

He tried again to touch the pushbar, but the attempt was half-hearted. He knew she was right: he would not be able to exit.

He covered the distance between them in three strong strides, gripped her arms and pulled her closer to him. "We have to leave. Have to. You don't know what I've seen."

"Tell me."

The tips of their noses were inches apart. Some remote corner of Lance's brain was informing him how surprising and wondrous it was to have drawn her so close, let alone to have found her at all. But other concerns had priority now. "It's... There's things that happen... in the Tower..."

"What things? What have you found?"

His thoughts were agitated, contradictory impulses smashing into one another, but as they settled they took on a single, immutable shape. There was something he had to do, and he had to do it now. "Come with me," he said.

As they descended the stairs, he told her everything he could think of. Memories came back in a jumble; his words gushed, flooded, eddied; he jumped from stream to stream and let her questions guide him back, and by the time they were in the depths of the Tower it had all tumbled out— the drink and how it solved his problem; Furlanetti and the radiator and the shameful lie that had landed the man on floor three; the revelations in the cellar. The story of Emberton's infancy and what the Tower did to him. The tales from outside, language leaching from the world in sudden spurts. Ms. Shillingsham's dreadful revelation.

And he told her what he now must do. He must return to that furrowed patch of wall; he must reach in and seize it and tear it apart. He had to kill the Emberton project.

It was hard to read her reaction. She nodded, made a serious face, muttered that yes, this was for the best; but he could also see a foretaste of grief—the object of her long quest might be destroyed before she did more than glance at it.

He found the door that led to the torchlit passage. A smooth yellow light spilled from the crack at its base. Lance remembered now that Emberton had used a key to open it.

He tugged the black metal ring that served as a handle, but the door would not open—he could feel the resistance of its bolt. He kicked at the decayed planks, but they weren't so thoroughly rotted as to yield.

Elena stared at the door. Disappointment came off her like body heat.

Lance tried again, throwing himself into the work, ramming his heels on the wood, which dented but did not splinter. He tried to wrench the metal bands away, but they were immovable. He ran his sleeve over his forehead. It came back sopping.

The yellow light under the door flickered. Lance watched its lazy surge and retreat. When he looked at Elena, she was watching it too.

"It's okay," she said. "You're exhausted. This can wait. Tomorrow we'll figure out a way through. We'll find Emberton. He's bound to come down here again with his key." Her cool hand touched Lance's brow. "But you need rest. Food too, I'll bet. When did you last eat?"

In all this madness, he had forgotten to be hungry. But now, reminded of its duties, hunger got busy announcing itself. A punishing sensation swelled in his stomach, a glob of bread dough flecked with shrapnel, and rising. Dizzy weakness infused his skull. He swooned. Elena held him, propped him up.

He wanted to let consciousness drop away, to stay in her grasp and abandon all worry. But his brain would not stop bothering him; insistent thoughts bubbled along its surface. If he could not get in to destroy the thing in the room, then he must turn his attention to Mr. Furlanetti. Yes, Ms. Shillingsham had gone to get him out—but she was relying on Lance to call for help. Which he had not done.

Elena was repeating her question: "Lance, when did you eat?"

Hunger finally eclipsed the pestering thoughts. He wouldn't be much use to anyone until he dealt with it. "Too long ago," he said.

"Let's go." Elena's voice was serene. "I'll take care of you."

The cafeteria lights were off, but the goldfish pool gave off a slight glow. The chairs were tucked neatly into place around the circular tables. The sneeze guard protected empty serving trays from nonexistent patrons. Elena led Lance through the swinging door and into the kitchen. Its big metal machines were shut, showing lids and sheaths instead of working surfaces. No food was in sight.

"Normally," said Elena, "I sneak into the break rooms of various departments. Microwave a pizza, swipe a sandwich someone left behind. But I'm guessing you're too hungry for a scouting expedition. So you get the finest I can offer: cafeteria cuisine." She noticed Lance's expression. "Don't worry—it'll be better than what they sell. They cook fast, for convenience, and the product sits for days. But the ingredients are actually pretty good, if you pick out the freshest ones. Just takes a bit of thought."

She set quickly to work, unsheathing stovetops, hauling open cupboard doors, homing in on the foods she needed. Soon a huddle of aluminum containers and bottles occupied a corner of a counter, and she was heating a pot and laying things out on a baking sheet, and the greasy institutional room began to fill with the smell of cooking.

Elena moved with the quick, darting certainty of a bird constructing its nest; she seemed to know her way around every cupboard and fridge, even if this was only her special-occasion kitchen. There was one exception—against a far wall lurked a tall, thin refrigerator, claw marks of rust defacing its door. It was gunmetal grey, and its door was secured with an ostentatious old padlock. Elena did not look at or acknowledge this fridge; Lance, already unnerved by his first cafeteria experience, was not inclined to ask too many questions. Instead, he helped as best he could, chopping carrots, taking down a high hanging pot, whatever Elena could find for him to do. The simple toil, so much more purposeful than the uselessness of his "job" up on floor four, was comforting. He let the trauma of the last few days fall away and forgot for now his weariness and aches.

The cooking done, he and Elena carried their full plates into the cavernous dining hall. They chose a table near the waterfall, where they could make out the swim paths of the goldfish.

"Chicken à la Emberton," Elena announced as they sat. It was good. She'd coated the meat with some sort of glaze, and assembled a pretty killer salad. But in his hunger Lance barely registered the details, and it was only as an afterthought that he found his manners and uttered a "Delicious!" before spearing another slab of chicken.

"Just a question of mixing things a little better," she said, looking pleased. "Choosing more carefully. A bit of imagination." She jabbed absentmindedly at a lettuce leaf. "Imagination is not prized here. You do whatever job you're assigned, and you do it with precision and rigour. You don't vary from the designated path. And don't you dare indulge any curiosity about what's really going on in the Tower."

Lance felt he'd had his fill of that subject. Sure, there were holes, gaps in the fabric, questions yet unanswered.

But how much more revelation could he take? Each new discovery was more sickening—*nauseous,* Mr. Tradd would say—than the last. And yes, there were important matters to attend to. But for now, Lance was content to sit and eat, enjoy the elementary pleasures of taste, texture, of chewing and swallowing. Of Elena's company.

And there lay another mystery, one that at this moment allured him far more. Who was Elena Wright, really, and why was she here? "So," he said, cautiously, "I learned some other interesting things."

"Uh huh?"

Lance decided he should start with the less serious matter. "Well, for one thing, the etymology of *hazy* is listed as unknown."

She laughed, a loud, abrupt burst that almost choked her. "Tell me you didn't... I mean, no offence, but you didn't think that whole *hazy* yarn was accurate, did you? All that detail? I was just... I made that up as I went. Just having fun with it."

The laughter irked Lance. He took another bite of chicken but this time didn't really notice its flavour. "Sure," he mumbled. "I figured as much."

"I mean," she said, "if it was convincing, that's great. I'm flattered. But it's a hobby of mine; I enjoy making up stories. It beats doing etymology."

"But etymology! I would've thought it was cool. Like a dig at an old tomb."

"You ever been on a dig? It's all tedious sifting and measurements. Or so I imagine."

"And etymology's like that too?"

"You try spending a few hours trying to deduce an origin based on Grimm's law of consonantal decay."

"There's a Grimm's law?"

"Yep. Named for one of the brothers Grimm. The fairy tale guys."

"Huh." Lance looked away. He didn't feel ready for the next round of questions. He sized up the waterfall. The strands of water braided as they fell, lit from behind by a bulb embedded in the fake rock.

"Etymology's dry," Elena said. "Theoretical. It's not a bunch of tales; it's not magical fog and vengeful spirits. Even if I wish it were."

"Whatever," said Lance, annoyed again. He'd believed the story, however far-fetched it actually was. Her voice, her eyes, had invited him into it, and now he was being told that she was just playing around. *Magical fog and vengeful spirits.* He felt like a gullible child. A chump. "It was a neat story, sure. But now you're going to need a better one."

She chewed slowly, watching him. "What does that mean?"

"I've been up to floor nine, Elena. They don't even know who you are. Mr. Emberton, he says you used to work here. Used to."

She looked at her half-eaten chicken. "Well done. You busted me."

"What's the story?"

"I was fired three years ago. They have a high turnover up there; many of the current staff never knew me."

"Then what were you doing in that office?"

"It used to be mine. I'm up there all the time after hours. And sometimes in the daytime, if I know they're in a meeting. I look something up in one of my old books, check a website. Make like I still have a... like I'm still useful."

"What happened?"

Elena shook her head. "It's a long story."

"I don't mind."

She looked around. "We're pushing our luck. This is a long time to stay in one spot, out in the open like this. We need to destroy our evidence, clean up, get out. Then I'll answer your questions."

"Fine." The light through the waterfall was tedious now; a headache crept up Lance's temples. A change of scene would be welcome.

"But you must be exhausted," she said.

"Elena." Lance swallowed his last bite of chicken. "I spent all week going up and down Emberton Tower trying to find you, after they told me that you don't even exist. I sat in my office every day, staring out the window, feeling like... I don't know. Like my rib cage was filled up with ash. I sat through *meetings*. If you had any idea what the meetings are like on that floor... All I could think about was you."

She blushed and stammered.

"Point is," continued Lance, "now you're here, and you have something to tell me. I'll stay awake as long as it takes."

They bundled their dishes into the commercial-grade dishwasher, its vertical sliding doors rising and falling like guillotine blades, then hauled out the tray of glistening clean plates and cutlery. Elena slotted everything swiftly back into place.

She led him back through the tunnel to the lobby. From its shaded mouth they scoped the security desk. A night guard eyed one of the screens, green light splashed over his rigid face. Elena drew Lance back into the shadows and led him across the dining area to the waterfall. At the edge of the fish pond, a small doorway was set into the fake rock. They entered a dark, musty space. To their left, as they inched forward, a Plexiglas sheet revealed a heavily grimed view through the waterfall and out beyond to the tables. At the end of the passage was yet another small door; this one opened to the stairs. They descended in a silence that Lance found strangely unsettling—until he realized what it meant. The presses, which he was accustomed to feeling in his feet and being comforted by, were idle.

They emerged from the stairs into a room filled with long, low worktables. Teeming bookshelves lined the walls, alternating with tall cupboards, their varnished wooden doors closed and clasped. Large rolls of paper and other, thicker materials sat on a metal rack. Near that, perched on steel scaffoldings of varying size and complexity, were several machines that most reminded Lance of medieval torture devices. They had baton-shaped handles and descending screws and square metal plates and numerous other bits that suggested tightening, stretching, slicing.

"The bindery," Elena said. "This is where they take the printed pages and turn them into books. Still done by hand. They modernized the printing, but the binding remains traditional."

She approached one of the tall cupboards. Its door was gorgeous, if chipped and dulled with age. Varnished oak. She stood before it, framed by its elegant lines. "When the dictionary was founded in the nineteenth century, Emberton Publishing lured the best bookbinder in England to come here and bind their dictionary."

"This is... uh, part of how you got fired?"

She examined his face with something like hopeful sadness, as if she were a doctor and he were a mortally wounded patient who could not be rescued but perhaps could be offered comfort. "What I'm doing right now," she said, "is why I got fired."

"Going into other people's departments?"

She shook her head. "Hang on. Just listen. This book-binder set the template for the dictionary. Today, the deluxe edition still follows it. The spine, the cover, the marbled endpapers—nothing has been altered since. But he's long gone. He lived out his final years in a home for the criminally insane."

Anyone who worked at Emberton Tower, Lance figured, was liable to end up criminally insane. "What happened?"

"Love happened. As it always does. My mother liked to say it arrives like an unwanted fire. Things warm up, and then they soften, and then they are destroyed."

"Your mother taught you *that*?"

"She had reasons to be cynical. Anyway, shortly after the Tower was built, a young woman came to work for the master binder. A female apprentice would have been rare at the time, I think. But she had a way with gilding—applying gold leaf to the page ends and embossment."

"So they fell in love," said Lance.

"He would have been a lot older, and of course he was her boss. Who knows how mutual the passion was, but they did become lovers."

"How do you know this?"

Elena smiled. "The archives. All those hours. Anyway, then a young man came to the Tower. A labourer. Carried boxes of bound dictionaries out from this room. Poor, uneducated, a boy of no account. But he caught her eye, and she caught his." Elena laid a hand on the cupboard door. "She probably longed for escape at this point, felt the constraints of her situation, the long hours stitching and gilding to meet demand, the endless days in this one room, hardly stirring from her seat... and this guy represented the outside world, escape. And he was young, whereas the master binder was ailing, and the age difference was ever more apparent to her. So an intrigue developed... God knows where, or how, but in some quiet recess of the Tower, they managed a tryst. But the secret could not last."

"They got caught?"

"They did. The master flew into a jealous rage. He attacked the young man with one of those." On a nearby table was a rust-coloured pair of heavy shears. "They're meant for cutting board stock, but they work pretty well for carving up a stomach, as it turns out. The poor guy was carted up to the infirmary, where he died. What happened to his remains, I haven't been able to discover. The master then made it clear to the girl that her terms of employment had changed. She was restricted to the bindery, forbidden to leave. He stayed here with her, watched her every move. Had minions bring food, drink, fresh chamber pots. Soon, overwhelmed by sadness, she died—whether by her own hand or by merely wasting away, I don't know. The master found her one morning, slouched at the work table, her golden hair fanned out around her."

Lance looked around this windowless workspace. With its orderly array of implements, it did not seem a suitable stage for such drama. "This all really happened?"

"More or less, from what the records allowed me to piece together. I connected a few dots myself, but I believe my account is close enough to true. But now..." She turned to the tall cupboard and unclasped the doors. Inside, a honeycomb of cubbyholes. Some held stacks of paper cut into various sizes; others were crammed with tools, handles thrust out; others held small plastic containers or glass pots filled, Lance supposed, with glue, glaze, varnish, whatever else was involved in assembling a book. She took out a thick glass pot and examined its black lid. She overturned it and squinted at the heel. "Some of these materials have been here for a very long time; they're no longer used for making the dictionary. But the binders wouldn't dream of tossing anything out. It's like a museum in here." She replaced the pot in its nook. "Makes you wonder what we might find if we combed through it all."

"Bunch of old chemicals?" Lance offered.

"Maybe. Maybe that's all. Who knows?"

Lance surveyed the height of the cupboard. Nearby, a footstool was tucked under a table; otherwise, the top shelves would be beyond human reach.

"The timing of the young woman's death was awkward. A special order had arrived for a custom-made edition of the dictionary, and the binding was to be as lavish as possible. A very powerful person had placed the order."

"And this powerful person wanted the words changed?"

"Sorry?"

"Back in the day, I mean *really* back in the day, like hundreds of years ago, in England, the Emberton family printed Bibles. Rich families paid them to change the words."

"You're kidding."

"That's what Mr. Emberton told me."

"Wow. Perfect." She bit her lower lip and concentrated. Wheels turned behind her eyes. "Okay, so the answer to your question is yes. He wanted some words altered, and he wanted some words added—his own name, for example. A biographical entry." She took down another jar from its nook, surveyed the label. "Only one copy would be made. The binder saw his chance. He could create his masterpiece, and he could immortalize the young woman he'd loved." She turned the jar over in her hands, inspecting its murky contents. "He hid the body in a closet to which he had the only key. He worked quickly, in the dead of night, to outpace her decay. He was a resourceful man, truly a master of materials, and he found ways to preserve parts of her and dispose of the rest. The soft skin of her belly encased the book. Threads of her golden hair, finely intertwined, stood in for gilding." She slid the jar back into place. "Dead centre, in the crux of the book, one page was different from all the rest. The page that listed the entry for *love*. He arranged with the printers that they omit the middle signature—the central batch of pages—and allow him to sew in an insert. He borrowed the plate they'd set for the signature, and impressed the words himself. Instead of paper, he used the stretched and cured skin of her very heart."

Lance stepped back from the cupboard. "Really? That's true?"

She was amused. "Not the last part, no."

"Good."

"There was indeed a love triangle, a murder, banishment to a criminal asylum. We don't know what happened to the two bodies. But there was no wealthy client. And there was no book built from a body... Do you think I pushed it too far, with the heart thing?" She frowned like a furniture buyer making up her mind about a pricey piece. "Yeah, too cheesy, I think. I shouldn't have gone that far. Anytime the heart sneaks in like that, you have to be suspicious." She closed the cupboard door, latched it. "But when I arrived at Emberton Tower and discovered the archives, you can imagine—I spent more and more time there, less and less doing my job. And I wanted to build on the stories I found. I wanted to live in them."

"Why?"

She made for the door, Lance in tow. She stopped by something that looked like a long vise, except it was made of wood rather than metal, and had nailheads protruding from its length and bulbous glazed handles jutting from each end. Scissors, thread, and rulers lay haphazardly beside the device, and in its long jaw it held a fat Emberton, spine-up. She ran a finger along the book's length. "My father read to me, every single night before bed. Books intended for older kids—adventures, history, quests and battles and miraculous events. And then, when I was six, he was gone, and that other realm was gone with him."

"I'm sorry. My dad died too."

"He didn't die. He was just... *gone*. Vanished. No explanation. There *was* an explanation of some kind—another woman or something—but my mom protected me from knowing, and I never asked. I made my own interpretation and stuck with it: he'd been called away on a magnificent adventure, and he was fighting battles to keep us safe. But no, the fact was I'd lost him. And my mom was never going to carry me into the stories like he had. She got all bound up in the betrayal, crabbed with it. She hated anything romantic. Told me to *be sensible, stop throwing yourself at rainbows.*

"But those stories! He took the chaos of real life—the mean kids at school, the smashed cars on the highway—and he gave me a pattern I could fit it all into. And without him, it felt like the chaos had won."

"I'm sorry," said Lance.

"Well, life goes on. We grow up."

She looked up: directly above them was a black hemisphere housing a camera. "This," she said, "is another place where it's unwise to hang around too long. We'll go get you set up with what you need for the night, then head up to floor ten. I know a good place for us to sleep." With that, she shut off the bindery lights.

Chapter 13

For *us* to sleep. Lance tried to wrestle his excitement to the mat. Instead, he allowed his conscience to speak up. "I have to go to the infirmary."

"Not recommended. There are better places."

"I don't mean for sleeping. I mean Mr. Furlanetti. Ms. Shillingsham. I have to get them."

She shook her head. "If Ms. Shillingsham couldn't get in and out safely, neither will we. And if she did, we're wasting our time. What we have to do is rest, and in the morning we will find Emberton and convince him to let us in downstairs. Then you'll do as you said and kill the thing down there. That's the first priority. After that we'll collect your friends. Okay?"

It made sense, but misgivings gnawed at Lance. He remembered the moan from behind the frosted glass door. He remembered all of Elena's own warnings about that infirmary. Could he turn in for the night when people were in there on account of his lies?

Yes, he could. His tiredness surged, and Elena was

glancing again at the security camera, and he let her lead the way to the elevator.

"In university I took a linguistics major," she said as she pressed the up button. "That seemed close enough to a science to be sensible, to keep my mom happy. I took a shine to etymology because it took the snake's nest of language—so messy, tangled, confused—and drew out a story." The doors opened and they stepped inside. "But then I grew up and got a job and realized: the rules are dull. To follow them is to plod through probabilities; there's no leap of imagination. I wanted the stories back."

On floor two, they entered a corridor lined with bright yellow mop buckets.

"The archives fed me stories," Elena continued, keeping her voice down now, "but I always ran up against walls. Where was the labourer buried? What happened to the remains of that poor girl? Why did words vanish from the language?"

They passed shut metal doors emblazoned with warning graphics—lightning bolts, triangles enclosing exclamation marks. The concrete walls were festooned with pipes and bundled lengths of cord.

"My frustration spilled over into my work. I started to falsify. Just the tiniest bit—nothing extravagant like that improv on *hazy*. I threw in little tweaks that I was sure my bosses would catch and correct before the files went up to the editors. Like citing a root as Old English that was really Old Norse. And when they found the mistake-on-purpose, I pretended to be embarrassed. Pretended it was a typo."

Up ahead, a night janitor slumped in a chair, his belly rising and falling in slumber. "Don't worry," said Elena.

"He sleeps through anything. If he wakes up, just smile and nod."

"Might work for you," muttered Lance. "My smile's not nearly so pretty."

"Nonsense." She elbowed him gently. "You have a lovely smile."

Past the guard—whose nap, as promised, was undisturbed by their passage—they turned into a long room filled with racks of maintenance coveralls.

"So," said Elena, "here I was, tinkering with etymologies. The tiniest tweaks. But even that got boring, so I tried something bolder."

Another doorway, and they emerged in a bunker occupied by laundromat-grade washers and dryers.

"I changed the meaning of a source word. It was in the entry for *fiction*—a conspicuous choice, I know. Ultimately, *fiction* derives from the Latin *fingere,* a verb that means 'form' or 'mould.' I added one word to that definition. Suddenly *fingere* was a noun, and its meaning was '*true* form.'"

Elena swung open a dryer door and pulled out a heap of clothes, testing them for dampness. Lance recognized the brown cardigan she'd been wearing when he first saw her; he spotted the tan corduroy skirt she'd worn in the garden.

"Dumb, I know. Really dumb. But it was like a compulsion, and it gave me such a high... And of course I got caught. Some diligent copy editor spotted one of my tweaks. A bit of poking around, a pinch of forensics, and the bosses realized this was no error. This was a thing I did."

She pulled something from a shelf, gave it a shake, and it billowed into a canvas laundry sack. "Sorry about the detour," she said, "but if I leave my clothes in here overnight, I'll lose them."

She started tossing the garments into the sack. "They fired me. I went down to the lobby with a little cardboard box of personal effects. And then I discovered I literally could not leave. I convinced my security escort that I needed a moment to sit by the fire and get organized before stepping out—it was raining, I had some story about an umbrella buried in my box. And then I slipped away. Back into the Tower's innards."

She pulled a cord, and the sack was cinched shut.

"You had all those clothes with you when you were fired?"

"Nope. I had to scavenge. That's nicer word than *steal*, isn't it? Now that you're stuck here, we'll have to scavenge for you too. It takes time. You have to go through the uniforms, pick through the lost and found, find what fits. Anyway, we're dawdling."

She hurried to a cupboard set into the wall and took out folded sheets and a pair of quilts. Lance accepted the bundle of bedclothes and Elena slung the laundry sack over her shoulder. "There are showers on this floor too," she said as they started out. They made their way back through the racks of uniforms, past the snoozing guard, to the elevator.

"Didn't anyone notice that you'd stayed?" Lance asked.

"I've learned how to flit under the radar. People see me from time to time, cameras catch the odd glimpse, but no one really notices. I'm a ghost."

An elevator arrived. The middle car—the one on which Lance and Elena had first come face to face, she in her worn brown cardigan, he in a stew of anxiety, heading into an interview he had no business taking. "I noticed you," he said as they shuffled in.

Pressing *10,* she gave him a look that said *cut the crap.* "I'm not as eye-catching as you think."

"Hell yes, you are."

"I suspect," Elena said, so quietly that Lance had to move closer to hear her, "that it wants you to feel that way."

"*It*? What *it*?"

"The Tower."

"Oh, come on. I saw you, I liked you. End of story."

The elevator gave out onto a raised walkway looking out over a long grid of cubicles. "Proofreading," Elena said. "Vital to the dictionary's success. This is the one book where a typo could be cataclysmic."

Lance had a clear view of some of the workstations: family photos, cartoons, and computer printouts were pinned to the padded dividers, but the desks themselves revealed no idiosyncrasy. There were no computers. The desktops were worn shiny from use, and each surface was entirely clear except for a black cylindrical pen holder with two red pens jutting from it. Desk after desk, this detail did not vary.

Elena led him down carpeted steps—their edges were a vivid, soul-sucking institutional green, but the inner track had been trampled colourless.

"Surely," Lance said, "a typo's not the end of the world? Can't people figure out what you mean?"

"Not always," said Elena. "Besides, authority is vital, right? People turn to a dictionary for the absolute truth. They use it to settle disagreements—how a word's spelled, what it really means. Even court cases have been decided by flipping open an Emberton. I'm surprised they don't make witnesses swear on it."

She wound through the labyrinth, and each desk

conformed to the pattern: empty save the black holder with its two red pens.

"Once," she said quietly, "a headword was misspelled."

"Headword?"

"The main word, in big bold type—the one being defined. Instead of *hemoglobin*, the typesetters had it as *hemogoblin*."

"What does that even mean?"

"It's a component of the red blood cell. Carries oxygen and nutrients. But somehow this error, *goblin* for *globin*, slipped through the proofreading net and into the third edition. Can you guess what happened?"

"People wrote angry letters?"

"Nope. That's what they do when they see a cuss word or new slang they don't approve of. What happened was that *hemogoblin* entered the language. A few speakers picked it up from the Emberton, and when they were corrected they said, 'It's in the dictionary. Look it up.' Teachers used it in biology lessons. It must have appealed to students' imaginations—these little goblins lurking in your blood, doing its work. The word even appeared in a few newspaper articles. The mistake was caught before the next Emberton edition was printed, and after a while *hemogoblin* died out. But this floor was in crisis for a while."

They had reached the far end of the room, which terminated with a glass wall. Vertical blinds concealed what lay beyond. Elena located a door—also glass, distinguished only by its seams and its discreet metal handle—and tugged it open.

Chaises longues and cots lined each wall, interrupted every ten feet or so by a sink and mirror. The air wafting from the ceiling vents was cooler, less oppressive. The light was dim; rather than strips of fluorescence, pot lights were embedded in the ceiling.

"The proofing is so important, so intense, so tough on the eyes," Elena explained. "These people stare down printed pages eight hours a day, even the finest of the fine print. It's not regular reading—they have to comb the text for errors, for the slightest infelicity, for a comma instead of a dot. It's hell on the eyes and facial muscles. So they come here to recuperate. Doze, rehydrate, freshen up."

The beds, Lance noted, were only large enough to sleep one.

She led him to the far end of the room, where she set her sack on the floor and directed him to drop the bedclothes on a cot. She burrowed through the heap, extracting one quilt and one set of sheets, and threw them on a cot across the aisle. Each bed already had a small pillow; Elena directed Lance to a nightstand, where disposable paper pillowcases were stowed.

Their beds made, they sat facing each other across the aisle.

"So," said Elena. "Welcome. Your new lodgings."

"Looks good. Now what?"

"What do you mean? We sleep." She stood and crossed toward him in what seemed acutely slow motion. She stood over his bed, placing her fingertips on his cheek. "I feel it too," she said, her eyes unfocused. "But we have to be careful. The Tower is strong, but we have to be stronger."

Lance gripped her wrist. "Why would it be wrong?"

"It doesn't come from us. It's not our own impulse."

"Is the Tower always wrong?"

"You know how wrong the Tower is. You've seen what happens here."

"But I know what *I* want."

Her hand did not move from his face; he wouldn't let it. "Let's do what we have to do tomorrow," she said. "If our feelings are still there after that... then maybe there's something to them."

She stood abruptly, shook her forearm free of his grip, and went to the wall, where she swung open a grey metal door, exposing a panel of switches. She pressed a button, and the meagre light faded to nil. Only the faintest glow from the proofing room seeped around the edges of the curtains. "The cameras won't see us here," she said.

"But they'll see that the lights are off." He could hear her moving toward her cot. Then the sound of two shoes worked free and dropped to the floor.

"Don't worry. If we're invisible, we're safe."

The rustle of clothes sliding off.

What would Lance sleep in? His suit? He slipped out of his jacket.

She was rummaging in her laundry hamper. Lance could not see any hint of her. Only the outlines of the windows. He heard clothing slipped over her head and wriggled into. Lance could only imagine what it was, how loose or tight, how sheer, how its fabric lay against her, what it hid and what it revealed. He tried to keep his pulse down; the hammering was in his ears and surely resounded through the whole room.

Our feelings, she had said. Not *your* feelings. *Our.* And *I feel it too.*

More rustling of cloth; a hoarse croak of springs; a small fist beating a pillow encased in paper. Then her voice, which seemed to smoulder as it crossed that gap in the darkness: "Good night, Lance."

"Wait." He sat upright, and the springs on his own cot gave away his motion.

She stirred. "Whatever you're thinking," she said, "it's probably a bad idea."

"I just want one more etymology from you. An imaginary one."

"You haven't heard enough from me today? That performance in the bindery wasn't adequate?"

"A word whose real etymology is unknown," he pressed. "A totally open field. You can do whatever you want with it."

"Okay," she said quietly. "You win."

"Thank you," whispered Lance, unsure if his voice even carried.

There was a long pause; Lance wondered if she'd conned him and simply gone to sleep. But then her voice returned: "*Conundrum.*"

"That's the word?"

"Yes. *Conundrum* is the word." In this darkness, at this distance, it was hard to tell where her voice came from. She could have moved farther away; she could be speaking close to his ear; her voice could be a quality of the air itself, like coldness or heat.

"*Conundrum* originates in the Wars of the Roses."

"Who fought that? England versus France?"

"England versus England, mostly. With French involvement. Different groups of nobles, vying for the crown."

"Okay."

"A Lancastrian soldier got separated from his regiment. He heard the sounds of approaching troops, the marching feet." Her words started to come faster. "The clank of armour plates, the jangle of chain mail."

Lance lay back. His imagination was splitting in half.

One part was there, in some reeking battlefield of yore, listening as the metallic jostle of an army drew near. The other was right here, in this dark room, with Elena.

She spoke as if she were actually remembering this event, plucking scenes one by one from the swamp of memory. "So this poor soldier is shivering behind a hedge in the rain, soaked to the skin, his muscles aching from tramping over the countryside in battle gear. He doesn't know whether these guys are friends or foes. Should he run out and join them, and have his wounds tended to? Or should he hide?"

Lance's imagination could not juggle the two scenarios it had conjured. They were starting to merge. He was there, soaked by rain and blood and sodden earth, gripping a heavy medieval spear, feeling the soldier's keen dilemma. And she was there too, soaked to the skin as well, and they lowered themselves into the mud to avoid detection.

A sound of rustling cloth. Her springs creaked to punctuate her words. "They draw closer. They are just on the other side of the hedge. He tries to peek through, but the foliage is too thick."

More noises. It sounded as if she had risen from her cot, as if bare feet were padding on the carpeted floor, as if her voice—already so hard to locate—might be inching closer to him.

"But there's a safety check: a particular drum signal the Lancastrians would use to communicate their presence. A kind of password: *It's us. We're here.* Two sharp raps on a drum, a huge, monstrous, loud thing." Elena knocked on something. It sounded wooden. Nightstand? Wall? "So there he is, waiting for the signal. And he hears it. Two loud booms. And then the traditional response, a rousing yell and the clatter of swords on shields. Your typical fifteenth-century battle cry."

"So he's safe," said Lance. "Everything's okay."

"Everything's okay," Elena whispered. And Lance gave a start as her fingers found his face, brushed his nose and lips. And her other hand reached his hair; the fingers slid through it. "Or not," she said. "The drum was *too* loud, *too* strong. Maybe it was not a drum." Something on his cheek now. Her lips, barely brushing it. One hand now gripping his shoulder, the other cupping the back of his head. "So maybe," she said, "it's not his friends at all. Maybe it's the enemy, under fire. He's lying there in his ditch, wounded, losing blood, longing to return to his comrades. But who's on the other side of that hedge?"

Her hands had stopped moving. He could feel her breath on his face. He realized her question was directed at him.

"I don't know," he answered.

"Neither does he," she whispered. "He doesn't know what to think." She gripped his face with both hands. "Are they friendly on the other side, beating the drum? Or are they enemies, shot at by a cannon? Cannon or drum? He lies there, stuck in that mud, muttering to himself, over and over again: *cannon or drum? cannon or drum?* The years pass. The words bleed together." Her lips must be inches from his. "*Conundrum.*"

Their mouths met too fast, too hard; teeth collided. But when Lance pulled his head slightly away, she followed, her tongue seeking his. His hand fumbled for some part of her face or head to hold, but then she was drawing it down, past her shoulder, to her breast. Through the thin cloth—so it was thin, after all—he felt her nipple stiffen at his touch.

Then she pushed his hand aside. Though he could not hear her move, he could sense she was backing away; he detected a distance lengthening between them. "I don't think," she said, her voice choked, "that this is a good idea."

"It's not."

And they were kissing again, and his lips were on her neck as her head arched away, and his fingers had cleverly found buttons down the front of whatever she was wearing.

Three buttons in, she laid a hand on his and stopped him. "Lance." She had to say it again before he pulled his lips from her neck. "Lance. This isn't us."

Lance opened his mouth to say no, this *was* them, the Tower had nothing to do with it. With every tendon of his body, he wanted to set such nonsense aside and continue what they'd been doing.

"Because, I mean, come *on*," she said. Her voice had lost its huskiness; it no longer smouldered as if her chest cradled embers; she was speaking in the rational tones that he was accustomed to hearing from Elena Wright, etymologist. "I tell you a story, the darkness between us is bridged, we slide closer together... It's cheap. This isn't how you and I would really end up together. Our story's not this tacky. Is it?"

Lance allowed his pulse to subside. Blood eased back to its normal distribution throughout his body. She was right. This was too... it was too something. They were succumbing to a force outside themselves.

But wasn't that love? Wasn't it supposed to be this way?

Lance didn't know. He had no experience in such matters.

"I really want to see what can happen with us," she said. "I want to know the possibilities. But not this, not now.

Let's do what we have to do. Then we can get out of this accursed place, and—"

"How? It won't let us leave."

"Its power will be destroyed. That's what he told you, right? You kill this thing, it releases its hold on us. We're free. And then we find out if we really belong together."

Lance jabbed an elbow into his pillow, propping himself up. Was she really going to want him, in the end? He was an outcast from the world she treasured so much. A leper in the kingdom of the written word. What did it matter if the Tower seduced her on his behalf? If there was any future for them—and now he guessed there probably was not—it had to be pursued outside. Staying in the Tower was madness. So there was only one thing to say.

He lowered himself back onto the bed. He peered up into the darkness above. He spoke to whatever was up there: panels, bulbs, wires, the halved eyeball of the security cam. "Yes," said Lance. "Yes, Elena. You're right."

He waited for her answer. Waited to see if she might revert, change her mind, touch him again.

But he waited for only a moment. Before she had a chance to speak, the Tower gave its most convulsive tremor yet. The sound from the walls was horrific, a deep and agonized rending, as if the stone flesh of the edifice had been gashed, from lobby to penthouse. Then a crack and a whoosh, and dust was swirling around his head. He coughed violently and swatted the air. He heard Elena's feet patter on the floor, and the lights came on and she was at the wall panel in a small white nightie.

Another shudder through the Tower, and a curtain rod broke free of its moorings and crashed to the floor, the curtain flapping above it like a cape, and the pane it exposed was webbed with cracks. Beyond that, a groan, a crunch, and something fell from the high ceiling and smashed onto a proofreader's desktop. A lamp fixture.

"It's not safe here," said Lance.

"It's not safe anywhere," Elena answered.

"We've got to find Emberton. Talk him into taking us down. His key lets us in, and then I go and I kill this thing."

"Where will we find him? We'll have to hunt up and down the whole Tower."

Hunt. What was it Emberton had said? Something about lodgings?

Another judder. Another window splintered with fissures. A sound like the crack of a gargantuan whip.

"*The Hunt!*" shouted Lance.

Floor twelve showed the effect of the latest tremor: wide cracks in the walls; cracked windowpanes; doors half off their hinges. And it was strewn with the remnants of books. Their covers were bent or torn jagged; some pages had been shredded into almost microscopic fragments; swatches of text had been slapped onto the walls, glued in place with God knew what.

A violent ripping sound burst from behind an open office door. Lance poked his head around the edge.

Mr. Tradd stood alone in an office, a heap of books on the table in front of him. He had one book in his hand—a gorgeous antique volume, leather-bound and gilded—and was grabbing pages by the fistful and wrenching them free. When the last batch had been torn out, he flung the gutted cover aside, threw back his head, and howled.

"What are you doing here? It's the middle of the night."

No answer; Mr. Tradd reached for another book.

"You need to get out."

Severely bloodshot eyes regarded him. The scent of booze was prominent.

"The Tower's coming apart."

"I told them it would," slurred Mr. Tradd. "Told them time and again. Permit the language to fall apart, and civilization too will collapse. Everything will fall about our ears. But no one listens to the truth. Who wants it? All it does is poison their pretty illusions."

"Okay, but you shouldn't be in here. It's going to—"

"I know. I welcome it. Let the edifice collapse! They abandoned their duty. They destroyed the language they were meant to *protect!*" Simultaneously with the last word, Mr. Tradd wrenched free a great hunk of book. "*Uphold!*" Another hunk. "*Guide!*" Another. He threw the binding, hard. Lance flinched as it slammed into the jamb behind him. "When they return to this vaunted floor," snarled Tradd, "there will be *no more books.*"

"You really have to—"

"Barbarisms in the lexicon! Errors canonized! No structure, no sense, no scheme. Why should buildings stand, or traffic flow, or the beautiful idea survive? I embrace this. I endorse the destruction. Let the Tower fall!"

"Decay is essential." Elena had stepped into the room. "The leaf browns, it falls from the twig, it rots, and new growth is fed by the rot." Her tone was immensely soothing, but she wasn't wasting time—an odd fusion of hypnotist and auctioneer. "I don't need to tell you this. There are dozens of examples. Like, I don't know, the word *not.*"

Mr. Tradd sighed. It was the sound of a man who knew what was coming, knew it was inevitable, knew it would defeat him.

"*Not*," said Elena, her pace picking up, "began as a redundancy—the simple, useful *ne* was embellished as *ne-a-whit*. Needless linguistic inflation used for emphasis, the way we use 'totally' today. If you'd been around in the tenth century, you'd have railed against it. But out of it we got the word *not*, and now it's vital to our grammar. You'd never propose to banish it."

"I don't really follow any of this," Lance cut in, "but I think Mr. Tradd better—"

But Mr. Tradd was not listening to Lance. "Language is structure," he said. "It is built by accretion, a great coral reef. Its desecration is anathema."

"Language is a species," answered Elena, her auctioneer's pace flagging. "A beautiful one, yes—but it must not stop evolving. Beauty is not locked inside the flower; it doesn't die when the blossom fades. Beauty is the entire cycle, the petals falling off and rotting, the new flowers arising from their decay. And the mutations that make a better-adapted plant."

Mr. Tradd's red-spangled eyes took her in.

"You have all kinds of reasons to keep on living," she said. "See where the language goes! See what new glories emerge from the rot, see how your beloved creature evolves. If you care about something, you stick around to watch it grow."

"I see." All argument had been wrung from him.

"And if you're going to live, you need to adapt to what's going on, right here and now. You must leave the Tower."

He nodded. "Thank you," he mumbled. He stood, tucked in his shirt, smoothed his hair, and made an unsteady foray toward the door.

"Elevators are still working," said Lance. "You okay to get down?"

"Yes," said Mr. Tradd, "I'm *okay to get down*." There was acid in his voice. He was mocking Lance's choice of words. With that, Lance knew for sure that Mr. Tradd was going to be all right—he was back to his old self. They watched him lurch to the elevator and press the button, then stagger into the arriving car.

"Okay," said Lance. "To the penthouse."

In the anteroom, the bare bulb flickered, showing intermittent glimpses of a floor strewn with dead flies. Lance tried the door, which was locked. He buzzed. Nothing. He was examining the hinges, trying to find the best place to ram his shoulder, when the buzzer crackled awake. "Yes?" The voice that had summoned him to the Tower all those weeks ago—but broken now, drained of its pep.

"Lance Blunt. Please let me in."

They found Miss Fairburn a wreck, makeup smeared, beehive unravelling. A thin white blanket was wrapped around her shoulders. "Yesterday," she said, voice quavering, "he dismissed me. Told me I would not be needed at the Tower anymore."

"But you stayed," said Lance.

"How can I leave? Half a century I've served him. How could I turn my back?"

"So you're just waiting here."

"Waiting for him to come back out. He'll have some use for me. I'm sure of it."

"I need to see him," said Lance.

"No one disturbs Mr. Emberton in his private lodgings. He will come out when he is ready."

"This is an emerg—" Lance was cut short by a new spasm of the walls around them. Plaster broke loose in chunks.

Miss Fairburn's *Smooth Sailing* poster, he noticed, was gashed; its top half curled from the wall like peeled skin, the poster's words now veiled by its own back end. The rumble faded in a slow decrescendo.

Miss Fairburn wrapped her blanket tighter around her shoulders.

"We have to stop this," said Lance. "This quake, or whatever it is. We need his help."

"Private lodgings," she whimpered.

"This is going to kill him too," said Lance, "unless he helps us take care of it."

Under the blanket's threadbare protection, her shoulders sagged in surrender. She beckoned mutely and led them into the office.

Chapter 14

Beyond the windows was the inky blue of early daylight—clear, no encroaching fog, no trace of haze—and it showed Mr. Emberton's office as shabby. Pitiful. Sure, the furniture was fine, the paintings old, the bookcases resplendent with antique leather volumes. But the carpet was threadbare in places; dust touched everything and swirled mid-air; cobwebs colonized the high corners.

Miss Fairburn made straight for *The Hunt*. The hunters' faces focused ahead, ruthless. Hands brandished whips. Foam crowded horses' nostrils. The fox's legs were extended in its fastest possible sprint, nose thrust forth like an arrow, light glimmering on its black eye.

That eye harboured more than fear. Something else was there in that tiny patch of surface and reflection, an emotion that Lance was sure he could identify if he had a minute to ponder it. But the chance was taken away: Miss Fairburn jabbed a thumb into the eye.

The painting groaned and trundled aside, revealing a patch of brick wall and a plain wooden door. Miss Fairburn opened it. "Sir?" Her voice eased nervously into the dark space beyond.

"I told you to leave," came the eventual reply. "Your work for me is finished."

Under the white blanket, her shoulders heaved. Her words were interspersed with sobs. "Why? Half a century, sir. Why now?"

Now Emberton came into view. He registered no surprise at seeing Lance and Elena lined up behind his loyal secretary. "Things are changing. I can't appease the Tower fast enough."

"What's going on?" Elena asked.

Without a word, Emberton flicked on a light and shuffled deeper into his room. It was squalid: scuffed tile floor, no wallpaper, no decoration of any kind. Not even a window. A rudimentary kitchen was lined up along one wall—basin, stovetop, tiny fridge. The opposite side of the room held a double bed, its sheets and blankets a rumpled heap.

The far wall was broken by a wooden door. "Come," said Emberton, "and see what the Tower is doing in the world." He opened the door and led them through to a stone patio bound by a crude iron railing. He leaned on this, looking out over the city. The others came and stood abreast of him.

Far to the west, a few dark clouds loitered, but they seemed to be in slow retreat. In the other direction, where business towers subsided and the lower-level sprawl began, the sky was a wash of pink. Enough to see by; enough to make out the scene at the Tower's feet.

The streets were scrubbed of traffic. It was early, yes, but not even a taxi or a delivery truck prowled by. No one on the sidewalks, not even city workers in reflector vests collecting trash, or cops on the beat. After a few blocks, though, this changed: a border was marked by the lights of emergency vehicles. Crowds of people milled beyond the cordons.

Within those boundaries, the Tower would be doing the ominous work that Ms. Shillingsham had described. Swallowing language. Within those boundaries, the police radios would spew nonsense, the maps and GPS screens would be devoid of text, conversation would fail, street signs would give no names. Within those boundaries, the world was the same as the one in which Lance had grown up, a world where nothing written made any sense—but worse. Far worse. Not only the written word but the spoken too was confiscated. A world without language. Robbed of the greatest thing that humans had devised, or stumbled on, or been granted by a god—the thing that empowered them to thrive, to chisel out their place on the planet. *In the beginning was the Word.*

Craning his neck, Lance spotted a pair of cars crunched nose to nose at a corner. But there was no knot of onlookers, no wounded driver staggering or prone, no paramedics dressing wounds. A breeze picked up, ruffling Lance's hair, and far away he spotted a newspaper rolling like tumbleweed down an empty street, its pages scattering as the wind peeled them apart.

Lance was working on a question for Emberton. But he couldn't quite put the words together. So he kept his silence, surveying the city and the beautiful sky and the approaching warmth of dawn.

Emberton led them back into his shabby apartment and closed the door. Lance found his question was no longer encumbered: it burst fully formed from his lips: "What is going on out there?"

"The Tower is drinking language. Siphoning it from the city."

"Why?"

"Because it is agitated, restless, mad with hunger. It is hungry because I have not fed it recently enough—the intervals, I'm sorry to say, grow shorter; its demands are more frequent every week. It is agitated by a new development. Something changed at Emberton Tower to hasten its awakening."

"Take me down, sir. I want to understand this. Take me down and show me the final depths." *And then I will destroy it.* "I want to learn everything, sir. Everything there is to know."

Emberton regarded Lance. His jowls, under their crosshatch of wrinkles, were spreading. An emotion was transforming the old man's face: pride. He was looking at Lance with pride. "Very well," he said. "Down we go."

The lobby showed signs of hasty departure by whatever staff had been on the night shift: an abandoned mop bucket lay on its side in a dark, foamy puddle of water; a buffing machine hunkered idle on the marble floor. The row of Emberton dictionaries had tumbled from the mantel; they lay in front of the sluggish fire, dust swirling over them like a host of drowsy flies. But the night guard held his post, staring impassively at his screens as if nothing strange had occurred, as if no upheavals had ruptured the building he was paid to protect.

Emberton gave an approving nod and murmured to his companions: "My guards are models of loyalty. They do not flinch in the face of the unexpected." He laid a hand on his secretary's shoulder. "As for *your* loyalty," he said, "it has been most deeply appreciated, Miss Fairburn."

Her finger sneaked under her cat-eye frames to dab something away.

"I have seen to it," he continued, "that you will be cared for out there."

"I have no reason to go, sir. Nothing to live for."

"Yes, you do, Miss Fairburn. You have the remainder of your days to enjoy in the comfort you have earned. But first, you face a brief but difficult ordeal. You will go through this revolving door into the immediate vicinity, where the damage is heaviest. You must endure the shock when your language evaporates. You will be unable to articulate a word. But you are a strong woman. You will find the courage to walk on, until you see the lights and crowds, until you hear the flowing of articulate voices and you can read the words on unscoured signs. And you will step forward into the mass of people. You belong among them now. You are released from your service."

"I don't want freedom, Mr. Emberton. I want to be in the Tower, with you." She tightened her grip on her handbag. "I wish to serve. Sir."

"There is no further service you can provide. There is no longer an Emberton Dictionary. There is no longer a need for twelve floors of staff. I have an infirmary, and I have guards. I have young Lance and the girl. I have what I need. You, Miss Fairburn, have become extraneous. I wish you to go."

"I'm... what?"

"You are *extraneous*, Miss Fairburn." He pointed at the heap of fallen dictionaries. "Do you need to look it up?"

Another shudder passed through the room, and this

one seemed to pass through Miss Fairburn too. She covered her mouth. "No," she said.

"Good. Now, my cherished Miss Fairburn, do as I say and get out of my Tower. Loyalty demands it."

She watched Mr. Emberton for a half-dozen seconds. Just as she seemed ready to formulate her answer, a nasty tremor shoved her and Emberton and Lance and Elena off balance. Everyone staggered. Miss Fairburn showed no further desire to speak. When the tremor abated, she gave the slightest hint of a curtsy and made her unsteady way to the door.

Just as she reached the cusp, Mr. Emberton cried out: "Miss Fairburn!" Her hand touched the door. "Ruth!" She turned. "It's the best for you," he said. And, to her questioning glance: "I want the best for you."

She lowered her eyes and pushed through.

Emberton turned on his heel and headed into the cafeteria, Lance and Elena scrambling in his wake. He passed the dull gleam of the sneeze guards, navigated around the cash register, and stole through the swinging door. Lance and Elena did the same. A fug of old meals enveloped them.

They passed a backsplash tarred with runnels of grease; they ducked under a rack of spoons and spatulas dangling like wind chimes; they arrived at the tall, padlocked refrigerator with its claw marks of rust. Emberton inserted a key from his old ring, undid the padlock, and swung open the thick door. A smell wafted over Lance, a mix of freezer burn and old meat. Emberton extracted a large metal briefcase.

The floor moved. The dangling spoons and spatulas clattered without harmony.

Emberton handed the metal case to Lance. It was

heavier than it looked. "The Tower is impatient," he said. "Let's move."

They rode the elevator so far down that they left the modernized system behind. When the car opened at its destination floor, an antique metal grille confronted them; Emberton separated it by hand. They were level with the rotted wooden door. The ancient key went in, and they proceeded into the torchlit corridor.

"These flames," Elena said. "They give no heat." She stopped at one of the torches, passed her hand through the light. It came out gilded.

"Does it hurt?" asked Lance.

"No." She gazed rapturously at her hand. "It doesn't hurt, but it feels... my skin feels *brighter*."

But they couldn't linger; Emberton was pressing ever ahead, and they had to scurry to keep pace. Once they had passed through the vast metal door with its mutable designs, Lance hurriedly pointed out details of the extraction room, murmuring his explanations to Elena; Emberton stood impatiently at the far side of the vat, and finally roared at them to *hurry up, we cannot keep it waiting any longer.* So they followed him to the small iron door set into the wall beyond the vat, and the third and last of his keys slid into its place. They entered the final tunnel.

It was long, low, narrow, apparently chiselled from rock. It sloped relentlessly down, and every so often it curved slightly to the left—they were descending a spiral. No torches were mounted on these walls. Faint light shimmered from the trickle of fluid leaked from the vat, which flowed in a runnel along one side. The passageway was still and silent but for breathing and feet and the susurration of the liquid beside them. Lance shifted the heavy metal briefcase from hand to hand as one arm and then the other began to ache. After what could have been a long or a short time— time itself seemed to bend with them as they traversed the spiral—a stronger light appeared up ahead, brightening as they approached it. With it came a wash of sound like gentle surf, or perhaps many voices whispering.

They eased around a final curve and entered a cavern of astonishing size. Its jagged roof soared fifty feet overhead. Its floor was a plain of scarred, grooved bedrock with loose stones and boulders strewn over its expanse. Except it wasn't all rock. Farther ahead, in the centre, it was moving. Swaying, or breathing, or—*rippling*. It was liquid. A viscous lake, big enough that Lance would exhaust himself if he tried to swim to its opposite side. At his feet, the trickle of vat-leaked fluid ran between chunks of rock, snaking its way forward until it flowed into that lake. But unlike the clear, bright substance that fed it, the lake was mottled with dark patches.

"Down here," said Emberton, "the corrosion is wanton, unbridled. It's eating its way into the depths of the earth, seeking what lies at the bottom of everything."

"And what's at the bottom?" said Lance.

"The limits of language. The final boundaries of thought and expression."

"I would have thought," Elena interjected, "it would just be more rock."

Emberton chose to ignore this, or maybe he hadn't caught it. "It's what they've always pursued," he continued, "the priests, the mystics, the chanters of curses, the cantors of prayer. They've tried to push against the boundaries of language, discover where words end and the divine begins. But they don't have the means that I have. Down there, underneath all that distraction of stone, down there is the ultimate truth."

"But that isn't language," Elena said, looking out over the gold and grey expanse. It shrugged and rolled as she spoke; it had the speed and consistency of a stream of lava. "The words you withheld from the dictionary... nobody's *saying* them. Nobody even knows they existed."

"So," said Emberton, "the etymologist speaks." This time he'd heard her. "You, claiming the roots of language as your vocation—who, if not you, ransacks the dead words, the dead tongues?" He took a menacing step toward Elena, and Lance moved to her side. "You fail to understand what we've created here. You studied my family's project—snooped around, pawed feebly at our past—but you understood nothing. You may be an intelligent girl, but you lack wisdom." He gave her a once-over, a slow, geriatric version of the inspection a man might give a woman in a pickup joint. "But you're young. You have your health. You'll serve."

Elena was about to lash out with an answer—Lance too was trying to summon a sharp word on her behalf—when a disturbance caused all three of them to turn: a flurry of high-pitched squeals, then a sudden incursion of black flapping creatures from a hole in the wall above the lake's opposite edge. Bats.

"There," said Emberton, "is an accident of the cavern's expansion. As the fluid ate farther into the earth and reached fingers up into the Tower, tendrils of corrosion broke through to the city's network of tunnels. Now when it gets hungry, its vapours reach beyond the Tower's confines, out into sewers and subways, up into the wider population."

A growl moved through the rock below and around

them. "And this is what happens," said Emberton, as the walls began to quake. The lake churned, waves moving across its surface, colliding with effusions of foam, heaving up the walls to sear the rock before plunging back down.

Lance opened his mouth to ask a question, but the words that emerged were garbled. He tried again, but more nonsense emerged. He looked helplessly at Elena, who was working her own mouth to no avail. Emberton nodded gravely and headed for the lake.

They clambered over the rocky shore. It was delicate work, picking a path without turning an ankle. But they made their way to a flat-topped boulder that jutted out over the surface of the lake. Emberton took the metal briefcase from Lance, laid it on the ground, and unlatched it. He pulled out what appeared to be a slab of raw meat, pinkish, marbled, laced with blue veins.

Something thin dangled from it. A hair. Swallowing his revulsion, Lance plucked it free. Beads of slime adhered to its length, but Lance paid these no heed. What got his attention was the colour of the hair. Blond, with an ash-grey root.

Emberton lifted the meat over his shoulder and flung it into the lake. It hit the surface with a slap. The fluid around it began to seethe and mutter. As it sank, a steam arose. The lake's hunger subsided; relative calm returned.

Emberton turned his back to the lake and produced a handkerchief with which to wipe his gleaming fingers. When he spoke, nothing garbled his words. "Down here, we are not protected as we are in the Tower. When this lake gets hungry, it steals our speech."

"That was Jeanine!" hollered Lance. "You were feeding it part of Jeanine!"

"That is what she's for," answered Emberton.

"That's... that goes way beyond..."

A rustling sound above them, and a change in the light. The bats were filing back into their hole. On the distant ceiling, their shadows were outsized negatives cut from the golden glow.

"We must feed this, Lance," Emberton said. "We must harvest flesh and give it to this lake. Otherwise its hunger will cast tentacles further into the world. Drain the human race of language. The imbeciles up there will revert to a mob of marauding beasts."

"There has to be another way," said Elena. Dismay soaked her features; she looked ready to cry. Her dreams of uncovering Emberton's secrets had come to this. She'd plumbed the depths of the story, and this was all she'd found. Hunks of marketer tossed in a puddle.

"I suppose," said Emberton pensively, "we could simply let its hunger rage. I can't say I care whether our sorry species keeps its languages. Letting them amass in the Tower may be the best culmination of the project. In the kingdom of the wordless, the man who speaks is king."

"But no one understands his commands," muttered Elena.

Emberton had only a withering stare for her. The lake seemed to sigh, a slow wave passing wearily over its shining skin. "It has been such effort, such toil, performing my duties," Emberton said. "When you kill as a matter of routine, when you harvest flesh and blood, it gnaws at you. I am not without conscience. But I have succeeded in my work. I've kept this thing contained. Can the containment go on? I don't know. The upheavals grow worse by the day."

"Why?" asked Lance. "What's different now?"

"You."

"What?"

"You. Lance Blunt. You have arrived at the Tower, and it recognizes its own. It senses the quickening of fate."

Lance looked out at the lake's mottled face. "I don't understand."

"What is your earliest memory?"

Lance did not want to play whatever game this was, but his brain couldn't resist the question, and automatically he scrolled back as far as he could. The earliest he could come up with was a glimpse of the wares at Blunt Furnishings, which towered over him, tabletops like ceilings, chairs' armrests like high cliffs. He toddled toward something tall and flat, perhaps the glass door of a cabinet, before being scooped up by a maternal hand.

That was the earliest image he had. But he did not want to share it with Emberton. That little movie was his, and his alone. No one else had any right to it. "Don't know," he said.

"Think hard. Is there a place, a location, way back in the depths of memory?"

"The store, obviously," said Lance. "Furniture."

"Earlier than that."

"There is no earlier. I grew up there."

"Is there a sound that takes you back in time? A particular lullaby, soothing you into the past?"

And, in a flash, there it was. The press room. Its endless grumble. As if on an old and scratchy film, Lance could envision crawling on the rough ground, the noise encasing him, filling his tiny skeleton. Some giant thing was beside him—the corner of a machine. And he was crawling toward it, the ground advancing under him, and around that corner was something he wanted, and his crawling brought him inexorably closer. He could only move so fast with just two hands and two knees to propel him, but the angle was changing, he was rounding the edge of the machine, dragging himself toward something hideous and inevitable, something like fate.

Emberton rested his weight on his cane. Behind him, the lake rippled. "Late one night, twenty-five years ago, I was doing my rounds, checking the Tower's pulse. I came to the press room. And there I heard something that had not resounded within the Tower walls for a long time: the cries of an infant. I found you in a corner, naked, abandoned, skin smeared with fresh ink. You fell silent as I approached."

Ahead of baby Lance, floor met wall. A strange sound emitted from that spot: a kind of gurgling. He hurried forward, limbs furious. He reached the wall and did the thing he was compelled to do. And after that he lay on his back, glutted. And a shadow loomed, a figure drew near. A human face, creased with many wrinkles.

"Something grey and foamy leaked from the corner of your mouth and spilled down your plump cheek. And you turned from me and opened your mouth, and from a fissure in the wall bubbled the grey substance that rises through the Tower. The filthy obverse of my beautiful fluid. And you drank. My old heart—yes, I was old even then—hammered my ribs. Here was a creature with the same curse that had afflicted me: a baby suckled by the Tower itself!"

Infant Lance was plucked from the ground, hoisted up. The wrinkled face loomed. The dry lips parted and a gust of air came out, and with it came sound—Lance of course could not understand the sound, could not understand even that it was a word, but he felt the warm breath and smelled its corruption and understood that the sound it made was meant for him.

And the mind's screen faded to black. His new earliest memory was complete.

But Emberton was not finished. His voice droned on, and Lance could barely grasp its substance. He was too shaken, his mind a frenzy of questions and denials, all afloat on an undertow of fear. If he was from the Tower, why did the Blunts raise him without ever saying a word? If as a fragile baby he had drunk the same poison that the hulking Mr. Furlanetti ingested today, what did that mean for his brain, his insides?

"I had to rescue you," Emberton was saying. "You'd lived by creeping about and evading discovery. With no mother, no milk, you subsisted on what the Tower fed you. The substance is too damaging, its allure too strong. You've seen your vice-president. You had to be removed from the Tower, but I had to stay to do my work. So I struck a deal with a furniture seller who had supplied some of our offices. He was getting on in years, his business was failing, his marriage barren. They dearly wanted a child. I gave them that, and I gave them money to sustain their inept store. In exchange, they would return the child to the Tower when he was ready."

Lance was desperate to demolish Emberton's tale, but he knew, with an inexplicable certainty, that it was true. Still, if truth itself was too awful to accept, then it had to be savaged, torn down, denied. "But I always talked fine," he tried. "Mr. Furlanetti sucks that stuff, he can barely speak.

You said you couldn't talk as a kid. Not me. I'm a good talker."

"Lucky I rescued you when I did. The damage to the higher functions was deep enough to be permanent—you will never acquire the ability to read through natural means. But your abundant expressive skill, which drew on the elemental speech centres—this could be nurtured back to health. I left you in reliable hands until I could take you back."

Reliable hands. Lance thought back to the Blunts, their stolid, diligent life. They never harmed him, never failed to be there when he needed them. Reliable, yes—except that they were living a lie. *Always tell 'em the truth. But never tell 'em the whole truth.* The hallowed words of Blunt Sr. *I love you,* he'd said. *You were the sweetest baby. Loved you the second I saw you.* But he never said *I am your father.* He left it as obvious; no need to say the damn words.

That furniture dealer, with his thick eyebrows, the constant shading of stubble, the coarse black hair; that gruff man who loved his dictionary, revelled in the etymologies. So much older than Lance—what was it, fifty years? And Mrs. Blunt, with her stern grey eyes and fine bones. She was forty-five years Lance's senior. Sure, he'd always known they were a bit old, but that gets overcome, people find a way, there are medical options, probability gets defied. He had come to his parents later in their life than he should have, and he resembled neither of them. But he had never imagined he wasn't theirs.

Lance did not know what his fury might lead to. With an enraged cry, he turned his attention to the briefcase that had conveyed Jeanine's meat. He kicked it as hard as he could; it slid along the rock and came to rest by the lake's edge, on a slab of rock still shiny and wet from the last upheaval. "Who?" he flung his question out over the mottled surface. "My parents, who were they?"

"One of the pressmen. I don't know which. He got mixed up with a woman working in the cafeteria. Yes, the cafeteria once had a staff of more than two. And customers. My father had a purpose for it, and he gave it a generous budget. When the girl got pregnant, the pressman tried to distance himself from her. But she would have none of that. She came down to the press room constantly—what do you call it these days? She stalked him."

Lance looked at Elena. She was watching the conversation, transfixed. He couldn't gauge what effect all this was having on her opinion of him, whether his link to the Tower appalled or attracted her. Her cheeks were flushed, her hair cascading in mad strands about her temples. Her eyes blazed with something, though Lance did not know what.

"She was fired from the cafeteria, but rather than going home she found some obscure nook and bedded down. She vanished, poor girl. I would have tried to salvage her, put her in the infirmary. But we never found her hiding place. God knows, she may be somewhere down here still today, a skeleton in the tunnels above us. But before she went away, she left us a precious gift."

"I'm not your gift."

"You belong to the Tower. You are a child of the Tower. It is your birthright, your destiny."

Lance turned his back on the lake and faced the old man. "No," he said. "No, it is not."

"I will not last much longer, Lance. The fluid has

extended my years, emboldened my body to thrive and work. But time is running out. You will take over for me."

"Elena is right," said Lance slowly. "There is another way. No one needs to die to placate this thing."

"You cannot escape this," said Emberton. "I know you have tried. I know you have gone to the lobby, approached the revolving door, strained to push through. But you have failed. The Tower wants you, and it will have you."

"No," insisted Lance. "When I had my hand inside the wall, you warned me to be careful. You said if *it* dies, its power dies. The fluid in your blood would be useless. The vat would dry up and stop leaking down here. Right? And this thing, this lake... it would lose its powers too, wouldn't it? All the fluid is connected. All of its strength comes from the same place."

Emberton edged forward, cane raised. "I don't like this line of speaking, Lance. Be very careful what you say next."

Lance could not exercise that kind of care. He no longer had any facility for playing along. "I'm going to go up there right now, stick my fists in the wall, find that tube, and tear it to shreds. I'll kill it with my bare hands."

"Imbecile," said Emberton. "You'll never read again."

"I don't care," Lance answered.

"He's wrong," Elena said. Some sort of breeze had caught her hair; its uppermost strands twirled above her as if she'd laid her hands on an electrified sphere. "If the Tower loses its power, you'll be freed from it. You can learn to read and write."

"Foolish girl," bellowed Emberton. "The damage to his brain is physical. Permanent. The power of the fluid is what *cures* him. Once he discards this juvenile rage and accepts reality, he will not dare destroy that power."

Lance hadn't torn his eyes from Elena. The boldness in her face as she spoke, the certainty, the investment in Lance's future—these had absorbed his attention entirely. And now she was about to reply to the old man, but her face changed. Alarm flashed across it. Lance tried to step toward her, but Emberton's cane thudded into his chest. With his free hand, the old man took a swig from his flask. "I recommend," he said, "that you retract your threat."

"No."

"I order you," said Emberton, "to retract."

"No. I'll kill your Tower."

"Very well." And, with three strides forward, the cane still jammed in place, Emberton had successfully set Lance off balance. Lance stumbled backward and ran into something on the ground behind him. The briefcase. Another shove from Emberton's cane, and he toppled over the case onto the sloping shore. He was stuck there, the cloth of his shirt adhering to the rock face. Then the cohesion gave out, and he was sliding backward. He put out his hands to halt his descent, but they slid on the wet rock.

His head hit the surface of the lake first.

Chapter 15

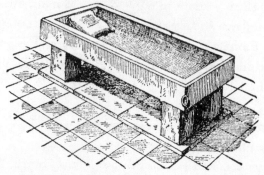

Sound warped. It was like he'd been shoved through a barrier of sound waves all crunched together. A roar baptized him on entry, then everything was quiet. Time stretched.

The surface of the lake was palpable, a line of heat that descended his body in slo-mo. It crept down his throat, slid over his Adam's apple, made a snail's charge for the base of his neck. The hairs there crackled.

Despite the pain sliding down Lance's body, the parts of him already submerged did not burn. This slow, quiet place—the subsurface realm—was not going to cause him any harm. Not yet.

Open your eyes. The command seemed to emanate from the fluid surrounding him. But it did not take the form of those words. It was some other form of address, ancient and alien—yet Lance understood it, instinctively, even though he had never heard it before.

Open your eyes.

He gathered his courage.

His collarbone was slipping under the surface, in increments.

Open— The sentence did not finish. His eyelids had already parted.

He was suspended in a glittering, golden translucence. A sound vibrated around him—a hum that rose from the depths and cradled his head. It was a vowel, the sound someone makes when they don't know what to say: *Uh...* And suddenly, like a swift school of fish, syllables and sounds rushed past him, through him, around him. Then they were gone.

Far below, in the depths, a cloud of murk was gathering force, billowing, rising. It sent no voice ahead of it; silence was its envoy. It was remarkably thick, bursting upward in clouds. It was, Lance realized, the source of the mayhem: the entity that gurgled through the pipes and addicted Mr. Furlanetti; the essence whose vapours seeped into the city and stole its language. Lance had a sudden, vivid vision of what would happen if he obeyed Emberton and cared for it, cultivated it, fed it, helped it grow. It would bully up through the Tower—not just the pipes and ducts; it would bubble up through the open spaces, clog the corridors, flood the rooms, rise to the top, and eat the Tower from within, rotting its carpets and chairs, digesting its books and all their millions of words, corroding the walls and doors and partitions that defined the Tower's interior. The Tower would become nothing but a suction tube, rotten inside and thirsty for all the world's language. It wouldn't need human minions to feed it words. It would take its true form, and it would guzzle words at will. It was pure greed—no plan, no purpose, nothing but the blind fulfillment of its own yearning.

And it was speaking to him. Nothing audible, only a stirring in Lance's mind, one intelligence calling another.

Flesh of my flesh, it said. And, with these hungry words, it billowed closer. The golden fluid holding Lance boiled in anticipation, its dark heart no more than a dozen feet away. *Flesh of my flesh.*

But in that plaintive, acquisitive cry, Lance heard also the shadow cry, the unspoken second half, the culminating complement: *Blood of my blood.* The lake recognized Lance's body—his damaged tissue, his compromised brain—as quasi-kin. But it wanted something more, which Lance could not give. It would never be satisfied, Lance realized, would never cease its restless upheavals, until it consumed the family that spawned it. It needed Emberton blood. Unless Lance completed his plan—which, it seemed, he might not survive to do—unless he shredded the tender tube that pulsed within the cellar wall, this thing would survive down here, ravenous for its own creator.

The billowing darkness was closer. The surface of the lake had advanced to Lance's upper back. But all burning had subsided now; the golden fluid was almost a balm against his skin. The truly damaging stuff was coming next.

So he was going to be claimed by the lake. For a while, it would be soothed—flesh of its flesh, a feast to be digested for an age. Long enough, perhaps, for Emberton to cultivate a new heir, find someone else to prolong the nightmare. The approaching darkness was a seduction: it wanted him, needed him like no human ever had, was ready to bestow on him a significance that he had never known in his short and inconsequential life. He was ready to let it roil up and seize him. *Flesh of my flesh,* he thought as it advanced like a sandstorm.

Something had him by the legs. He was being pulled back, away. The sound waves scrunched together again, and with a thudding detonation he was up through the surface, and time ticked along at its normal pace. His hair felt singed. The skin of his upper body felt bathed in flame. He fell. Someone was beneath him, someone smaller than he was. Lance rolled off his rescuer and yelped as his tender skin collided with the rock.

A cough racked his chest, filled his throat with a hot, viscous gorge. He opened his mouth, and a pearled mess of fluid—gold, black, and clear components, jellied together like oil and vinegar—slid from his mouth and caked the rock.

Staring at this unholy mess, Lance was overcome by a fierce dizziness. Darkness rushed around him in a frantic host of hovering blacknesses, an obliterating swirl of batwings.

And he fell into an unconscious void.

And was yanked back into bright lights, noise, commotion. Someone was yelling something. He was being dragged; his feet seemed to slide over a rough surface. He opened his eyes. Upside down, her face: Elena. Her mouth moving frantically to get a syllable out. The same sound, over and over. His name.

Darkness returned, and was lifted again, ever so briefly. He was laid on a cold floor. His cheek was on the ground. He could see armchairs, their feet, dust on the floor underneath. And beyond that, the slow sway of the yellow flames in the lobby fireplace. The unburning wood.

Elena's voice again. Frantic, loud. Protesting. "No!" she was saying. "Don't— I have to—" And suddenly she was muffled. Heavy boots were hammering the floor. He wanted to raise himself, turn his head, see what was happening, but he could not move. Pain gripped his skull, paralysis the rest of him.

He went back under.

The world returned, breaking in like a burglar, kicking down the dreamless void. Bright light and copious noise. He was on his back on a soft, flat surface borne swiftly forward. He became aware of bodies flanking it, clad in mint-green scrubs, hands gripping the sides of the bed. He raised his head, chin to chest, to see where the stretcher was headed. For a second he held out hope that he would see an emergency ward, a waiting room with beam chairs and old magazines, ambulance lights blinking beyond the glass doors. The legitimate world, a valid hospital, his body given over to the care of professionals whose aim was to cure him. But instead he saw a pair of frosted glass panels, the familiar red cross dividing itself in two.

Empty beds were arrayed on each side of the central corridor, some of them sheathed in curtains that hung from curved rails. Lance was steered into the alcove beside one of the veiled nooks and dropped on the bed, sending a new flare of pain through his tender shoulders.

"Don't worry, we know what to do for you," said one of his attendants. The other yanked the curtain, enclosing them in a pus-coloured husk. Now he could see their faces in full: a man and a woman, wearing a sheen of professional compassion. The woman brushed a sweaty strand of hair from Lance's forehead. "Only a short stay," she said, "and you'll be good as new."

"You're in the right place," said the man. "We have a handle on some of the... *unique* complaints you get at

Emberton." As he spoke, he tapped a forefinger, hard, on Lance's knee, six or seven times in rhythm. Lance hardly absorbed what the man said; he was staring at the knee in wonderment, trying to understand what that tapping was about.

It was about distraction. Lance didn't notice until it was too late that the woman had jammed a substantial needle into his right bicep. The needle withdrew with an unhealthy slurp. A violet tinge came over everything in the room. It thickened, and Lance was in darkness again.

Images arose intermittently. Hazy glimpses of the deserted Tower. But it wasn't quite deserted—figures flitted on the periphery of sight, disappearing around corners, ducking behind desks. All the pipes were alive with noise; every opening frothed with luminous fluid. The building shuddered and plaster fell from walls, disintegrating on a marble floor, exposing the Tower's flesh, subcutaneous and pulsing. And again Lance was in the men's room on floor four, the flesh contorting itself into a mouth, a mouth that stirred and gaped and wanted to tell him something.

But when the Tower spoke, no words came out. Lance had expected a revelation; he had expected the Tower would tell him its secrets, indoctrinate him. But it was the opposite. When the mouth opened, it did not give; it took. Everything in that grotty john—the air, the light, the ambient rush of water in bathroom pipes—was being warped in its very fabric, pulled by a great inhaling force, and the room began to distend and dissolve and finally to flow, sliding like thick soup into the widening gap between the lips. And Lance's own flesh stretched from him, grew soft like beef boiled and loosened from the bone, and drifted toward the mouth, which even now was widening, even now was swallowing more of the living realm with a great, gasping, scarfing slurp, and the sound grew in intensity, and every last trace of the world was consumed.

He woke to a blazing incandescence, but as he adjusted, it settled to a cool glow. He felt a pinching sensation at a few points on his torso. Glancing down, he saw he was wearing a hospital gown. In three spots it was torn, and from those gashes emerged clear plastic tubes glutted with liquid—red or clear or yellow flecked with grey. Another tube puckered the skin of each arm.

Beyond his curtain wall, a voice—old, familiar, rich like tea in honey—was delivering a tirade. "I pay you an excellent living. Why? To feed your cowardice? No. You are not paid to quail and flee every time the ground shakes. Stay here and do your job."

Another voice, female, barely audible, replied in plaintive tones.

"Nonsense," replied Mr. Emberton's voice. "It is a trifle, and I will have it fixed. As long as you do your work, the Tower will be stable."

Now a male voice cut in with what sounded like a string of medical jargon, peppered with queries.

"Yes," said Emberton, "she's done. Dispose. We're fine with the new one."

The female voice piped up.

"No, no," remonstrated Emberton. "The *fat* new one."

Both additional voices babbled overtop of each other.

"Fine," said Emberton. "Now leave me be."

Shuffling feet, and a corner of Lance's yellow curtain was pulled aside. "Feeling better?"

"Get me out now!" spat Lance. "You're not going to feed my... *meat* to that thing!"

Emberton laughed, a tired, voiceless gust. "No, I'm not. You have a far more glorious fate, my boy. And I want you to be intact for it."

"Then why am I *here*?"

"Lance, settle. This infirmary does function as an actual hospital, whatever fanciful stories your marketers may have cooked up. We are capable of curing injury. You spent a few seconds too many in that lake." Emberton patted Lance's leg. "You owe your life to Elena," he said. "After the blasphemy that passed your lips, I would have been content to see you die." The hand closed on Lance's shin, very hard. Enough force in that hand to crush bone. "Abandon you to the depths, find myself another heir. But the girl was heroic. Pushed me aside—and my strength surprises those who test it—and splashed in after you, hauled you out. It must have hurt her a bit, going in like that. Nothing like what you've been through, of course."

"What have you done with her?" Emberton loosened his grip, and Lance tried to withdraw his leg, but something more than the old man's hand was restraining him. "You better not touch her."

"Oh, don't worry," said Emberton. "I don't want the girl harmed. I want her healthy and whole."

"You let her go?"

"Of course not, Lance. I need her. She's in the custody of protection services. In the holding cell."

"Fuck that." Lance tore at the tubes in his arms. "I'm going to get her." They were anchored deep, but he managed to work one free; it sprang from his flesh with a sickening pop, and blood spattered the sheet where it lay.

Mirth spread across Emberton's features.

"What's so funny?"

Emberton pressed a button on one of the machines. He studied the LED screen. "Young love," he wheezed. "So predictable. I think the future is in reliable hands."

Lance wrestled with a new tube. His flesh squelched as the plastic wriggled.

"Your passion," said Emberton, "is exactly what I hoped to see. I encourage you to hang on to it. Just long enough."

Behind him, the yellow curtain parted and the woman with the needle appeared. Lance writhed and twisted in his restraints, but he could not escape her persistent needle. It took her two tries, but she plunged it into the side of his neck.

As Lance went under, Emberton's voice drifted into his dwindling awareness. "The second procedure. You will go ahead with it, please."

This was a thick unconsciousness, murky, almost dreamless—though a few nightmares did intrude. At first they all took place in the infirmary. Lance watched the medics care for him; he was outside his body, but not floating above the bed as he'd heard people did near death. Instead, he had the point of view of a patient in a neighbouring bed, observing the show from mattress height. But the Lance he watched receive treatment was not Lance. The face resisted focus, dissolved into fragments, came back together incomplete or deformed or blurred to invisibility.

Marshalling all his power of attention, Lance forced the face into clarity. It was Emberton's. Large, humming machines stood beside him and tubes protruded from his body, a brood of them. Bags of red fluid hung haphazard from metal poles, too many of them, surplus pinatas at an overzealous birthday party.

His dream flitted to childhood parties and childhood pain, the inability to read the packaging on gifts he opened, to understand what he'd received.

But then he saw Emberton again, deathly pale on the bed, tubes filling and emptying with red. But it wasn't pure red, every time. Sometimes it had a golden tinge.

No one was taking care of anyone's injuries. Not that Lance could see.

He tried to speak up. His flesh throbbed. He felt pierced all over his body, a fleeing warrior caught by a hail of arrows. He tried to say something about wounds, about blood, about his brief communion with the anguished lake far beneath Emberton Tower, but bodies moved toward him and the darkness plunged over him again, and the dreams receded and twinkled away.

Lance awoke alone in his berth. He felt none of the grogginess that had followed his other needle-induced naps; now a peculiar vim infused his mind and senses. He could see his surroundings clearly. The details of the machines—the knobs and panels, the LED displays and tubes notched by the milligram—stood out in sharp detail.

He sat up. He had to get to Elena before Emberton did. He checked his arm. Several tubes connected him to humming machines or suspended bags of red or gold fluid. One by one, he worked them free, trying not to give voice to his pain. Little red gashes pocked his forearms. He braced his hand on the mattress and tried to spin around to a sitting position.

But his feet wouldn't come free. He flung aside his

blanket and sheet. Sturdy plastic ties secured his ankles to the foot of the bed. Not a surgical knife or a pair of scissors in sight. He tugged himself down the length of the bed to better examine his ankles. The bands were tight—skin welled up at their edges and flared red along their borders. They were vulnerable only near their anchor points on the bed. He tried to rip the exposed strips of plastic, but all he achieved was a torn fingernail. With a growl of frustration, he threw himself back on the bed.

A stir and a cough from behind the drawn curtain beside him. He recognized that sound. Thick, phlegmy, simmering with gurgles. Trying to keep his voice low, he called out through the curtain: "Mr. Furlanetti!"

The sound of a great weight shifting on a bed. Below the bottom of the curtain, Lance could see a pair of feet plant themselves on the floor. Then a laborious bout of muttering, and the feet began to walk. They padded alongside the curtain, and when they reached its edge Mr. Furlanetti's head peeked around it.

Lance beckoned him closer.

Mr. Furlanetti pushed through the gap between the curtains. He was wearing only a green paper hospital gown, his belly pushing its dimensions to the limit. His bare legs were very pale, accentuating their thick, dark hairs. His right arm, white and intermittently hairy, hung limp at his side. The other one, the one that would have been his left arm, was gone. Its shoulder was a meringue of cauterized flesh.

"Lance," said Mr. Furlanetti, after an introductory bouquet of burbles. He stood at the foot of the bed. His right arm was so big, its bicep lost in rolls of fat, that the other arm's absence was monumental too, a presence all its own. The vacant air sang with it.

"What happened to you?" asked Lance.

Mr. Furlanetti closed his eyes. "Questions. All these questions. He thought I was..."

Lance suddenly felt very cold. Bile was in his throat, a thick and acidic stew. He wanted to clap his hands over his ears, shout, do anything to drown out what Mr. Furlanetti had to say. But that would serve nothing. This was his fault, and he had to face the full consequences of what he'd done. "*Who* thought you were?"

"The boss. Mr...." The voice trailed fearfully away.

"*What* did he think you were?"

A tear descended Mr. Furlanetti's cheek. "Spy. I'm a spy." His one hand made a slow pass over his cheek to smear the tear away. "All I did was take what the Tower gave. I never pried. Never sneaked."

"Your arm."

"Infection. Because he burned me. Had my arm on the radiator, and it burned so bad. They told me it wouldn't heal. Arm had to go."

"This is insane."

"This is Emberton Tower."

"I'm so, so sorry." It came out sounding like condolence rather than remorse, but Lance let that impression stand. He didn't have the courage to admit what he'd done.

Furlanetti spoke at the ceiling. "Can't be avoided," he said.

"What do you mean?"

"In the end, Lance. Can't avoid it. We're marketers."

"Okay, listen. We need to get out of here. Like, pronto.

But they've tied my feet. I need you to find something sharp and cut me free."

Mr. Furlanetti's raisin eyes were uncomprehending. "Get out?"

"Yeah, like escape."

"But we don't come back." His voice was placid. "This is the final home for us."

"Not for you. Not for me. We're going to change that. Do you understand?"

Mr. Furlanetti did not understand.

"They took your arm," pressed Lance. "What's next? Do you want to stay and find out?"

"It's what happens to us, Lance. She already tried, anyway. Came here for me. To get me out, she said. But no. They kept her."

"What do you mean?"

"Ms. Shillingsham. She came for me. But they put a needle in her neck."

"She's here too?"

"Even though there's no meat on her. I heard him... I heard the boss telling the staff she's no good. 'No meat,' he said." Mr. Furlanetti leaned forward. "I think she thought she could avoid this, she could avoid coming here, if she kept herself very thin."

"Mr. Furlanetti, listen up. We're going to get you out. Out of the infirmary, and out of the Tower. Her too. The both of you." Lance waggled his foot to show its restraint. "First, I need you to find me something sharp."

Mr. Furlanetti blinked at the foot and its plastic band.

"Fuck's sake, Mr. Furlanetti. Look at your arm."

Mr. Furlanetti eyes tracked slowly from the bed to his right bicep. He raised his elbow, gawked at it. Fatty flesh dangled from the upper arm; dark moles nestled in the hairs of the lower. The fingers gave a slow wriggle.

"That arm," hissed Lance, "is a beautiful thing. Look at those fingers move. Think of everything that arm can do for you. You're going to let them take that one too?"

A few more wriggles of the fingers. "Something sharp," Mr. Furlanetti said.

"Yes. And hurry."

With Mr. Furlanetti gone, Lance twisted in place to survey his bedside table. Even with his feet held in place, he managed to turn onto his belly and yank open the top drawer. There he found his clothes, neatly folded. One by one, he pulled them free and laid them on the bed beside him. He fastened his wristwatch. It showed ten o'clock.

A rustle at the curtains: Mr. Furlanetti had found a small surgical saw. Lance's plastic restraints easily fell away.

"Get dressed," Lance whispered. Mr. Furlanetti retreated to his own alcove, and Lance could hear a drawer open and the rustling of cloth.

Lance was almost done—only a few more buttons on his shirt to do up—when footsteps resounded from the corridor. Voices too, hushed and indistinct. He slipped back into the bed and pulled the blankets up to his chin. In the neighbouring alcove, Mr. Furlanetti's bed creaked as his own bulk plumped back onto it.

The footsteps and voices swept past Lance's nook, and then past Mr. Furlanetti's. Then they stopped, and a loud clanging of metal filled the infirmary. The voices struck up again and faded from earshot.

Lance slipped to the top of his alcove and peered out. At the terminus of the main corridor, a metal door stood open. Wisps of mist curled around its edges.

Voices drifted from the gap.

A man: "Time of death?"

A woman: "Oh-eight-hundred."

"Can we get more from her?"

"Scraping the barrel now, I'd say. Boss says dispose. We have the big fella now."

"All right, let's shut this one down. Get Caitlin on it."

The shuffle of feet. Two figures clad in scrubs emerged around the edge of the door; Lance retreated behind his curtain. The footsteps passed out of earshot.

Lance allowed a few moments to go by, his ears pricked for any hint of the medics' return. But all he heard was the ambience that had been with him since he woke up here: the humming and bleeping and chuffing of hospital machinery; the usual Emberton Tower whispering and sighing of ducts and vents; the occasional gulp of fluid traversing a pipe. When he was reasonably sure the medics were gone, he slipped into the neighbouring nook.

Mr. Furlanetti sat upright on his bed. "They were in the back room."

"I saw. What goes on in there?"

"No clue." Mr. Furlanetti pondered and gurgled. Then: "Don't want one."

Quiet had fallen over the infirmary; no one seemed to be around. Lance felt strong, indomitable where he had been wounded. A strange optimism coursed through him, a sense of mastery over this environment. He'd been shown the farthest depths—hell, he'd been *immersed* in the depths— and surely nothing in this Tower was beyond his reach. A keen curiosity, a desire to answer some kind of call, passed through him with each heartbeat. "Let's go in," he said.

Mr. Furlanetti's face shaped itself into a range of

expressions. Horror was there first, his mouth opening and his skin shading white. Then a sort of fearful respect, an appreciation of Lance as a brilliant madman. Then a nascent curiosity. "Yes" was all he said.

They stepped into a room with its temperature lowered to meat-locker levels. It was an operating theatre. Barely lit, but its metal surfaces glinted. The ceiling was domed metal, like the inside of a bullet's tip. Banks of lights lurked up there, switched off for now but ready to unleash great brilliance. Numerous trays and surfaces stood like onlookers at the room's fringes, tools of the trade laid on top of them— Lance noted a surgical saw, a shiny scalpel, a large pair of tweezers curved like the jaws of a shark and filed to deadly points. But the fringes of the room barely registered. The centre dominated Lance's attention.

There, a single bed was positioned, elevated at the pillow end as if to present the patient to Lance and Mr. Furlanetti for easy viewing. The only visible part was the head. A woman's head, with long, blond hair fanning out on either side. Her body was covered by some kind of plastic sheet. Something about the shape was just plain wrong.

They drew closer, Lance's breath suspended, Mr. Furlanetti's belly grumbling like a diesel truck. Lance knew the face of this woman—the slightly upturned nose, the worry lines down the sides of her mouth, the spattering of freckles. The blond hair showing its roots of grey. There was no doubt, but Mr. Furlanetti's dismayed moan provided the final confirmation: "Jeanine."

Lance placed his finger on her neck. Pure cold; not a hint of pulse. He mumbled an apology to the departed woman, knowing how intrusive this would be. But he felt he needed to see. He peeled back the sheet.

None of her limbs were left. Roughly cauterized patches marked where their roots had been. A paper gown covered her front, but on the uncovered sides it was clear that great furrows and craters had been gouged into her flesh. Hints of bone and organ showed through the deepest layers of meat, which was crosshatched with deep, wide gouges—they reminded Lance of the brushstrokes on *The Hunt*.

Mr. Furlanetti made a new sound, not a gurgle but something else, something more convulsive. It was only when the first clear drop landed on the bed that Lance realized Mr. Furlanetti was weeping.

"I have her office," Lance said. "I have her stuff, her pictures."

"She told me, before... before she went away. Things from her life. Keepsakes. Bring them into the Tower. She knew."

"Knew what?"

"She'd never leave."

"She was married, I think. There were wedding photos."

"On floor four," said Mr. Furlanetti quietly, "we're alone. Single, I mean. All of us are single. And we're not young. Unlikely to meet someone. But she... shortly after she started here, she met him. Sixty-three years old, and she married him right away. Head over heels, she said. I tried to warn her. Don't come to work. Not if you have some... something to live for."

"Where is he?"

Mr. Furlanetti shrugged, the jagged flesh of his left shoulder rippling with the motion, creases opening to reveal red, raw depths. "The marriage couldn't last. Not when the Tower had her. They broke up—he said she was 'married to her job.' He was right. Couldn't pull herself away."

Noises beyond the door. The soft slap of hospital slippers; the trundling of a cart.

"This way," Lance whispered. He led Mr. Furlanetti to the very back, where a small aperture was set into the wall. Its entrance was covered by thick black rubber strips like luggage passes through at an airport carousel. Lance poked his head through the rubber strips.

Beyond them was a small tunnel, about ten feet long, with a diameter of five feet. A conveyor belt ran down the centre, from front to back, toward a set of overlaid metal jaws like those in a garbage truck.

Fast as he could—not very fast, given Mr. Furlanetti's size and one-armed awkwardness—Lance helped his departmental vice-president climb up to the aperture and crawl through the curtain of strips. He hauled himself through next, pressing hard into Mr. Furlanetti's broad back as they squeezed into the space. The voices and footsteps got louder.

Lance and Mr. Furlanetti scrambled from the conveyor belt to the floor beside it. Nozzles jutted from the walls. The smell was a mix of rubber, metal, and chemical. Space was limited, and Lance found himself getting cozier than he would have wished with Mr. Furlanetti's burbling mass.

Machines wheezed and beeped. Feet shuffled periodically. Paper shifted and crinkled; cloth slid against cloth. Lance had to shift position, which he did as quietly as he could. Beside him, Mr. Furlanetti did the same. Bed wheels sounded on the floor outside. Jeanine was being pushed closer.

"Ready?" said a man's voice. "Count of three." Then he grunted, and something was thrust through the rubber flaps.

Lance raised his head to peek over the edge of the conveyor belt. A mummified bundle sat atop it.

"You'll finish up, Caitlin?" the man said.

"Yep," a woman replied.

The rubber flaps had fallen shut. The man made his exit, and Caitlin did swift and quiet work—maybe flicking switches on a panel or rearranging instruments on a tray. Footsteps. A loud click. The nozzles aimed at the conveyor belt spewed a fine steam that reeked of chemical. Sweet, sickly—an odour Lance knew he'd smelled before but couldn't quite remember when or where. It did not feel breathable, though.

He pressed his lips to Furlanetti's ear. "We have to move."

He was examining the belt, trying to strategize how to clamber with Mr. Furlanetti around Jeanine's body, when the belt groaned and juddered to life. And at once Lance remembered why he knew this smell. The garden. He'd thought it was fertilizer.

The metal jaws at the room's end opened, showing rusted fangs and interlocked threshers, and Jeanine lurched toward them.

Like a wrestler reversing a hold, Lance wriggled around Mr. Furlanetti to get behind him. Then he hoisted him up onto the conveyor belt, Furlanetti's one arm helping as best it could, and pushed him, against the movement of the belt, toward the rubber flaps. Outside, Caitlin shrieked as the entirety of Mr. Furlanetti slid through the flaps and crashed to the floor. Lance scrambled after him. From behind the flaps, a crunching, grinding noise signalled the arrival of Jeanine's body at the disposal contraption. At the other end of which, Lance knew, her soupy remains would emerge through a vent and land on a patch of soil, ready to be spread over the garden to nourish its moist grass, its flowers with their serpentine stems, its withered claw of a fruit tree.

Caitlin was backed up against a tray of tools, brandishing a surgical saw. Lance recognized her as the nurse who had plunged a needle, twice, into his flesh to conk him out. "What are you doing in here? This is a restricted..." She abandoned her spiel, apparently accepting that Lance and Mr. Furlanetti were now quite well versed in the nature of this room. "You have to get... Return immediately to your beds."

"How can you do this?" bellowed Lance.

Caitlin flinched from him even as she waved the saw more menacingly. "We do medicine here. Same as anywhere else."

The disposal mechanism gave an especially loud growl, followed by a staccato sound like a bough splintered by lightning.

"You take people's flesh! How is that medicine?"

"Infections have to be cut out. To save the patient."

"You didn't save Jeanine."

More gnashing and grinding and splintering noises, then the disposal machine fell silent.

Only then did Lance notice Caitlin was sobbing. "It's an old building. It's got unusual... infections are different here. They take hold." The saw drooped in her grip. "Emberton Tower has unique properties. We need to follow unique procedures. It's in the manual."

"This is sick," thundered Lance. "We're leaving. And we're taking Ms. Shillingsham. Come on, Mr. Furlanetti."

Caitlin tried half-heartedly to step into their path, but Lance shoved the saw aside and she shrank from him.

Her voice drifted plaintively in their wake: "I'm calling the boss. You can't just leave." Then, louder, bolder: "No one leaves!"

One by one, Lance tore open the curtains that were closed around beds. Caitlin scurried past him to a desk near the front of the room. "Yes, sir, they're trying to escape," she sobbed into a phone. Two beds were empty, but the third contained Ms. Shillingsham. She was asleep. She still had both her arms—they were crossed over her chest. Lance gripped her shoulders and shook her. No response. He shook harder.

"Let me," mumbled Mr. Furlanetti, who had arrived at the opposite side of the bed. Tenderly, he looked down at his president. A tear gathered on his downturned face, hung a second before detaching and landing on the sheets with a soft pat. He touched a hand to her brow. Then, burbling slightly, he planted a soft kiss on the middle of her forehead. Lance looked away; he felt he was intruding.

But the kiss must have done the job, because her voice chimed out, soft and weak but infused with something like hope: "John!"

"Lily," answered Mr. Furlanetti. "I'm here to get you out."

She made as if to say more, but her mouth didn't seem to work properly. A finger of drool seeped from one corner. It was frothy and grey.

"Why?" whispered Mr. Furlanetti, tenderly wiping it away with his thumb.

"I... thought..." She wasn't used to struggling with her words. The shame overwhelmed her, but she rallied: "...I was too late. For you. Gave up hope."

"Was it worth it? In the end?" asked Mr. Furlanetti.

She closed her eyes and shook her head, then let it sink back into the pillow.

"I always told you," said Mr. Furlanetti. "Not worth it."

Caitlin shrieked from the reception desk: "The boss is on his way. You'd better get back to your beds, or you're in for it."

"I'll handle the old man," said Lance. "You two have to leave. Fast."

"Are you strong enough to walk?" asked Mr. Furlanetti.

"Can try," said Ms. Shillingsham.

They helped lift her from the bed, and Mr. Furlanetti hoisted her arm around his shoulder. They made their way toward the frosted glass doors, ignoring Caitlin's threats.

Ms. Shillingsham looked mournfully at the elevator. A string of grey had escaped her mouth again and dangled, swaying, to her chest. "Now that I've tasted it... I don't want to leave it. I need it nearby."

"No, Lily." Firmly, Mr. Furlanetti pulled her into the car with him.

"Resist," said Lance. "You only need to fight for a short time. All you need to do is leave, and be brave, and wait. I think I know how to kill this thing, and your hunger with it." He remembered Emberton's counsel to Miss Fairburn. "It will be scary when you first step out of the Tower—you'll have no language at all, like you've taken a huge hit from the radiator. But keep walking."

The elevator door was sliding closed. Mr. Furlanetti's raisin eyes were slick with tears, and some sort of question appeared to be gathering in his thick, doughy features. Ms. Shillingsham's usual intelligence was returning to her face. She too seemed to have a question for him.

But Lance shook his head, and they let the door close.

When Lance stepped back from the elevator, the frosted glass doors slid back open. Caitlin watched him from behind the desk. The surgical saw was laid on top of it. "The boss is coming," she said.

"Good," answered Lance. "I'm ready."

Chapter 16

Emberton burst through the fire exit door and slugged
from his flask. Watching Lance watch him, he shook
his head. "No, my boy. No drink for you. It will ruin the
surprise." With three decisive steps, he triggered the glass
doors. He pointed his cane into the infirmary's depths.
"Caitlin. Give Mr. Blunt his patient report."

She produced a clipboard and slid it across the desktop.

"Take it, Lance," said Emberton. Then: "What does it
say?"

And Lance began to read it. "'Patient: Lance Blunt.
Sex: Male: Age: Twenty-fi—'" He broke off.

"Been a while since you've had a drink, hasn't it?" said
Emberton. "And here you are. Reading as if it were your
birthright."

"What," demanded Lance, "did you do?" His mouth
was suddenly parched; his tongue clicked coming free from
the roof.

"Oh, I don't have to tell you, Lance. Read it for
yourself."

Amid the scrawled notes, four words stood out starkly from the thicket: *Full body blood transfusion.*

Emberton unfolded his jackknife. "Go on," he said.

The blade did not reflect any light, as if it were stone instead of steel.

"Just a small incision," Emberton said. "Just enough to bleed."

Lance chose the plump flesh below his thumb. He aimed the knife and depressed the blade. The skin broke easily and the slit showed pink. But nothing flowed. Lance pinched the wound. And there it was: a bead welling through the slit, breaking its tension and streaming down his palm. Not entirely red. Distinct in that dark tone were bright threads of gold.

He couldn't bring himself to speak. But the face he showed Emberton was awash with the single question: *Why?*

"The written word, Lance! All your life you've coveted this. And now it's yours. As long as the fluid lives in the cellars, the power will thrive in your veins, and you will read. As I promised." He raised his cane, pointing its tip at Lance. "This is why you came to the Tower, Lance. You needed this power. Now it is yours for... for..." He grabbed his flask and drank. "For good." Lowering his cane, the old man stepped forward; his rough hand rested on Lance's cheek. "And the Emberton bloodline lives on."

Lance's unasked questions swirled like tornado debris, whipping in and out of his awareness too quickly to be spoken aloud. Emberton was saying something about his age, how Lance need not worry about taking the blood of someone so old, the fluid invigorated the blood, killed things that shouldn't be there, endowed it with strength and vitality. Lance would not suffer for carrying blood four times his age.

That's right, I won't. Because I suffered before. A soft utterance, the hint of a voice in the back reaches of his mind. *I don't need to suffer anymore. The Word is mine.*

Lance had to suppress an impulse to shake his head madly, slam a palm against it, dislodge this insidious whisper. His anger was his rightful master; horror and revulsion governed him; this quiet lie, singing from the cranial shadows, did not. He was not grateful. He was not tempted by this sham inheritance. He did not want to rule a corrupt, cursed tower where murder was rote.

Rote! Lance knew what it meant, the word that had stumped him in Elena's office during his tour. No corner of language, it seemed, would be denied him. All was within reach. He need never again misunderstand a word, need never watch as the woman he desired winced at his ignorance. He never again had to disappoint—

"Elena!" He shook his head, letting the warring thoughts scatter. "I want her out of your cell. Now."

"No need for raised voices, son. We will retrieve the girl, and then we will proceed to the cellars."

Good. Because that was the next thing to be done, once Elena was freed. Get down there and destroy the valve in the wall. Terminate the madness of the Tower.

The cell was on floor two, in an area with *Protection Services* stencilled on the wall at regular intervals. Which Lance duly read, as he did every swath of signage that came into sight. *I can do this now,* whispered the voice he'd rather not hear.

Elena's guard had abandoned her, leaving the door open and Elena handcuffed to a pipe. She sat on the floor, wrists raised above her. A tray of cafeteria food, partly picked over and long since congealed, lay nearby.

Lance spotted a pair of keys on a hook on the wall; they worked on Elena's cuffs. Her arms fell hard and she slumped forward with the movement. Lance knelt in front of her. "You okay?" He rubbed her wrists. "How long were you like this?"

She rested her head on his chest. "Since the last quake. The guard was too scared to stay, but too scared of the punishment if he let me go." She rose, Lance still holding her wrists, and tested her weight on her legs. "And you? What did they do to you?"

"I'll tell you later."

She was looking him up and down, trying to be discreet about it. An inventory. Checking for all the parts.

"Don't worry," said Lance, "the knives stayed in the drawer. For me, anyway—Mr. Furlanetti lost an arm. He got out, though, him and Ms. Shillingsham."

"The guard," said Elena, "before he left, he said the building was empty. Other than floors three and two, the cameras showed no action."

"That was unwise, Lance," said Emberton, "letting marketer meat walk free. Compassion may have been a virtue once, but it no longer becomes you. You face new responsibilities. You have a duty to the greater good."

Lance swallowed his retort—he had a charade to perform. Cooperate and get downstairs. "Don't worry, sir," he said. "Their addiction is strong. Both of them—she picked it up too."

Emberton smiled. This had never been a pretty sight, but nor had it ever been so ghastly. "So you expect them back."

"As long as the Tower is alive, it will call them back." *Except*, Lance did not add, *I will not let it live.*

"Good, Lance. Good." Emberton turned to Elena. His tone lost its indulgent warmth. "You can walk?"

"Yes."

"Lance will want you with him, down there."

"Why?" Her gaze flitted between the two men.

"The future of my family's lie..." Emberton scrabbled for his flask and drank. "My family's *line* depends on him. And on you, if you succumb to your affections. But he is not truly an Emberton yet. He faces one final test. To prove himself worthy of his blood. Down there, we will find out. Great glory awaits him—and possibly you—should he succeed."

"What do you mean about..." Elena looked at Lance, even as she finished her question for Emberton: "About blood?"

Lance swallowed hard. His rage at the transfusion was raw and overwhelming, but he had to tamp it down. To Emberton, he had to appear trustworthy, still onside with the old man's monstrous plans; and yet he had to show Elena that he was still Lance, that he had not crossed some transformational river. He didn't know how to do this with words. So he did the best he could think of. He drew her close to him and kissed her tenderly on the mouth. His touch, he hoped, would do the talking that he dare not do out loud.

"No time for lut," said Emberton.

Lance and Elena drew apart.

Emberton was fumbling with his flask. The screw-on lid seemed to be giving him trouble. "For luh," he said. "Fruluh." The lid came off; the flask leapt to his lips. He settled a ferocious look on Lance; droplets of drink were visible on his lip and chin. "No time for lovers' reunions," he barked. "The lake awaits us."

They stopped in the cafeteria kitchen, where Emberton retrieved another metal briefcase and handed it to Lance. And then back to the stairs. Their descent was accompanied by a series of escalating tremors. Near the press room, a pipe buckled, steam shooting from its gash—the three of them had to duck to avoid the hot vapour. In addition to the groans and grumbles in the walls, the occasional crash reached their ears as some fixture fell to the ground. One radiator had been dislodged from its anchor, and a familiar grey fount burbled from the exposed pipework.

On they pressed, through the torchlit passage, where the flames now guttered and flared, and into the room with the vat. The pile of dead words rippled. The vat's light burned brighter than before, swirled more rapidly.

Here, Lance tried to linger at the back of the procession—he released Elena's hand, which he'd gripped the whole way down. He was going to wait until Emberton was out of sight around the vat, when it would take more than a dozen seconds for the old man to turn and regain lost ground and wrestle him away from the wall.

But Emberton stopped beside the patch of rutted mud. He took a long slug from his flask. Then he fumbled for his old key ring, which he held out to Lance. "You, boy. You unlock the final door."

Lance had not foreseen this. "You go ahead, sir."

"Lance, I insist. I want you to unlock the door and take us to the lake. You are the leader of the Emberton endeavour. You must accustom yourself to leading."

The shadows of the mud's grooves slid and slithered in the swirling light from the vat. Emberton stood resolutely between Lance and the wall. There was nothing to do, for now, but obey.

After the long, silent descent through the spiralling passage with its luminous trickle alongside, Lance led the way across the shore to the lake's edge and set the metal briefcase on the altar-like protrusion of rock. Emberton unlatched it. The object inside was shaped like a malformed boomerang, one side heavier than the other. It was clammy and white, sprouting thick dark hairs. One end terminated with a pudgy hand, fingers curled.

With Mr. Furlanetti's arm exposed to the air, the lake shuddered along its surface. Lance tried to speak, but words were torn from his lips and went unsounded. A chunk of the ceiling broke off and plummeted into the hissing fluid.

The lake took a moment to settle, and Lance felt ready to speak again. But it was Emberton who got there first: "It needs flesh," he said.

"Why?" asked Elena.

Lance had to get his bit in, if only to test that he was able to talk: "This is not right, sir. Not right at all."

Emberton shrugged. "Maybe not. But it is necessary."

"Why?" repeated Elena. "How can Lance do this if he doesn't know why?"

Emberton glared at her with unalloyed disdain. But, after a thoughtful draw on the flask, he answered. "We never intended, my father and I, to become harvesters of flesh. When we discovered what was happening down here, we could not fathom how to quell the upheavals. And then one day we brought down a labourer to help us shore up the crumbling rock." Emberton pointed to a patch of lake. "Over there, the ground was still dry; the lake has expanded since. We erected scaffolding to put in some beams. A misguided venture; none of those flimsy supports lasted more than a year. The Tower stands, precariously, on this pocket of air." A moment of reverie, followed by a rapid drink from the flask. "All three of us were standing on it— me, my father, the hired man—when the lake went into one of its furies. The room shook. The scaffolding shuddered. We feared that a true... atruh..."

Another sip. Lance realized now what was happening. Because they'd swapped blood, Emberton's veins were no longer saturated with the fluid. If he did not drink, he would revert to his original condition—worse than Lance's. Without a continuous supply, the man could not even talk.

"We feared a true catastrophe," said Emberton. "We thought the Tower might come down around our ears. And then the labourer lost his balance, and he fell. Straight down to the rock floor. Burst his skull. The lake continued to heave. My father caught my eye. Together we clambered down, clinging for life to the scaffolding. We checked the man; he was truly dead. Sooner than planned."

"Sooner than *what*?"

Emberton took another deep drink, tipping the flask to vertical. He shook out the last few drops and flung it aside, where it clattered against rock. "The workers we brought down here were never meant to live. What could we do? Let them wander the city at will, telling all and sundry of the marvels below ground? These men were carefully chosen— vagrants, men of no account, nobody anyone would miss."

"Like the withhold words," said Elena.

Emberton produced a new flask from his belt. He watched Elena while he unscrewed it. "Thoun..." He took an angry swig. "That female," he said to Lance, "is overly proficient of mouth. You may want to see she doesn't use it too much." Another sip. "This was not our fault. We had good intentions. We could not have foreseen this consequence, this underside. But it transpired, and we had to contain it."

"So what happened to the worker?" asked Lance.

"We hove him into the lake. And then we made for the tunnel, hoping to flee before the ceiling collapsed. But then we noticed: the quaking had stopped. We tried, experimentally, to speak—and found we could. The hunger was appeased. The lake was calm. It was no longer stealing our language."

"Meat," said Lance.

"Blood, was what we thought. Language lives in the blood, the blood that feeds the brain, the blood that operates the lungs, engorges the tongue. At first, my father thought animals would satisfy it—they had blood, lungs, voices. So he built a cafeteria to justify trucking in animal carcasses. Didn't work." Emberton took a thoughtful sip. "The meat floated on the surface of the lake, decomposing. The lake was not interested in it."

"Why?"

"This is language, Lance. It can't survive without humans. The animals had no capacity for language, so they were useless to the lake. Next my father tried human blood. There were many opportunities, up and down the Tower, to extract it and divert it down here. But after a time, that was not enough. Today the lake demands a more substantial meal. Flesh. But even that no longer satisfies it. When it's ravenous, when it seeps out beyond the Tower walls, it has begun to feed on pure language. The real thing—not the old, dead words that created it. The living language that humans use."

The lake gave another heave, as if impatient, and it was a moment before any of the three figures on its shore were able to speak.

"The duty to feed the lake," Emberton announced, "has passed to my heir." He shoved Mr. Furlanetti's arm at Lance. Where it had been torn from its shoulder, unidentifiable shreds—grey-blue, rooted in a nest of what appeared to be blubber—dangled like festive ribbon. Lance took a hard step back as a strand brushed his shirt. He raised his hands, palms forward.

"You must, Lance. No chaw— chay— *choice.*" Emberton hawked and spat pearly phlegm to the rock floor.

It wasn't the hand, with its demurely curled fingers, that fixated Lance's eye. It wasn't the stark black hairs on pallid skin, or the crudely separated shoulder. It was the extruding blubber, like a clump of marshmallows dropped in a fire. In Lance's first, unkind assessment, fat had been Mr. Furlanetti's defining characteristic. That distended belly inching into Lance's office, lowering into a chair so Lance's computer habits could be probed. Tears trailing down the rotund jowls when Ms. Shillingsham lay on her infirmary bed.

Regret chilled Lance. He had betrayed the man. It was because of Lance's grubby, petty misdeed that Mr. Furlanetti's arm was severed.

"Wrong," moaned Lance. "So, so wrong."

He was talking about himself, about what he'd done. But Emberton heard differently. "This is necessary, Lance," said the old man quietly. "Right and wrong do not matter."

"No," said Lance.

"You will do this. You carry my blood."

Lance's laughter came out more hideous, more hysterical, than he had intended. "So?"

"You carry the Emberton bloodline." The old man's face was bereft of all colour. Astonishment consumed it.

"Do you not realize the significance? You *are* the Emberton line, Lance. You are it, and it is you. The family's project is yours." He was abject in his disbelief—no guile, no play-acting. Emberton had really believed the transfusion was his trump card.

"Sorry," said Lance, as gently as he could. "It's only blood. It just carries oxygen and food. It isn't fate."

Through all its flaws and folds, Emberton's face—his *paline* face—was a clear window. The scales had fallen from his eyes: where he'd envisioned a prince, an heir to this kingdom, all he had was some squalling baby ditched in the cellar. An urchin, unwowed by the glories of blood.

"You disappoint me," said Emberton. He raised Mr. Furlanetti's arm and flung it forward. The fluid received it with roiling and hissing. "I gave my life to this," the old man said, his voice a croak accompanied by a dribble of drink down his chin. He dropped his flask; no fluid spilled from its open throat. "You betrayed me, Lance."

"Sir, what are you—"

"Stay, Lance." The syllables oozed out slow and broken. "Rule the Tower. Prolong the line." He laboured to get each word out, to mould the appropriate sounds. Emberton's language was falling apart before Lance's ears.

"Come with us, sir. Leave with us. Live in the world."

Emberton knelt. Carefully, almost tenderly, he laid his cane on the ground. "The world," he intoned, "is the Tower's now." And with that, the last living Emberton launched himself from the overhanging rock.

In the air, muscular control relinquished, he looked like a ragdoll handled too much over the years, its stuffing beaten thin. He writhed and flopped and landed on the surface and stuck there—it was too viscous to admit him right away, or he was too light. He sprawled, his face thrust into the fluid. Then he rolled onto his back.

"Sir!" shouted Lance. He extended Emberton's cane, crook-first. "Sir! Grab this."

Emberton closed his eyes, crossed his arms over his chest, and began to sink. The fluid was frenzied where it received him, seething and bubbling like hot bacon grease. He lay motionless.

Lance flailed with the cane, trying to loop the crook around Emberton's leg. It snagged on a foot. Lance tugged, but the cane's end slipped from his sweaty grip.

Emberton slid from sight, the cane following him down. The lake's tumult increased, as if beasts were gathering underwater to tear apart the sinking body. A tongue of wave rose up the far wall, mauling the entrance to the bats' cavern.

"Get up," Elena said. "Lance, get up. He's gone, now. Let him go."

Flesh of my flesh. At last the lake had Emberton flesh. But it needed more. It tore at the shrunken old form it had admitted, sniffing in vain for the coveted Emberton blood. Lance could feel the lake's magnetic pull. It needed what he had. It sang to Lance's new corpuscles, sent out a piercing cry of longing, and his blood sang in reply. The obverse fluid, the grey cloud that amassed and billowed at the bottom of this pond, was beginning to understand the terrain around it, to deduce who these humans were on the rocky shore. It was getting wise, and it was coming for Lance.

He rolled away from the precipice. New sounds rose from the lake: a low cry, hoarse and intermittent, like metal under great duress, and snapping wisps of sibilance, whispers that started and stopped and overlapped.

Elena helped Lance to his feet. She did not need to tell him to run.

The lake grew more furious as they fled. It snapped at the shore, and each retreating wave burned a groove into the rock. With a sudden report, a crack appeared in the wall. Pebbles broke free and clattered to the ground. From high above came a terrific groan as the Tower resettled on its foundations. The lake heaved with even greater energy, little noxious coils rising off its skin. A chunk of wall came loose and fell into the lake, sending out foot-high ripples. The shore crackled with them.

They reached the tunnel. Here and there, chunks of rock had worked loose from the wall and lay spilled on the floor. Lance's strength flagged. Blackness swam at the edges of his vision, and then it flooded in, blotting everything. He sank to one knee.

"Lance!" screamed Elena.

She yanked him to his feet and tugged him forward. Behind him, the air was a lethal wall of noise. The tunnel was collapsing. A deluge of boulders and gravel and fine dust and jagged pebbles and all manner of rock fragment was filling the passage behind them.

And together he and Elena ran, hurtled up the spiral corridor, which now seemed endless, as if it would wind them around and around, higher than the penthouse, up into the clouds, and still they would have to sprint, lungs raw and aflame, knees weeping at the abuse. But fear dug spurs into their ribs; they did not stop running, and the tunnel's collapse, the lake's last frantic stab at possessing Lance, did not outpace them.

Back in the chamber, they swung the iron door closed. The tunnel had ceased its roaring; the collapse was done.

They edged around the vat, which gave off the heat of a raging woodstove. Lance approached the furrowed patch of wall. It too emanated heat. The clay yielded to his hand but also resisted, like tough sponge. He stretched his hand until the tip of his middle finger found what it sought. The texture of partially cooked cannelloni. The opening of the tube.

His arm thrust forward and his hand clenched around the vulnerable spot. It quivered, as if in anticipation of a new word. As if Lance were here to nourish, not destroy.

He balked. The wall squeezed and then released his forearm. The open tube quivered again. He realized that this oozing mud could crush him if it wished. He had to move decisively, or his bones might be pulverized. He thrust his other hand into the wall and pushed it through slime until it met the first. With two hands, he took the tube into his grip. He took a breath and began to pull.

The tube's skin was tough, fibrous, like canvas. His wrist ached with effort. But he could feel its tensile strength start to give. He could feel the fight go out of it. One more ounce of pressure, and he could open a tear.

But he couldn't. He felt the weakness of the thing now, the tender plea in its surrender. All it wanted was to live. It had shown none of the aggression he'd feared, had not crushed his forearms. It spoke to him with its caresses, its exerting and relinquishing of pressure, and it pleaded for its life.

What harm could come of something so delicate? Yes, the Tower caused problems; sure, it might imperil civiliza-tion. But it was a living thing, so simple in its need, and it was bound to him by blood. He could not kill it. He stood there like an aspiring thief whose arm got stuck in a vending machine, who had to crouch there in his failure until the paramedics came.

But Elena was close behind him. Her arm slid around his waist; her lips moved inches from his ear. "We have to do it," she whispered.

"I can't."

"You must."

"I won't be able to read anymore. It was so beautiful, Elena. I saw your note. I saw what you thought when you wrote to me."

"I'll help you," she said. "I'll be with you. Whatever you can and can't do, we'll survive. I promise." Her lips pressed against the tender skin along the side of his neck.

And he finished the job. Yanked and twisted and sweated until the tube's mouth was in shreds, until the pulsing died out spasmodically against his palms, until he felt the moisture in the wall dry up and the ruts on the surface go brittle, until the swirling light above the vat died out. The Tower did not tremble; there were no apocalyptic spasms. Just the quiet whimper, the last desperate twitch, as its tiny, crucial valve expired.

And from beyond the lightless vat, from beyond the sealed iron door, past the rubble the lake had dislodged, from the depths below the city's depths, he thought he detected something else, a message spoken directly to his blood: *I'm still here.* He had sealed off the lake, starved it of its feed. But it was down there, brooding, hungry. As long as it lived, it would thirst for his blood. As long as his heart pumped, the lake would serenade him.

Elena had gripped Lance's elbows and pulled his arms from the wall. Lance had another life to attend to now. A different future. He was going to go up to the ground floor, walk out of the revolving door.

The mayhem had scattered the pile of dead words. Some were strewn in the hallway, others had dispersed over the small room, littering the floor, sticking to wet patches of wall. Some twirled midair, like indecisive snow. Lance kicked at the centre of the pile, and the words stirred yet further, riding underdrafts and making for the hall. Something whirred, a duct of some kind, and as the air shifted they moved faster. A row of them lifted off, zipped up to the vent from which the noise had come, and slid through its grille. Fleeing from their ancient confinement and into the living world.

The torches on the corridor wall were sputtering. The way was growing rapidly darker. Joining hands and inter-locking their fingers, Lance and Elena hurried through the last choking remnants of light.

The lobby was in worse disarray than before. Everything was dusted with plaster or shards of glass. Fixtures dangled from the ceiling by thin wires. One whole wall was buckled, showing a diametric scar. Lance and Elena paused by the fireplace. The merest scrap of yellow flame licked around the useless wood. Lance picked up one of the Embertons that had tumbled from the mantel. He flipped it open and scanned the page. Nothing. He could no longer read. A last sad flicker, and the flame died completely. The power was gone.

He tried not to dwell on what he'd lost. He tried not to recall the exhilaration of those passages from the Bible leaping to life, the thrill of reading what Elena had jotted for him on that brittle Post-it. That was the past. A past that he had killed.

Tentatively, he reached for the revolving door. Nothing, this time, forbade his hand from touching the cool metal bar. He gave it an experimental shove. The door answered with a partial revolution. Here too the Tower had no dominion over him.

He turned to Elena. "You ready?"

She was squinting at the bright realm beyond the glass, steeling herself to enter it. She looked small and timid in the morning light, which drenched her chalky skin and tangled hair. Her eyes were narrowed to almost nothing. It had been years since she'd been out.

They would help each other. All this time she'd been trapped in her cave, sealed off from the jostling city outside. Lance could guide her, and she could guide him when written language stood in the way. Together, they could do this.

He put an arm around her shoulder and drew her close. "You ready?"

She closed her eyes and breathed deep. "I am."

And Lance stepped forward, gave the pushbar a shove, and whisked them through into the world beyond.

Epilogue

Sunday finds the city resting only partially. Traffic moves more sedately than it will tomorrow. Pedestrians throng the pavement, but a languor infuses the tide of bodies. Earlier this morning, a light rain, ushered in by heavy grey clouds, glazed everything. Only now are the clouds being brushed aside by a soft, insistent breeze; only now is the sunlight nudging through.

A young man folds an umbrella, gives it a shake, and lopes on, his shoes leaving faint imprints on the sidewalk's wet sheen. He passes a row of shops deserted and boarded up. Their signs appear vandalized, the letters mauled, as if a great corrosive claw had swiped across them, smearing away all text. Bold new graffiti occupies the plywood in the window frames. New street signs are bolted to poles, offering clear, sure guidance to the weekend cars. Some time ago, the old signs became blurred. And so they were replaced.

Confusion surrounds the events that occurred in this district. What's known is that there was a gas leak, and so the vicinity was evacuated, cordons were established, not a soul was allowed back in until things cleared up. As for the defaced signage, the mangled text, there are claims that more than gas seeped out, some kind of chemical which for obvious reasons the authorities will not admit exists. But those are paranoid urban legends. The elements are ferocious. Leave something out on the street, and who knows what shape it'll be beaten into. Things corrode. Even the letters printed on signs.

The young man stops in the shadow of a squat old tower. Many of its windows are boarded up. Others are opaque with grime. Something bright catches his eye. He approaches the entrance. A large orange sign is plastered on the glass face of a revolving door. *Condemned,* it says. The man can't read this—words on signs are meaningless to him—but he is aware of the building's fate; he has heard about it on the news. What he can see, looking at the sign, is that the word has something wrong with it. It wavers, or smears, lilts somehow just off true. Something amiss in the font. He turns away, ready to re-emerge into the city, step back into the flow of his life, forget this doomed old edifice.

Because his life does have a flow. It does have purpose and satisfactions and achievements to be proud of. To a reasonable extent, he can function in society. Progress has been sporadic and painful. He is helped along by a smart and patient woman who is also his lover, whose patience only occasionally gives way to fits of exasperation. Gradually, she is helping him overcome his lifelong difficulty.

He has learned to be frank about this, to ask for help when he needs it. Sometimes he is greeted by scorn or derision, but most people are eager to help. He has even held on to part-time work as a salesman in a warehouse outlet, paid on commission. After a brief probation, his boss was pleased with his numbers and was therefore willing to handle the paperwork side of things.

The young man is about to move on, descend the steps to the subway station, turn his back on the Tower, go home to the apartment he shares with his lover, unpack the shopping he's brought with him—groceries, toiletries, food for the plants; the necessities of a domestic life. They will share a light meal and a conversation. Maybe, if he's lucky, she'll be in the mood to invent an etymology and narrate it to him.

It's time to go. These visits to the Tower are more and more infrequent now; he's ready to forget the monstrous building ever existed; he's ready to banish it from his life. His lover, of course, does not know about these little detours he makes on his way home from errands.

But something halts him as he turns to leave. A tremor in the ground. The young man looks around. Towers are not swaying; power lines don't jog in place. This is not an ordinary quake. Something else has stirred the earth.

A few yards from the toe of his shoe is a sewer grate. Something rises from it, a gentle waft of mist, slightly golden. The man hurries to the grate. He kneels on the wet ground. The wreath of haze has risen several feet into the air, out of reach, dissipating as it heads for the sky, batted one way by a breeze, then dashed against a cross-current.

He crooks his fingers around the grate and peers down into the darkness. He leans closer to the cold and filthy metal, presses his face against it, aching to see what can't be seen. He breathes deep, as if to suck up all the air beneath him, as if the force of his inhalation were enough to draw into his lungs whatever is left of that ethereal mist.

But nothing lingers down there. Wherever the sewer ultimately leads is just a desolate cavern. The power it housed has died out. Surely it has.

But Lance kneels, and he breathes, and he waits.

Notes and Acknowledgements

The goings-on at Emberton Tower (even the supposedly professional ones) of course bear little resemblance to lexicography as it's practised in real life. However, I did glean valuable details about actual dictionary-building from several sources, notably the following: Henry Hitchings, *Defining the World: The Extraordinary Story of Dr Johnson's Dictionary*; Sidney Landau, *Dictionaries: The Art and Craft of Lexicography*; Lynda Mugglestone, *Lost for Words: The Hidden History of the Oxford English Dictionary*; and Simon Winchester, *The Meaning of Everything: The Story of the Oxford English Dictionary*. Many language and etymology books were generally helpful; the account of the origin of *not* was informed specifically by Guy Deutscher's *The Unfolding of Language*.

Very special thanks to Chris Labonté, who acquired this book for Douglas & McIntyre and guided it through several rewrites, and whose enthusiasm and insight were invaluable. Huge thanks also to Caroline Skelton, for her brilliant substantive and copy editing; Anna Comfort O'Keeffe, for deftly steering *Emberton* to the finish line; Mary White, Carleton Wilson and Megan Ferguson, for their fabulous work on the design; Pam Robertson for the sharp-eyed proofread; the Canada Council for the Arts, for financial help in the early stages; Anne McDermid and Chris Bucci, for feedback, guidance, and advocacy; Ian Weir, for story advice; Laurie Mack, Jane Mack, and Aaron Doppler, for making the ultimate sacrifice. And my utmost gratitude to Melanie Little—for casting an astute editorial eye over two different versions of the novel, and for her unflagging love, support, and faith over these many years.